CU00731070

MISS BINGLEY'S REVENGE

ELIZA AUSTIN

Boldwood

First published in 2013. This edition published in Great Britain in 2024 by Boldwood Books Ltd.

Copyright © Eliza Austin, 2013

Cover Design by Colin Thomas

Cover Photography: Colin Thomas

The moral right of Eliza Austin to be identified as the author of this work has been asserted in accordance with the Copyright, Designs and Patents Act 1988.

All rights reserved. No part of this book may be reproduced in any form or by any electronic or mechanical means, including information storage and retrieval systems, without written permission from the author, except for the use of brief quotations in a book review.

This book is a work of fiction and, except in the case of historical fact, any resemblance to actual persons, living or dead, is purely coincidental.

Every effort has been made to obtain the necessary permissions with reference to copyright material, both illustrative and quoted. We apologise for any omissions in this respect and will be pleased to make the appropriate acknowledgements in any future edition.

A CIP catalogue record for this book is available from the British Library.

Paperback ISBN 978-1-83603-190-1

Large Print ISBN 978-1-83603-189-5

Hardback ISBN 978-1-83603-188-8

Ebook ISBN 978-1-83603-191-8

Kindle ISBN 978-1-83603-192-5

Audio CD ISBN 978-1-83603-183-3

MP3 CD ISBN 978-1-83603-184-0

Digital audio download ISBN 978-1-83603-186-4

Boldwood Books Ltd
23 Bowerdean Street
London SW6 3TN
www.boldwoodbooks.com

1

'Oh botheration, this isn't going to work.'

Lizzy glanced through the open doorway. 'Is something wrong, Georgie?'

'Yes, everything.' A loud sigh accompanied this admission. 'Besides being lopsided, it's neither one thing nor the other.'

Lizzy put aside her lists and stood up. 'Let me see.'

'I'd much prefer it if you didn't look at it. You'll only laugh.'

'I promise not to.' Lizzy walked from the small sitting room she favoured directly into Pemberley's main entrance vestibule, where Georgiana was working on her floral display. 'You're far too creative for me to criticise anything you do. I'm in a permanent state of awe at your talent.'

'Thank you, but you have no need to be. There's such a thing as trying to be too creative. I thought the wild heather would reflect the rural nature of our locality, you see, and the beautiful roses are supposed to be a tribute to our gardens.' Georgiana grimaced at the bold arrangement. 'All I've managed to create is something that's completely ambiguous.'

'I disagree.' Lizzy studied the floral tribute to Derbyshire, knowing better than to mislead Georgiana with platitudes. 'It's different enough to be eye-catching, and the mingled scent of the roses and heather assails one's senses the moment one steps into the hall.'

'Do you really think so?' Georgiana bit her lip in evident indecision, but at least she was no longer frowning. 'My brother might not agree.'

'Your brother will actually notice your efforts, which means you've succeeded.'

'Well, he can hardly miss it. It does rather dominate this sideboard.'

'Gentlemen of your brother's ilk don't usually take much interest in the floral arrangements that surround them simply because they take them for granted. Your originality, on the other hand, will most certainly be noticed and talked about.'

'Or laughed at.'

'Never that.'

Georgiana released a long breath. 'Well, just so long as you're sure. I wouldn't wish to upset Fitzwilliam.' She sent Lizzy an impish smile. 'Not that I would find that very easy to do, even if I tried. Since you came into his life, he's been a changed person.'

Lizzy laughed. 'If you're implying I've wrought some remarkable alteration in his character then you're quite wrong, Georgie. He's merely becoming the person he was always supposed to be.'

'Because he's happy?'

'I certainly hope he is. If he were to regret marrying me I would feel wretched.'

'Now who's being a goose?' Georgiana covered Lizzy's hand with her own. 'You know very well he adores you, as do I. Life is so much nicer with you here at Pemberley.'

'Thank you.' Lizzy squeezed Georgiana's hand as she led her back into the small sitting room. 'I believe he does enjoy the change in his circumstances, although he's still terribly stiff and formal in company.'

'Give him time. Fitzwilliam takes his responsibilities seriously. Laughing at the world in general and himself in particular isn't an adjustment he will find easy to make.'

Lizzy squared her shoulders. 'Then I shall just have to redouble my efforts with Will.'

Georgiana grinned. 'I still wonder whom you're referring to when I hear you address my brother as Will.'

'Fitzwilliam is such a mouthful.' Lizzy flapped a hand. 'Besides, Will suits him much better.'

'I agree, but he's never permitted *me* to shorten his name.'

Ah, Georgiana, one day you will understand. 'In my family we shorten names all the time. Well, with five girls with so much to say for themselves, one learned from an early age to make verbal economies in order to retain the attention of one's listener.'

'Oh, how I would have liked to have had a sister.'

Lizzy smiled, thinking how lonely it must have been for one as delicate as Georgiana, growing up alone on this huge estate, her only relation a brother who was almost old enough to be her father. 'Well, you have one now in me, which I hope doesn't disappoint you.'

'Oh no, not in the least. I didn't mean to imply—'

Lizzy laughed and reached across to touch Georgiana's knee. 'I know you did not.'

'Your being here has made a world of difference to me, Lizzy, and in a good way.'

'Thank you.'

A footman came in with refreshments. Lizzy thanked him, poured for them both and then returned to her conversation with Georgiana.

'It's hard for me to tell if Will is less formal in his manner,' she said. 'I wasn't here at Pemberley to observe how he behaved beneath his own roof, although I could probably make an accurate guess.' Lizzy flashed an impish smile. 'Still, if you can see the changes in him, then that's a good start.'

'Certainly he's changed. You need to look no further than the coming week if you doubt me. We're about to have a houseful of grand people, and he's never shown the slightest inclination for such entertainments before. That has to be a good sign, surely?'

'House parties are *de rigueur* during the summer, Georgie. I'm sure he would have held one this year, even if he wasn't now wedded to me. It's expected of a gentleman in his position, but you were too young to act as his hostess before now, which is probably the excuse he used not to put himself to the trouble.'

'But now he has you to shoulder the burden.'

'Yes, but you must remember that I've never done anything like this before either, so I'm relying on your help. After all, you know Pemberley so much better than I do.' Lizzy indicated her endless list of last-minute arrangements which lay abandoned on the table. 'I only hope I'm equal to the occasion.'

Georgiana arched a brow. 'You've been married to Fitzwilliam for more than six months, Lizzy. I've never before seen you show the slightest sign of nerves.'

'Perhaps that's because I haven't been called upon to play hostess to some of my fiercest critics during that time.'

'Your critics?'

'Never mind.' Lizzy shook her head, aware that she'd said too much. 'Perhaps you can help me with the allocation of chambers. God forbid that I should insult anyone by giving them a room that's beneath them.'

'You mean Miss Bingley?'

Lizzy looked up from her lists, flexed her brows and put her pen aside. 'You're more astute than I realised.'

'I would never admit it to anyone other than you, Lizzy, but I do not care for Caroline Bingley. I have always been uncomfortable in her company. She so obviously wanted to marry my brother, and tried to befriend me in an effort to win his approval.' Georgiana tossed her head, setting her curls dancing. 'I might not know much of the world, but I can sense when I am being exploited for the benefit of others.'

'She certainly has a high opinion of herself. However,' Lizzy said emphatically, 'if she wishes to be admitted to Pemberley then she must adjust to my being its mistress.'

'It can't be easy for your sister, Mrs Bingley.'

Once again, Lizzy was surprised by Georgiana's perspicacity. 'No, I suppose not. Miss Bingley was forced to give way to my sister as her brother's wife, usurping her position as his housekeeper *and* tolerating frequent visits from our mother. If Miss Bingley has any sense, she will start to think about marriage herself. She has a good dowry, which ought to attract the sort of gentleman she would consider worthy.'

'Mrs Bingley is far too kind-hearted to say so, but that would make her life much easier.'

'I dare say it would. I shall be sure to interrogate Jane when she arrives and discover how things stand in that respect. If Miss Bingley is trying to undermine my sister in any way then I must find a way to prevent it from happening.'

'Well,' Georgiana said, arching her back. 'I'm so glad Fitzwilliam saw through Miss Bingley's ruse and chose you instead.'

'Thank you for saying so.' Lizzy smiled. 'But, now, let's talk about you instead. We haven't spoken much about the time we spent in London after Christmas. You were in much demand, but I couldn't see that any particular young gentleman won your favour.'

'I know you'll respect my confidence if I admit that I didn't enjoy society's ways. I felt out of place, and awkward most of the time, and didn't know what to say to people.' Georgiana nibbled on her lower lip. 'I know that makes me sound ungrateful, but really, I heard myself described as an heiress worth pursuing more than once and—'

'And you couldn't decide if the ensuing attention you received was for yourself or your fortune.' Lizzy sighed. 'That can't have been easy for you.'

'It doesn't matter. None of the gentlemen excited my interest. Besides, I prefer to be here at Pemberley.'

'That I can understand. We certainly won't be rushing back to town.' Lizzy instinctively patted her stomach, fairly sure there was a very good reason for her not to be rushing anywhere. Not that she'd told her husband about her likely condition, nor did she intend to until after the house party. He pretended not to be in any hurry to welcome an heir into this world, but Lizzy suspected the opposite was true. Once he was made aware of her condition he would likely treat her as though she was made of porcelain. 'I believe Colonel Fitzwilliam is bringing two young gentlemen with him. Perhaps one of them will appeal to you. Not that it matters if they don't. There's absolutely no pressure on you to find a husband, unless you wish to, of course.'

Georgiana shook her head. 'Perhaps not, but I *do* still feel pressured to consider matrimony.'

'Not because of anything your brother has said to you, I hope.'

'No, it's just... Oh, I don't know. It was all the other young ladies spoke about while we were in London. Who were the most eligible gentlemen? How well were they situated? How best to be noticed by them?' Georgiana expelled a disgruntled sigh. 'Honestly, Lizzy, I didn't hear ten words of sense spoken the entire time I was there.'

Lizzy laughed. 'You must bear in mind that most of those young ladies aren't in your enviable position of being able to please themselves.'

'Because I have a large dowry and a loving home, you mean.'

'Yes, I mean precisely that. Although we were never grand enough to enjoy the questionable pleasures of a season in full swing, my sisters and I are still a gentleman's daughters. We were expected to marry well, but our pecuniary situation made that ambition exceedingly difficult to achieve.'

'But you managed it.'

Lizzy gasped. 'Oh lord, now you're going to think I married your brother for financial gain, but I assure you that is not the case. Not that I would expect anyone to believe it, but I had quite made up my mind not to marry unless I fell deeply and passionately in love.'

Georgiana sighed. 'I don't need to ask if you achieved that ambition. I see the evidence daily with my own eyes.'

'Yes. It's just fortunate I happened to fall in love with a gentleman of means.' They both laughed. 'All I am trying to say, my dear, is that this is every bit as much your home as it is mine. More so since you were born here. Never imagine for a moment you must marry simply because it's what society expects of you. My advice to you is to enjoy being young and, with luck, you will find a gentleman one day who is worthy of your regard.' Lizzy picked up her lists. 'There, that's all I am going to say on the matter. Now, about these chambers.'

'You'll be happy to see Mrs Bingley,' Georgiana said.

'Yes, indeed. If having Miss Bingley and the Hursts here is the price I must pay for the pleasure of my sister's society, then I shall endure their presence with equanimity... if I possibly can.'

Georgiana giggled. 'And one of your other sisters is coming, too.'

'Yes, Jane is bringing Kitty with her. I know the two of you have only met once, and then only briefly, but you're of a similar age.'

And poles apart in all other respects. 'It might be pleasant for you to have a companion. Kitty's to stay with us for the whole summer, and so you will see a lot of one another.'

If even half of what Jane had told Lizzy in her letters was to be believed, then Kitty's behaviour had improved beyond recognition since the removal of Lydia's influence. In spending much of her time with Jane, apparently the manners and mores of good society had rubbed off on Kitty, and Jane was pleased with the improvements in her. Even so, Kitty shared some of Lizzy's rebellious nature, whereas Georgiana was far too timid and unwilling to express her opinion, even though she was intelligent and perfectly qualified to do so. It was Lizzy's hope that the girls' characters would intermingle. Lizzy continued to do what she could with Georgiana, but she was her brother's wife and certain boundaries existed in their relationship which wouldn't come between two young, unmarried girls.

'Yes, that will be nice. And then you won't need to worry about me and can devote all your attention to my brother.'

'Oh, Georgiana, that isn't what I meant at all.'

'Put Miss Bingley in the green room in the west wing,' Georgiana said. 'The Hursts can have the blue suite opposite. They are fine rooms in a good part of the house, but a long way away from the family's chambers in the main wing.'

'Good girl!' Lizzy laughed and made the appropriate notation on her list. 'There's hope for you yet.'

'Ah, my two favourite ladies.'

Darcy entered the room and smiled at them both. Lizzy revelled in the warmth of that full, uncontrived smile and returned it with an enticing one of her own.

'Your sister is very good indeed at allocating chambers,' she said.

'My sister's talents run deep.'

'You're biased,' Georgiana said, but Lizzy could see she enjoyed the compliment.

'Make a comment on the flowers in the hall,' Lizzy whispered in an undertone while Georgiana took up Lizzy's list and examined it.

To his credit, Will caught on straightaway.

'What's that pleasant scent?' He followed his nose into the entrance vestibule and stood back to admire the display. 'Your work, Lizzy?' he asked.

'Heavens no. Georgie is the creative one.'

Georgiana grimaced. 'You don't think it lacks... well, something?'

'Not in the least.' Will bestowed a brotherly smile on Georgiana, so different to the intimate one he'd treated Lizzy to moments ago, but equally heartfelt. 'Creative is exactly the right description.'

'Come along, I'll ring for more tea,' Lizzy said, leading the way back into the sitting room. 'You spent all the morning locked away in your library and rode out with your steward for hours this afternoon, Will. You must be parched.'

'Tea would be welcome, as would the opportunity to spend a pleasant hour with the two of you before our privacy's invaded by our guests.'

'We're looking forward to it, aren't we, Georgie,' Lizzy said with a mischievous wink for her sister-in-law.

'Absolutely,' Georgiana agreed on a gurgle of laughter.

Simpson, the butler, entered the room, not with the tea things but with an expression of mild disapproval on his face.

'An unexpected guest has arrived, ma'am.'

'A guest,' Darcy replied, even though the comment had been addressed to Lizzy. 'Who the devil—'

'Lizzy, you have to help me!'

A bedraggled figure burst into the room and threw herself into Lizzy's arms.

'Lydia! What on earth are you doing here?'

2

'Are you ready yet, Caroline?'

'Come in, Louisa.' Caroline Bingley screwed up her features. 'How one is supposed to make oneself presentable in such primitive conditions is beyond me.'

'Quite so, although allowances are made regarding one's standards when travelling.'

'I *always* maintain my standards.'

Louisa Hurst perched cautiously on the edge of Caroline's bed, wisely taking care not to crease her gown. 'Tomorrow will see us in Derbyshire, and the conditions at Pemberley certainly aren't primitive.'

'Thank goodness for that.' Caroline sighed. 'This inn is totally unacceptable. I would be the first to concede one must make sacrifices when travelling, but really, I'm surprised Charles couldn't manage something better.'

'This is the only posting inn on this stretch of road apparently, so he didn't have much option.'

'We could have gone on for a while.'

'We could but the horses could not.' Louisa straightened her gloves. 'And at least Mrs Bennet isn't here to spring herself upon us uninvited.'

Caroline made an unladylike grunting sound. 'That's something to celebrate.'

'It most certainly is.' Louisa's expression softened. 'Does the prospect of reaching Pemberley make you anxious, my dear?'

Caroline summoned upon a nonchalant smile. 'I shall be glad to have the travelling over with.'

Louisa touched her hand. 'That's not what I meant and you know it.'

Caroline averted her eyes. 'What would you have me say, Louisa?'

'Don't imagine I fail to appreciate how difficult things are for you. First of all, Jane has usurped your position within Charles's household, leaving you with nothing to do.'

'Oh, I don't in the least resent Jane, but I will admit to feeling underemployed and perhaps just a little undervalued, too.'

'Perhaps it's time for you to find yourself a husband? Then you would have your own household to keep you occupied.' Louisa squeezed her sister's hand. 'I know you had your heart set on Darcy, but he's gone and there's an end to it.'

'I don't believe I ever admitted to a preference for Darcy,' Caroline replied with a haughty toss of her head.

Louisa smiled. 'You didn't need to. I could see how deeply attached to him you felt. He's a very handsome, very agreeable gentleman and would have been a perfect match for you. I was in alt at the prospect of your being the mistress of Pemberley.'

'God forbid I should be so easily read.'

'You are my most beloved sister and I understand you almost as well as you understand yourself.'

'Yes, well—'

'We've never spoken of this before but you ought to be aware how deeply I feel for you, Caro. He should have been yours.'

Yes, Caroline thought malevolently, and he would have been, had it not been for that sly doxy, Elizabeth Bennet. Caroline seethed with the injustice of it all. Why, oh why, had Charles chosen to take a house in Hertfordshire, within walking distance of the Bennet household, when there were a million other, far more suitable locations?

'What's done is done.' Caroline had no wish to discuss the matter and even less use for Louisa's misplaced pity. 'At least it will be pleasant to see Pemberley again.'

'And judge for ourselves if Mrs Darcy is capable of managing such a place.'

'Oh, I'm perfectly sure she'll make a complete mull of it, for which Darcy only has himself to blame.' *And I shall enjoy seeing his disappointment in his fine-eyed wife.* 'I only hope her outspokenness hasn't adversely influenced Georgiana.'

Louisa shuddered. 'By all means, let's hope not, but I am not optimistic. Georgiana idolises her brother and probably considers she should emulate his wife's manner of conducting herself.'

'Indeed. We've had daily evidence of how Jane and Elizabeth's advantageous marriages have affected Kitty. She's grown full of self-importance and quite forgets herself at times.'

'This is about you, Caro. I'm perfectly serious in my advice to start looking for a suitable husband.' Louisa smiled. 'Colonel Fitzwilliam is to be at Pemberley.'

Caroline raised an arrogant brow. 'You think I'd take Darcy's lesser simply because he needs my dowry?'

'He's very easy on the eye, and he's a gentleman with an impeccable pedigree.'

This reminder that Caroline needed to marry a gentleman in order to distance herself from her family's connection to trade infuriated her, causing her to strike out. 'In the same manner that Mr Hurst is a gentleman?' she asked scathingly.

'Precisely.' Louisa remained infuriatingly calm, which was most disobliging of her. Caroline badly needed to pick an argument, if only to distract her thoughts from the morrow, but that was difficult when one's adversary refused to fight. 'Mr Hurst and I understand one another very well. He affords me the respectability I crave, and my money keeps him in the latest fashion.'

Caroline smiled through her bitterness. 'And Mr Henley?'

Louisa elevated a brow. 'You know about him?'

'I wasn't certain but you have just confirmed my suspicions.'

'It's perfectly acceptable for a married lady to take a lover. If Mr Hurst knew he would not raise any objections, just so long as I am discreet.'

'Not so very discreet since I guessed.'

'You are my sister.' Louisa allowed herself a delicate shrug. 'No one else is interested in my activities.'

Louisa's casual remark about married ladies taking lovers lodged in Caroline's brain, re-igniting a half-formed plan. If Mr Darcy was so very disappointed with the choice he'd made... but no, she refused to be second best. Besides, if she harboured any ambitions to marry then she couldn't risk her reputation. It was marriage or nothing. Unfortunately, the man she loved with a single-minded passion was already married.

But there had to be a way to alter that situation – permanently.

There was a tap at the door, and Jane put her head around it.

'Dinner awaits us in a private dining room, ladies,' she said, smiling.

'Thank you, Jane, we'll be there directly.'

Why could Eliza Bennet not have been more like her sister, Caroline thought sourly as she took her place at the dinner table. Jane was so sweet, so unassuming, and played the part of hostess with becoming modesty. Even Caroline, who was in the mood to criticise everything, could find no fault with her manner. Jane made no effort to draw attention to herself, and seemed content to share the sort of intimate glances with Charles that made Caroline ache with envy. What she would give to find a gentleman who valued her in the way that Charles clearly worshipped Jane.

Recalling that she *had* found him, before a presumptuous little nobody stole him from beneath her very nose, fuelled Caroline's sour mood. If Eliza's character had been similar to Jane's self-effacing modesty, Darcy wouldn't have noticed her. How the devil was Caroline supposed to know Darcy enjoyed having lively discussions about subjects quite unsuitable for a woman or, worse, didn't object to having his opinions publicly challenged?

Caroline retired as soon as she reasonably could, anxious to avoid Louisa's well-meaning empathy. The very last thing she needed was to be pitied. Solitude, albeit in this cramped chamber situated immediately above the noisy taproom, would allow her to prepare for the ordeal of the following day. Seeing Darcy would be both a pleasure and a torment. Seeing his new wife corrupting Pemberley with her forthright ideas and outspoken views would be pure torture.

Caroline wondered for the fiftieth time what she was doing here, and why she was putting herself through this nightmare.

Because, she supposed, the alternative would have been to remain alone at Netherfield, within range of Mrs Bennet's interference. Really, everywhere she turned she tripped over the wretched Bennets. Louisa was right. The only escape for Caroline would be through marriage. Louisa certainly appeared to have the best of both worlds – a bore of a husband to lend her respectability and the freedom to do as she pleased.

Caroline was now in the same category as Georgiana Darcy and, God forbid, Kitty Bennet – unmarried and generally presumed to be in want of a husband. She was a good few years older than Georgiana and Kitty and would soon become the focus of general pity if she didn't make an effort to get married. She suppressed a snort. Did her critics really imagine she couldn't have been married many times over by now had she chosen to accept one of her many suitors? She had rejected them all, waiting for the only proposal she was prepared to entertain, convinced it would soon be forthcoming.

Caroline trembled with rage as she recalled how Eliza Bennet, spawn of the devil that she was, had breezed into her life with her saucy tongue and lively wit and ruined everything.

She would never recover from the total humiliation she felt when obliged to sit in Longbourn's church, pretending to be pleased and excited as she watched her brother wed Jane *and* Darcy pledge himself to Eliza. She had felt a combination of sympathetic and triumphant glances being sent her way as she smiled until her face hurt, wishing all the while that the earth would open up and swallow her whole.

Perhaps she would follow Louisa's example, Caroline mused as her maid braided her hair. If she could only find an obliging male who took no interest in her activities, she would then be able to do as she pleased. The only difficulty with such a plan was that it would take her no nearer to becoming the mistress of Pemberley, which was the only position to which she aspired.

Caroline dismissed her maid and slid between the sheets, wondering what she'd done to be dealt such an unfair hand in life. *God helps them who help themselves*, was her last conscious thought before drifting into a disturbed sleep. She was through with being patient and would find a way to get the only thing she had ever wanted from life.

Somehow.

Otherwise, what was the point?

* * *

'Lizzy, oh Lizzy!' Lydia wailed. 'What are we to do?'

Lizzy shared a glance with Will over Lydia's head, unsurprised to observe that his body had become rigid with tension. Anger swirled in the depths of his eyes when only moments before they'd been alight with laughter. She could scarce blame him. Any reminder of Wickham sent him into a rage. Of all the times for Lydia to descend upon them, Lizzy thought despairingly. Still, she *was* Lizzy's sister, she was here, clearly upset about something, and Lizzy could hardly send her away again until she knew what had gone wrong.

She shot Will an apologetic shrug and closed her arms around her sister's shaking shoulders, tilting her head to indicate that Will should leave them alone. Lydia would never speak freely in front of him since even she, with her forthright character and self-centred attitude, was intimidated by Lizzy's formidable husband. Scowling, Will nodded, collected Georgiana and quit the room.

'Sit down, Lydia.' Lizzy took a seat in the corner of the settee and pulled Lydia down with her. 'Compose yourself and tell me what you're doing here.'

Lydia's eyes were red-rimmed, her blotchy features rendered ugly from crying. She was a fine actress and frequently fell back on that skill when there was something she desired. Lizzy could see that this time her sister was genuinely upset and her dramatic appearance was no act. She'd never set foot in Pemberley before, and its splendour ought to have both intimidated and delighted her. The fact that she hadn't made a single comment about her salubrious surroundings, and didn't appear to have even noticed them, confirmed Lizzy's suspicion that a serious rift had already occurred in Lydia's hasty marriage.

'Are you here alone?' Lizzy didn't imagine Wickham would have the gall to encroach upon Pemberley, but she needed to be sure.

'Yes, don't worry. I'm all alone.'

'Then have some tea.' Lizzy nodded her thanks to Simpson as he delivered the tray and quietly withdrew. 'And tell me what brings you here in such a state.'

'Wickham's left the regulars,' she blurted.

'What!'

'Soldiering doesn't suit him after all.'

Lizzy did her very best to contain a sigh. It was a difficult ambition to achieve. 'I'm very sorry to hear it. Presumably, he made alternative arrangements to earn a living before selling the commission that Mr Darcy went to so much trouble to purchase for him.'

'There's no need to emphasise your husband's charity.' Lydia's attempt at superciliousness was spoiled when she sniffed rather inelegantly. 'I'm sure it's less than he deserves, given that he was old Mr Darcy's favourite.'

Lizzy wasn't sure of any such thing. Lydia clearly still didn't know the truth and, for Georgiana's sake, she was glad. Georgiana's fragile self-confidence had blossomed since Lizzy had married her brother, but Lizzy could think of few subjects more qualified to knock her back than her unfortunate history with Wickham.

'You still haven't explained what you're doing here, Lydia. We're expecting a houseful of guests tomorrow.'

'Well, I'm sorry if my life falling apart interferes with your social plans,' she cried dramatically.

This time Lizzy's sigh defied her best efforts to hold it in. 'Tell me it all,' she said with commendable patience.

'Wickham's gone to London. He's decided to talk to friends about resurrecting his career in the law.'

Lizzy wasn't aware that his legal career had been anything other than a passing fancy. As far as she knew, there was nothing to resurrect, but she refrained from saying so.

'Why did you not remain in Newcastle until he sent for you?'

'If we're to remove to London, there was no point in keeping up the cost of lodgings.'

In other words, they'd left a string of debts behind them, but trying to get Lydia to admit it would be a waste of breath.

'Wickham will send for me when he's established himself.'

'Forgive me, Lydia, but I find this surreal. You just assumed you could come here, knowing we were about to entertain, and remain indefinitely?'

'You *are* my sister. I would have gone to Jane since Hertfordshire is closer to London, but she's coming here so it seemed sensible to do the same thing.'

'Without bothering to inform me?'

'We left in a hurry.' Lydia focused her gaze on her folded hands. 'There was no time for letters.'

Which confirms my suspicions about debts. 'Then you should have gone to Longbourn.'

'I'll be no trouble.'

'Lydia, if things are as well arranged with Wickham's new career as you imply, why all the drama and tears? Why are you here at all, for that matter?'

'Can I not visit my newly married sister?'

'Lydia!'

'Well, I... There was some unpleasantness, if you must know. Wickham was falsely accused by a brother officer of...' Lydia broke off, fresh tears swamping her eyes. 'I can't tell you. It is too wicked an accusation to bear repeating.'

'Mr Darcy will need to know.' Lizzy fixed her sister with a firm look, in no mood for her histrionics. 'Would you rather tell him yourself, or have me act as your intermediary?'

'Wickham wouldn't have touched the horrible woman!'

'Ah, now I understand.'

Lydia's body stiffened. 'You sound as though you believe Wickham was in the wrong.'

Lizzy was perfectly sure that he must have been. 'Wickham was invited to sell his commission and save the reputation of the lady in question, to say nothing of the regiment's good name?'

Lydia tossed her head, her tears no longer in evidence. 'If you put it like that.'

Lizzy took a moment to digest what she had just learned. Of all the abominable timing! She was anxious enough about the house party without having Lydia's worries visited upon her too. Still, she couldn't very well turn her away. Will wouldn't be best pleased, but what else could she do? He had been more than generous of his time and fortune in covering up Lydia's shocking elopement and arranging her marriage. He was unaware that since then, Wickham had frequently applied to her and Jane for additional funds. Perhaps Lizzy had been wrong to help her sister in such a way, encouraging her to think the Darcy largesse was limitless.

In some respects, Lydia couldn't be blamed for that. She had been spoiled and indulged by their mother since the day she was born, and knew nothing of economy. Vitally, she also didn't know the true reason for Wickham's rift with Will.

She therefore had every reason to suppose her sister would be sympathetic to her plight. Lizzy *did* feel for Lydia, but she also felt for herself. She had so wanted to make this party a success and prove to her critics – namely Miss Bingley – that she was well able to manage her new home. Will would be furious when he learned all his efforts on Wickham's behalf – efforts that had been so distasteful for him – had already crumbled.

Lizzy dreaded telling him but knew the moment couldn't be delayed. She rang for Mrs Reynolds and had Lydia installed in a chamber in the west wing, far away from the family rooms. She then took a deep breath and sought out Will in his library.

He looked up when she walked in and smiled a devastating smile, all the annoyance she had seen in his eyes when Lydia appeared no longer evident.

'Not the sort of intrusion you need today of all days,' he said sympathetically.

Lizzy flashed a wan smile. He was always so intuitively understanding. She did not deserve him. She walked around to his side of the desk. Anticipating her, he pushed his chair back, and she fell onto his lap. His arms circled her waist, and his lips pecked delicately at her neck.

'My family are such a trial to you.'

'You make it all worthwhile.'

'Don't you even want to know why Lydia's here?'

'I'd much rather kiss you.'

And Lizzy would much rather be kissed, but what she had to tell her husband overcame even that desire.

'Wickham has quit the regulars,' she said abruptly.

'Hmm, I thought it might be something like that.'

His mild reaction stunned her. 'And you are not angry that he has so quickly thrown your generosity back in your face?'

Will shrugged. 'I know him too well to waste the energy it requires to get annoyed.'

'It seems he was encouraged to sell his commission. Something to do with an inappropriate liaison with another officer's wife which, of course, Lydia claims is impossible.'

Will's lips quirked. 'Well, at least she is proving to be a loyal wife.'

'Wickham has taken himself off to London to make enquiries about the career in the law he once aspired to.'

'And chose his moment to leave.'

'What do you mean?'

'I dare say he's left a trail of debts in Newcastle.'

Lizzy sighed. 'Yes, that thought occurred to me, too.'

'Wickham would also have known from Lydia's correspondence with you and Jane that we were planning this party.'

'Ah, now I understand you. Will, don't do that.' She tapped the hand that had drifted towards her breasts. 'I can't think coherently when you distract me so.'

Will chuckled. 'There's not much to think about. We are stuck with your sister for the duration of the party, and there's an end to the subject. Wickham made sure of that by sending her here at this time, knowing you would use your feminine wiles to persuade me to let her stay.'

Lizzy laughed. 'I haven't had to try very hard.'

He sent her a flirtatious glance. 'Ah, but I haven't been persuaded, yet.'

She playfully thumped his arm. 'Then I must work upon my conniving ways.'

'Certainly you must, but I ought to warn you that I'm a difficult person to influence.'

'Is that so?' She canted her head and regarded him from beneath a fringe of lowered lashes. 'Then it seems only right that you should give me a few hints about how to succeed.'

'Where would be the fun in that?'

The long fingers of one hand tangled with the curls at her nape as he put pressure on her neck, persuading her to lower her head so he could claim her lips. Given his very understanding attitude, Lizzy decided obliging him was the least she could do.

'I don't wish to see Georgiana overset by the mention of Wickham's name,' Lizzy said when her husband finally stopped kissing her.

'Nor shall she be. I'll reassure Georgiana. I assume Lydia doesn't know about—'

'No, she doesn't.'

'Right. Then Lydia will behave herself when she's beneath my roof simply because she is too afraid of me to do anything else. I shall glare at her if she sets one foot out of line.'

Lizzy laughed. 'That ought to do it, but what of afterwards? We have no idea how long Wickham will be detained in London, or how long it might be before he remembers he has a wife.'

'Let us face one hurdle at a time. We'll get the party out of the way and then decide what to do about your sister.' Will's hand rested protectively over Lizzy's stomach, as though he sensed her secret. 'Are you all right, my love? You look a little pale.'

Lizzy laughed. 'Lydia is enough to make anyone pale.'

'Go up to your room and rest,' he said, putting on the stern husband voice that thrilled but failed to influence her. 'I shall wake you before dinner.'

'Well, in that case...' She slid from his lap and walked towards the door. 'I look forward to being woken,' she said, sending him a speaking look over her shoulder.

3

Lizzy and Will stood together beneath Pemberley's grand entrance portico. Lizzy felt a contradiction of nervousness and anticipation grip her as she observed the carriage bearing the first of their guests wending its way up the long driveway.

'You look charming.' Will's eyes burned with the hot intent Lizzy was starting to recognise. 'And far too distracting. What madness persuaded me to open up my house when I could be spending my time far more profitably alone with you?'

Lizzy smiled. 'You always seem to know when I need reassurance.'

'Do I?' Will elevated one brow, looking genuinely surprised. 'Is that what I am doing? I must take your word for it since I have never known you to be unsure of yourself before now.'

Lizzy glanced down the winding drive and saw a second carriage closely following upon the heels of the first. She shuddered, beset with a whole array of unsettling feelings now that their guests were almost upon them, and she would be firmly in the spotlight for the next week. She expected, at any moment, to be asked what she thought she was doing, pretending to be a grand lady capable of running such a vast establishment, when really she was nothing more than a shameless interloper.

She was perfectly sure at least one of their guests would be asking herself the same question. Miss Bingley would doubtless watch Lizzy like a hawk, ready to criticise the moment she put a foot wrong. That realisation strengthened Lizzy's resolve. She glanced up at her handsome husband, his dark eyes still reflecting his wicked thoughts, and felt reassured. Will loved her passionately, and proved it to her every night with increasing inventiveness. Lizzy had become accustomed to falling asleep in the circle of his arms afterwards. Will explained that he saw no reason to disturb her by quitting her bed, and so the linens in his own chamber were seldom slept upon.

Will had come a long way from being the rigid, fastidiously correct, rather arrogant gentleman she had met and so disliked in Hertfordshire. He was now the caring, thoughtful, and intensely passionate husband she adored. He might not show his feelings for her in public, but Lizzy knew they ran deep. That knowledge would just have to sustain her through the vicissitudes of the coming sennight.

'I can see that you're going to force me to admit to my shortcomings,' she said, 'so I might as well confess I'm petrified, shaking like a leaf. I'm sure half your friends are only joining us so they can criticise your choice of a wife.'

'In which case, they will no longer be friends of mine.'

'Thank you.' She sent him a sparkling smile. 'But by not denying their intentions you have only succeeded in reinforcing my argument.'

'Say the word and I'll send them all away again.' The corners of his lips lifted into a deliciously tempting smile. 'I am perfectly sure they will understand.'

'I very well might,' she replied mischievously.

Georgiana joined them, looking vibrant and fresh in pink sprigged muslin. Lizzy linked her arm through the younger woman's, pleased that Lydia's unexpected arrival didn't appear to have overset her. There was a new-found maturity about her new sister, for which Lizzy claimed partial credit. She had taken considerable trouble to get to know Georgiana, who had blossomed like a flower beneath Lizzy's open friendliness.

'Ready?' she asked.

'Actually, I'm looking forward to it. Entertaining at Pemberley no longer frightens me since the lot of hostess now falls to you.'

'You don't escape that easily.' Lizzy smiled as she wagged a finger at Georgiana. 'I'm relying on your help.'

'Helping is very different from having to make all the decisions.'

Will's smile encompassed them both. 'The two of you are a formidable pairing. I fail to understand why you are so nervous.'

The first carriage rattled to a halt. It saved Lizzy the trouble of trying to explain to a man who'd been born into a position of wealth and privilege just how frightening it was for someone of Lizzy's ilk to take up the mantle of hostess at such an imposing establishment as Pemberley. Georgiana had been born to it as well, of course, but didn't possess her brother's forthright character and so better understood Lizzy's nerves.

Will's servants – *her* servants too, she reminded herself – ran to let down the steps and Lizzy's fears gave way to a gasp of pleasure when the first person to emerge from the conveyance was Mr Bingley. He waved to them good-naturedly and then held out a hand to his wife. Lizzy broke free from Will and Georgiana, ran lightly down the steps and straight into her sister's arms.

'Jane, you're here!'

'Lizzy!'

The sisters embraced, laughing, crying and talking all at the same time. This was the first occasion upon which they had seen one another since their wedding day six months previously. They were diligent correspondents, and so Lizzy was fully aware of her sister's activities, but had still missed her dreadfully and rejoiced to see her looking as lovely as ever.

'You look well,' Jane said, pulling back and eyeing Lizzy critically.

'Thank you, as do you. Married life clearly suits you.'

Jane smiled. 'I believe it does.'

'Mr Bingley.' Lizzy curtsied and allowed one of her hands to be clasped by both of Bingley's. 'Welcome to Pemberley.'

'It's certainly grand,' Jane said in an awed tone, glancing up at the imposing building. 'Are you getting to grips with being its mistress yet?'

'It took me a full month to find my way around without getting lost,' Lizzy admitted.

Jane laughed. 'I'm sure it must have.'

Kitty emerged from the carriage more decorously than Lizzy would have anticipated. Jane's influence was clearly rubbing off, reinforcing Lizzy's regret at Lydia's unexpected arrival. Her youngest sister's depressed mood was unlikely to stand the test of time now that she had an ally in Kitty. It would be a pity to see all Jane's hard work undone, and Lizzy vowed not to allow that situation to arise. Lydia would behave herself while at Pemberley or suffer the consequences.

Will and Georgiana joined them, more hugs and greetings were exchanged and, caught up in the excitement of her family's arrival, Lizzy could no longer keep track of what was said by whom. Lizzy relaxed, until the second carriage pulled up and the Hursts emerged from it, Miss Bingley on their heels. Lizzy's heart lurched. Why she was so wary of the woman, she couldn't have said. Even someone as self-centred as Caroline Bingley must realise she could no longer pursue Will. But she had seen one of their neighbours in

Hertfordshire make a considerable nuisance of herself when the gentleman she had set her heart on failed to return her regard. God forbid that Miss Bingley's nature was similarly vindictive. Not that there was anything she could do to cause trouble, but still...

Lizzy was secure in the strength of Will's affection for her. She blushed as she recalled the robust manner in which he'd reminded her of it the previous night. But what was apparent to her wouldn't necessarily be so to outsiders. She knew Miss Bingley would be watching her, ready to either criticise or interfere, according to which course of action would show her in a better light. Lizzy gave herself a mental shake as she squared her shoulders and stepped forward to greet the new arrivals. Perhaps she had got it wrong, had done Miss Bingley a disservice, and perhaps her mental perambulations were merely the result of her own paranoia. She would give Caroline Bingley the benefit of the doubt and wait to see how things developed.

'Miss Bingley,' she said, offering the lady her hand. 'You are very welcome to Pemberley.'

'Thank you, Mrs Darcy.'

The antipathy in her adversary's tone, the grudging manner in which she pronounced her name, and the way in which she almost flinched when Lizzy welcomed her to Pemberley, caused Lizzy's fledgling hopes of a truce to wither.

So be it.

Pleasantries completed, Lizzy gave her attention to the rest of the new arrivals. She glanced at Will and inwardly groaned. His relaxed pose hadn't slipped with Bingley and Jane's arrival, and the distant expression he more habitually wore in company was firmly back in place. She could see Miss Bingley had noticed, and his aloofness appeared to afford Lizzy's nemesis some satisfaction if the tight smile she struggled to contain was anything to go by.

Oh, Will!

Matters weren't helped when they entered the drawing room and Lydia made another of her dramatic entrances. Lizzy sent her a scolding glance, but Lydia pretended not to see it.

'Lydia!' Kitty's eyes flew wide. 'Whatever are you doing here?'

Lizzy chanced a glance at Will. He was standing in front of the fireplace, in conversation with Mr Bingley and Mr Hurst. He looked detached and gave no outward sign that he had even seen Lydia walk into the room. But Lizzy knew better. The infinitesimal tightening of his lips made his anger with Lydia apparent, at least to her. When the matter of their guests' arrival had been mentioned at dinner the previous night, Lydia had agreed to remain in her chamber until sent for, and Will had heard her make that promise. Lizzy had wanted to warn Kitty of their sister's presence and caution her against being pulled into any of Lydia's schemes. Lizzy should have known better than to imagine Lydia would keep her word.

'I have come to stay for a short time,' Lydia replied, embracing Kitty. 'What fun we shall have. It will be quite like old times.'

Not if I have any say in the matter.

'Mrs Wickham.' Miss Bingley fixed Lydia with a gaze of candid appraisal that caused Lizzy's heart to sink. 'This is indeed a surprise.'

'Miss Bingley.' Lydia greeted her cheerfully but had nothing further to say to her. 'Kitty, you must tell me all about your activities since we last met,' she said, leading her sister aside. 'And I have so much to tell you.'

Tea was brought in, and the ladies took their seats. As Lizzy poured, she noticed Miss Bingley's self-satisfied smile whenever her glance happened upon Kitty and Lydia, still with their heads together, giggling as they spoke to one another in exaggerated whispers. Lizzy inwardly sighed, taking comfort from the fact that at least Lydia hadn't attempted to pull Georgiana into their conversation.

'Miss Georgiana,' Miss Bingley said. 'I long to know how your performance on the pianoforte progresses.'

'I believe I have made a little headway since Lizzy arrived at Pemberley, Miss Bingley.' Georgiana smiled at Lizzy. 'We practise together most days, which makes it much more fun. And my brother loves to listen to us.'

Lizzy noticed a shadow pass across Miss Bingley's eyes. The conversation moved on to more general subjects, and Miss Bingley didn't try to single Georgiana out again.

'Who else are you expecting to arrive today, Lizzy?' Jane asked.

'Colonel Fitzwilliam and two of his fellow officers should be here before dinner,' Lizzy replied. 'Our aunt and uncle Gardiner will be here tomorrow.'

'Officers?' Lydia's head shot up from her conversation with Kitty. 'How jolly.'

Lizzy didn't need to glance at Miss Bingley to know she would be looking impossibly smug at Lydia's inappropriate response. Lydia was Lydia still – barely seventeen, married for almost a year, and yet still a child in so many respects, with no proper idea of how to behave in good society.

'What news from Longbourn, Jane?' Lizzy asked, desperate for a change of subject.

Jane smiled. 'I bring letters from Mama along with our father's very best wishes. Mary is obliged to put aside her books and bear Mama company now that Kitty spends so much time at Netherfield.'

Lizzy smiled. 'That comes as no great surprise. Mama has never cared for her own company.'

Jane smiled. 'I don't think Mary finds the change as disagreeable as she would have us all believe.'

'I'm sure she does not. Mary always did spend far too much time with her nose buried in a book. It cannot be good for her.'

General conversation brought the tea interval to a close, and Lizzy's guests dispersed to rest before dinner. She was alone with Jane at last, and the two sisters could finally talk openly.

'Tell me about Bingley,' Lizzy said, smiling. 'I can see the two of you are very happy together.'

Jane beamed. 'Indeed, we are.'

There was a slight wariness in Jane's eyes.

'And, yet?'

'Well, Charles is thinking of purchasing an estate in this part of the country. Indeed, he's already made enquiries and plans to look at a few places while we are here.'

'Oh, Jane, that would be wonderful! The only part of married life I dislike is the lack of your society.'

'Yes, I feel the same way about not being able to run to your room and tell you about my day.' Jane smiled. 'I had not realised how much I'd come to depend upon your wisdom and sound advice until it was no longer there.'

'Wisdom?' Lizzy offered her sister a self-depreciating smile. 'I would hardly describe myself as wise. Outspoken, impetuous, self-opinionated, quick to judge perhaps, but—'

'Lizzy!' Jane laughed and threw up her hands. 'It's me you're talking to.'

'And so I need hardly remind you how quick I was to judge Mr Darcy and brand him aloof and unfeeling.' Lizzy shuddered, adding softly, 'I was so wrong about him.'

'I can see that you are genuinely happy just by looking at you, although he still looks very severe.'

'It's just the way he seems in public.' Lizzy felt heat invade her cheeks. 'I can assure you he's very different in private.'

'Well, that's all right then.'

'I assume Netherfield's close proximity to Longbourn is one o
your husband's main reasons for wishing to remove himself from
the district.'

Jane grimaced. 'Yes. Mama will insist upon calling almost ever
day. Her persistence is even starting to wear upon Charles's eas
going nature.'

'Well, if it means that you will remove to the north then I an
glad for it.' Lizzy wrinkled her brow. 'Perhaps if you live so far awa
from town, Miss Bingley and the Hursts will remain in London.'

'Possibly, although I don't mind them spending the majority o
their time with us.'

No, Lizzy thought, *you're far too sweet-natured for it to bother you.*

'I feel particularly sorry for Caroline. Louisa has her ow
household—'

'But doesn't seem to spend much time in it.'

'No one of consequence is in London at this time of the year.'

Dear Jane! 'Yes, but even so.'

'Caroline, on the other hand, has had to give way to me as he
brother's hostess and really has nothing much to do with it herself.

'The same could be said of Georgiana.'

'Georgiana is younger than Caroline and, I think, she i
delighted to make way for you. It's different for Caroline, but she'
been very good about it.'

Lizzy suspected that Jane knew of Caroline's attachment to Wil
but didn't feel able to raise the subject. Lizzy had no intention o
making it any more real by doing so herself.

'Miss Bingley could do worse than find herself a husband.'

'Lizzy!' Jane opened her eyes wide and then laughed. 'You hav
certainly changed your tune. I remember a time, not so very lon;
ago, when you were extremely averse to the idea of marriage jus
for the sake of it.'

Lizzy laughed as well and patted Jane's hand. 'Very true, but suspect few other young ladies in England share that view. Certainly not Miss Bingley.'

'Perhaps not, but I have never heard Caroline talk of the subject, and I don't feel I can raise it myself for fear of making her think I want rid of her.'

'Of course you cannot.'

'What is Lydia doing here?' Jane asked after a short pause in the conversation.

Lizzy explained the reasons for their sister's unexpected arrival.

'Oh dear God!' Jane clasped a hand over her mouth. 'Wickham is behaving like a cad so soon after their marriage. Lydia doesn't deserve that.'

And I don't deserve to have Lydia foisted upon me, not now of all times. 'No, Lydia for all her faults doesn't deserve to have a philanderer for a husband.'

'Poor Georgiana. I assume Lydia knows nothing of her history with Wickham.'

'No. Mr Darcy and I have both reassured Georgiana that she has nothing to fear from Lydia's presence here. Darcy is being munificent in allowing Lydia to remain for the time being, but Wickham knows better than to set one foot on the Pemberley estate, and we have made sure Georgiana is aware of that.'

'Do you imagine Wickham has abandoned Lydia altogether?'

'Darcy and I spoke of the possibility last night but think it unlikely. If he still aspires to a gentleman's occupation then he must acknowledge his wife, even if he doesn't spend much time with her.'

'Poor, foolish Lydia.' Jane shook her head. 'Still, she was determined to have Wickham.'

'And now we must finance her lifestyle. It seems a year of marriage hasn't done much to improve her sense of responsibility or maturity.'

Jane flashed a wry smile. 'Did you really imagine that it would?'

'No, unfortunately her character too closely mirrors our mother's for there to be any possibility of that.'

'Yes, that's true.'

'Still, there is good news. I've barely had a chance to speak with Kitty, but I can see vast differences in her manner just by looking at her.' Lizzy smiled. 'You're to be congratulated, Jane. You've worked wonders on her.'

Jane shook her head. 'Thank you, but I can hardly claim any credit for that. You know as well as I do that Kitty is a follower.'

'And now the only example she has to follow is yours and your Mr Bingley's.' Lizzy sighed. 'Let's hope Lydia doesn't undo all your good work.'

'Poor Lizzy. You have to entertain your guests *and* ensure that your sisters behave themselves. This ought to be a time for triumph, not anxiety.'

Lizzy frowned. 'Triumph?'

'You attracted one of the wealthiest and most eligible bachelors in the country. You have every right to feel triumphant.'

'Yes, I suppose I do.' Lizzy sighed. 'Don't worry about Lydia. She is too afraid of Darcy to step out of line.' Lizzy eyed her sister more closely. 'But enough of this gloomy talk. Let us consider your situation instead. Do I imagine things, or is there something different about you, Jane?'

Jane's responding smile was radiant. 'We are not telling anyone yet, but you have obviously guessed our secret, and so—'

'Oh, but that is wonderful!' Lizzy threw her arms around Jane. 'I am so happy for you. How far along are you?'

'Not very, otherwise Charles wouldn't have permitted me to travel. It's one of the reasons why he wants to settle the matter of his estate as quickly as he can.'

'You know very well your secret is safe with me.' Lizzy thought about her own suspicions and was tempted to confide in Jane. What pleasure it would give Lizzy if the two of them went through their first confinements together. However, telling her now, when she wasn't even sure herself, would be akin to stealing her sister's thunder, and so she remained silent on the point. Besides, Will ought to be the first to know – when there was anything for him to actually be told. 'Now, come along, Mrs Bingley, you ought to go up and rest. We shall have plenty of time to catch up, especially if you're planning to stay in the district after this party.'

'Yes, Charles is going to ask Mr Darcy if we could remain here for a few days when everyone else leaves.'

'Oh, I would love that.'

'Yes, so would I.'

Jane had no sooner left the room than Will rejoined Lizzy there.

'You ought to be taking some time for yourself as well,' he said sternly.

'I am not in the least tired,' she replied, smiling up at her husband.

Will pulled her to her feet and into his arms. 'Nevertheless, as your husband I know what is best for you.'

Lizzy threw back her head and laughed. 'Heavy-handed tactics won't work with me.'

'But my hands most certainly will.' He brushed one across her derriere, causing her to gasp. 'Point proven, I believe.'

'Mr Darcy, need I remind you that there's a time and a place for everything?'

Will's eyes lit up with laughter and something more fundamental – a deep, yearning desire that stole Lizzy's breath away. 'I was about to remind you of the same thing. Your reaction to the slightest connection with my hands isn't quite the thing, you know. I was never more shocked.'

Lizzy bit her lower lip, trying hard to appear contrite. 'Then perhaps your suggestion of a rest before dinner isn't such a bad one.'

'Huh-hum.' Simpson stood in the open doorway, discreetly clearing his throat. Lizzy turned in Will's arms, looking for the cause of the interruption. It wasn't the first time he had come upon Mr and Mrs Darcy embracing in one of the public rooms, but Lizzy was still embarrassed to be caught and removed herself from the circle of Will's arms.

'What is it, Simpson?' Will asked.

'Colonel Fitzwilliam, Major Halstead and Captain Turner have arrived, sir.'

'Excellent. Show them in.'

Lizzy was truly delighted to receive Will's cousin, a gentleman whose society she had always enjoyed.

'Colonel Fitzwilliam.' She offered him her hand when he walked through the door and he bowed in front of her. 'It is a great pleasure to see you here.'

'And a greater pleasure for me to see you again, Mrs Darcy. May I make my friends known to you? I have the honour of presenting Major Halstead and Captain Turner.'

Lizzy curtsied to the gentlemen, appraising them as she did so.

'Your servant, ma'am,' Halstead said, bowing over her hand.

Will was already acquainted with both gentlemen and had told her that Halstead was in a similar position to his cousin – he was the younger son of a gentleman and obliged to make his own way in life. He was perhaps thirty years of age and easy on the eye with his shock of light hair, sparkling blue eyes and a happy manner of address.

'Welcome to Pemberley, sir.'

Lizzy turned her attention to Captain Turner. Lizzy had been told this gentleman's father was actually Lord Turner, the younger son of an earl. Thanks to a forward-thinking paternal grandfather, he had independent means but still chose to take the King's shilling. Less fortunately, he didn't share his friend's easy manners or good looks. Stiff and formal, with a long nose and weathered face, he bowed over Lizzy's hand and spoke with a slight stammer.

'Too k-kind of you to invite me, ma'am.'

Life wasn't fair, Lizzy thought as she had Simpson show the gentlemen to their chambers and then repaired to her own. Halstead had all the manners and allure to make himself agreeable but would be obliged to marry for reasons of financial expediency. Turner had plenty of money but none of Halstead's physical attributes or natural charm. No wonder he sought to hide himself away in the military. He probably felt more secure in all-male company. She thought of Mr Hurst, who could certainly be classified in a similar group to Halstead, except he had none of Halstead's charm or good looks. Even so, he had managed to attract an heiress of Louisa Bingley's standing. Perhaps there was hope for Captain Turner yet. Lizzy got the impression that he was shy, but the right woman would probably draw him out of himself.

'I'm turning into my mother,' she said aloud, smiling as she realised she'd just mentally paired off Miss Bingley and Turner. 'I'm also turning into the world's greatest optimist,' she added.

4

The party reassembled on the terrace before the dinner hour. It was a fine enough evening for Caroline to be able to dispense with her shawl, thus providing her with the opportunity to display her new shimmering, yellow silk evening gown to its best advantage. Hopefully her host would approve both her taste and good figure. He had been deprived the opportunity to enjoy both of those pleasures during the months of his marriage, to say nothing of intelligent and stimulating conversation.

Colonel Fitzwilliam and his friends had arrived during the afternoon, and Caroline couldn't decide if that was a good thing. She enjoyed the colonel's society and liked what she had seen so far of his friends. Their impeccable manners confirmed their status as gentlemen, and their presence lent much-needed sophistication to a party dominated by inconsequential Bennets.

Had their arrival been delayed, Caroline would have enjoyed the opportunity to observe Eliza performing her duties as hostess with only her immediate family around her. Lydia Wickham would have felt less inclined to behave herself under such circumstances. Not that her current behaviour could actually be described as seemly. Mrs Wickham batted her lashes at Major Halstead, talking over anyone's attempts to join their conversation as she demanded particulars of his regiment's deployment. It was an unsuitable topic of conversation that clearly made the major uncomfortable, but he appeared too well-mannered to rebuff her.

Eliza Bennet – Caroline refused to think of her as Eliza Darcy and only addressed her by that name when she couldn't avoid doing so – had noticed her sister badgering Major Halstead and clearly wasn't happy about the situation. More to the point, Darcy had seen it also. He looked so handsome, yet so remotely severe, that Caroline's heart went out to him. This situation was his own fault, but he wasn't the first man to fall victim to lust, and the consequences of his folly far outweighed his impulsive actions. Even his aunt, Lady Catherine de Bourgh, had apparently disowned him. Caroline understood she had given him ample warning of her intention to do so if he went through with the infamous marriage, and yet such was Eliza's influence over him that he married her anyway. Act in haste, repent at leisure, Caroline thought vindictively, still unable to understand what Darcy saw in the rather ordinary woman who was now his wife.

Unfortunately, Caroline didn't know the particulars of Darcy's dispute with Wickham and had long been curious about the reasons for it. Wickham had grown up at Pemberley but was no longer welcome there, and Darcy refused to recognise him. It could only be a matter of time before Lydia mentioned her husband's name publicly, even though everyone had so far studiously avoided raising it, further arousing Caroline's curiosity as to the nature of that gentleman's crimes against Darcy. She sipped at her peach ratafia in a contemplative frame of mind, deciding that she really ought to find out. Knowledge was power, and if she was in possession of all the facts, who knew where it might lead her?

Caroline was surprised to notice Kitty Bennet not following her younger sister's lead. The two of them had been hellions before Lydia's marriage, which hadn't taken place long enough ago for that situation to have changed. And yet, instead of joining Lydia in her inquisition of the handsome major, Kitty was conversing quietly with Captain Turner.

It was obvious to Caroline that the captain was uncomfortable in mixed company, but whatever Kitty had said to him appeared to have drawn him out, and she noticed him visibly relax. Caroline took personal credit for that situation. Kitty had virtually lived at Netherfield since Charles's marriage to Jane. As she'd continuously been in Caroline's and Louisa's company, it was inevitable that their good manners would rub off on Kitty and her conduct would improve. Curious to know what subject occasioned such animated conversation, Caroline moved closer to the pair.

'I d-do assure you, M-Miss Bennet, it would be n-no hardship.'

'But I understand the gentlemen are planning a fishing expedition tomorrow, Captain Turner. I would not have you miss the sport for my sake.'

'I d-don't m-mind at all. Fishing h-has never enthralled me.'

'Well then, I shall accept your company with pleasure. I am sure my sister will be able to provide us with all the materials we require. Miss Darcy is fond of drawing.'

Ah, that would explain it. Kitty showed a little talent for sketching – a talent that was ignored while Lydia still bore the name of Bennet, apparently, since the girls had more pressing matters to engage their attention. Jane had encouraged Kitty to pick up her charcoal again, and even Caroline had grudgingly admitted that she possessed some skill. How clever, Caroline thought, drifting away from the pair without interrupting their discourse. Captain Turner was independently wealthy. He was also reserved and nothing to look at, but if Kitty sought a husband to keep her in style, then she acted wisely in avoiding the handsome yet impecunious Halstead, saving her smiles for Turner.

It grieved Caroline to even think it, but Kitty would be deemed an acceptable match, mainly due to her older sisters' advantageous marriages. She briefly considered putting herself between Kitty and Turner. If pushed to choose between them, Turner couldn't fail to prefer Caroline. She had more sophistication, poise and conversation in her little finger than Kitty possessed in her entire body. Then again, if Kitty did manage to secure Turner, it would be one less Bennet hanging around Charles's establishment.

No... let Kitty do her worst. Caroline wasn't in the market for a husband. Instead she owed it to Darcy to help him extricate himself from the mess he had foolishly landed himself in. That thought took her by surprise since she hadn't been aware that she had made a conscious decision to actually do anything about his unhappy situation. It had just been a possibility, but seeing Darcy so unhappy made it impossible for her not to rescue him.

Darcy was briefly alone, staring sightlessly across his gardens, hands clasped behind his back. Caroline hadn't yet had an opportunity to exchange a single word with him in private, and she hastened to alter that situation.

'It's unpardonable to have serious thoughts with a houseful of guests, Mr Darcy,' she said in her most agreeable tone. 'For a deep thinker such as you are, and with your intellect, that must be a torment.'

'I deserve no such compliment, Miss Bingley, since my thoughts were entirely mundane. I was wondering, you see, about the arrangements for our fishing expedition tomorrow.'

'But surely that is your keeper's responsibility?'

Darcy had turned to face her, but she could sense he was still keeping half his attention on the rest of the party. His eyes seldom strayed far from his wife, but that only reinforced Caroline's deci-

sion to liberate him. Even the most impartial observer could not
have been fooled into believing he was looking upon her with a
tolerant eye. Obviously, he was afraid she would say or do something to embarrass him. Eliza happened to glance towards him at
that moment and smiled. Darcy did not return the gesture, making
do with a curt nod. Caroline chose to interpret that as an encouraging sign, which helped to quell the jealousy she felt at the sight of
the superb emeralds decorating Eliza's throat and ears. She had
seen those same jewels worn by one of Darcy's ancestors in the
portrait gallery here at Pemberley. The thought of them now being
owned by a mere Bennet filled her with anger.

She stole another glance at Darcy's fierce countenance,
convinced she was right to assume he already regretted his hasty
marriage. What precisely could she do to help him extricate
himself from it? While there was no child to complicate matters –
Caroline had taken careful stock of Eliza's figure and was satisfied
she wasn't yet increasing. That being the case, anything was
possible if one had the will, the funds and, most importantly of all,
the support to bring it about.

She glanced again at Lydia Wickham and a germ of an idea
took root in her brain.

'Indeed it is, but one must still ensure the correct instructions
are given.' Darcy appeared to collect himself and offered her a half-
smile. 'Tell me, how did you leave our acquaintances in Hertfordshire?'

'Sir William and Lady Lucas dined just before we left. Their
delight in Mrs Collins's baby daughter knows no bounds.'

His expression darkened and Caroline regretted mentioning
the Collinses. It had obviously caused Darcy to think about the rift
with his aunt, which hadn't been her intention. She searched her
mind for a different subject, but before she came up with anything,
others joined them and the opportunity was lost.

Louisa appeared beside her and the two of them watched Lydia Wickham's conduct with smugly superior smiles. She was getting increasingly loud, frequently drawing the attention of the rest of the party to her and causing poor Darcy to frown in her direction. Halstead repeatedly tried to instigate a conversation with Georgiana, but Lydia was having none of it. Georgiana's attention was eventually claimed by Kitty and Turner.

'Marriage has done nothing to improve Mrs Wickham's conduct,' Louisa remarked, looking down her nose at the offending party.

'I wonder what brings her here. Has Jane mentioned anything to you, Louisa?'

'No, not a word, but I do know she was not expected.'

'Poor Darcy!'

'What's done is done.' Louisa waved away a footman when he approached them with a tray of glasses filled with champagne. 'Anyway, why are you so interested in Mrs Wickham?'

Eliza summoned everyone to the dining room, saving Caroline from the trouble of forming a response. Louisa would have been shocked if she knew Caroline intended to befriend Lydia Wickham. She needed to discover everything she could about Wickham's rift with Darcy so she could use it to create a rift of her own – between Darcy and his fine-eyed wife.

* * *

Why, oh why did Lydia have to descend upon them now of all times? Lizzy had feared Caroline Bingley's scathing disapproval but would now gladly settle for that as her only source of discomfort. Seeing the manner in which her nemesis so enjoyed Lydia's unbecoming conduct tore Lizzy's confidence to shreds, especially since she agreed with Caroline's opinion. The party Lizzy had anticipated mostly pleasurably was rapidly turning into a disaster.

But Lizzy was nothing if not resilient. What couldn't be altered had to be endured. It may not be obvious to anyone else in the room, but she knew she had Will's unmitigated approval and support. With that thought in mind, Lizzy straightened her shoulders, determined not to disappoint him, and oversaw the seating of her guests. She had placed Jane on Will's right, Mrs Hurst on his left. She was seated at the foot of the table between Mr Bingley and Colonel Fitzwilliam. She was fiercely determined not to put herself through the ordeal of Mr Hurst's non-existent conversation. She had once had the misfortune to be seated beside him at Netherfield. Upon discovering she preferred a plain dish to a ragout, he lost all interest and had nothing more to say to her. Her culinary tastes had not changed, and she doubted whether Mr Hurst's social mores had improved.

Deciding where to put Lydia had caused her considerable consternation. Fortunately her arrival made the numbers uneven and there was one additional lady in the party. That gave Lizzy the perfect excuse to seat Lydia beside another female. Thus Lydia found herself between Mr Hurst and Miss Bingley. When Lydia discovered this, she cast Lizzy a censorious glance which Lizzy chose to ignore.

Lydia had only been with them for a day but had already broken her firm promise to behave with decorum. The manner in which she had flirted with Major Halstead before dinner had been deplorable, and Lizzy could tell from Will's features, taut with disapproval, that he had noticed too. No doubt Caroline Bingley thought that disapproval was directed at Lizzy. Dear God, whoever said married life would be easy?

The sound of refined voices conducting polite conversation,

and the fact that the meal was superbly prepared and served, helped to sooth Lizzy's jaded spirit. She toyed with her own food, her insides rebelling at the thought of actually eating anything. Lizzy was unsure whether that was because of her suspected condition, or if it could be attributable to nerves. Charles Bingley engaged her in light conversation and Lizzy gave him her attention, forcing herself to stop obsessing over his sister's opinion of her. The two of them didn't like one another and there was an end to the matter.

'I hear my friend Charlotte Collins is enjoying motherhood,' she remarked to Mr Bingley.

His smile lit up the room, causing Lizzy's own lips to quirk. He and Jane were so transparent in their delight at the prospect of parenthood, their secret wouldn't remain… well, a secret, for long.

'I believe so,' he replied. 'Sir William has a great deal to say on the subject.'

'And does Lady Catherine approve? You must forgive me for asking, but she no longer acknowledges my husband, so my only news of her opinions must come through my correspondence with Charlotte and through Longbourn.'

Mr Bingley dipped his head. 'I'm given to understand Lady Catherine is free with her advice when it comes to child-rearing.'

Lizzy rolled her eyes. 'That I have no difficulty in believing.' She paused to sip at her wine. 'Lady Catherine and I are not the best of friends, but it grieved me when she put Mr Darcy in the position of having to choose between us.'

'She'll undoubtedly come round.'

'Yes, I dare say she will.' Lizzy flashed a wan smile. 'But will Darcy?'

'Lizzy, will there be dancing later?'

Lydia's loud enquiry caused all conversations to cease. It wasn't done to speak across the table, much less shout down half its length. Lydia had always behaved thus at Longbourn, ignoring Jane's and Lizzy's efforts to improve her manners. Lizzy had briefly relaxed in Mr Bingley's undemanding company, but now Lydia's faux pas had spoiled the mood and all her uncertainties returned. She dealt Lydia a severe glance, but her sister merely shrugged.

'I only wished to know,' she said peevishly.

Lizzy glanced at Will. His features were set in stone, as was the frown that decorated his brow. Worse, Miss Bingley had noticed and was making no effort to hide her self-satisfied expression.

'Do you still enjoy dancing, Mrs Wickham?' Miss Bingley asked. 'I recall the ball we threw at Netherfield at which you danced every dance.'

'Oh yes, I love dancing above all things. My, how long ago that ball seems, and how much has happened since.'

'How long do you plan to remain at Pemberley, Mrs Wickham?'

Lizzy quietly seethed. Caroline Bingley was doing this deliberately, hoping to make Lydia blurt out the circumstances of her removal here and mention Wickham's name. If she was so very attached to Will, why go out of her way to discompose him? The answer was obvious. Lydia's bad manners reflected upon Lizzy, painting her in an unflattering light. Lizzy hadn't thought Caroline to be quite as vindictive as all that.

'Oh, I am not too sure. A week or two, I suppose. I am waiting here for now until I hear from—'

Lizzy, seeing everyone had finished eating, hastily rose to her feet.

'Shall we, ladies?'

The rest of the ladies followed suit, and Lydia's response was drowned out by the sound of chairs scraping across the floorboards. The gentlemen stood as well, as Lizzy led the ladies from the room. She passed Will's place at the head of the table, and he sent her a reassuring smile accompanied by the ghost of a wink. Glad as she was for his reassurance, a small part of her brain demanded to know why he couldn't do such a thing in Miss Bingley's sight.

'Kitty,' Lydia said as the ladies took tea in the drawing room, 'perhaps we could go into Lambton tomorrow? I saw the dearest little milliner's shop we ought to visit.'

'No, Lydia,' Kitty replied with more maturity than Lizzy would have given her credit for possessing. 'You must exclude me from the excursion. I am engaged to do some sketching with Captain Turner.'

'Captain Turner?' Lydia looked scandalised. 'But he is not the least bit handsome.'

'Lydia!' Lizzy and Jane cried together.

'Well, it is true,' Lydia said with a casual shrug.

'But he is a good artist, apparently. Will you join us, Georgiana?'

'Thank you, Kitty, but no. I have a music lesson in the morning.'

Once the ladies started to chat amongst themselves and before the gentlemen joined them, Lizzy took Lydia aside.

'Remember where you are, Lydia,' she said sternly, 'and the promises you made.'

Lydia widened her eyes, her astonishment apparently genuine. 'But I have kept my promise and not once mentioned Wickham's name.'

'That is the *only* part of your promise you have stuck to. How many times have Jane and I told you that you simply do not shout down the length of a dinner table?'

'Oh, that.' Lydia flapped a hand. 'I forgot.'

'Well, please don't forget again. And if you want to go into the village, talk to me about it first. A carriage *is* required to transport you there, and one cannot just be summoned out of thin air.'

'But you must have hundreds of them.'

'Which are not necessarily at your disposal. Besides, you don't have the funds to visit milliners' establishments.'

'You have changed, Lizzy.' Lydia's expression became accusatory. 'You have so much, but you are not the least bit generous with your relations.'

Lizzy sighed. Had she really supposed Lydia would pay heed to her? 'No more flirting with Major Halstead,' she said sternly, turning back to the rest of the party. 'You are a married woman, and you bring shame upon your entire family with your behaviour.'

'You are so strange. It is as though I no longer know my own sister.'

'Nor will you have the opportunity to know me if you continue to behave so loosely. Mend your ways or Wickham will not be the only member of your family barred from Pemberley.'

Lydia gaped. 'You would not be so heartless.'

'Obey my rules and you are welcome to stay.' Lizzy paused, determined to get through to her headstrong sister. 'For now.'

Lydia's lower lip protruded in a manner Lizzy recognised from their childhood. Lydia was not getting her way and was considering throwing a tantrum. Lizzy hoped common sense would prevail, because she was perfectly serious in her threat. If Lydia's behaviour didn't improve, Lizzy would not scruple to send her on to Longbourn. Their mother was responsible for Lydia's unconventional attitude. Let her deal with the results of it.

The gentlemen rejoined them, and the card tables were placed. Lydia managed to inveigle her way onto Major Halstead's table, but Lizzy joined that table also and kept her sister's more boisterous outbursts under control. Lizzy hated every minute of it. It was as though Lydia and Miss Bingley between them were deliberately testing her. Her disposition wasn't helped by the fact she felt permanently queasy. She wanted to ask Jane if that was a symptom of her condition too, but she could hardly do so without giving her own suspicions away.

By the time the evening broke up, well after midnight, she was exhausted and a headache threatened.

5

As soon as Lizzy dismissed her maid, Will slipped through the door that connected their two chambers.

'I'm so sorry about Lydia,' she said immediately. 'I really am trying to keep her under control, but she still appears to be very much a law unto herself.'

'You did really well tonight,' Will said at the same time. 'I was so very proud of you.'

Lizzy widened her eyes, aware that Will never paid false compliments. 'How can you say that after Lydia made it such an agony?'

In shirtsleeves and breeches, his feet bare, Will seated himself on the side of her bed and sent her a devastating smile. He ought to smile more often, she thought for the thousandth time. It lit up his entire face, enhancing his handsome features and dispelling the remote expression he habitually wore. She went to him and sat on his lap.

'Lydia's behaviour is not your fault.' He slid an arm around her waist and pulled her body against his torso. 'If our guests don't like it, then they are perfectly welcome to leave.'

Lizzy wrapped her arms around his neck and sank her fingers into his thick hair, her headache and nausea all forgotten. 'What have I done to deserve you?'

'You are my sanity, Lizzy.' He buried his face in her neck, his words now muffled but still intelligible. 'My life was incomplete until you came into it. You have taught me so much about myself I never would have discovered otherwise.'

Lizzy laughed, embarrassed by praise she did not deserve. 'Sometimes ignorance is bliss.'

'Nonsense.' His lips played with her earlobe. 'Seeing you in my mother's emeralds tonight, I was never more proud.'

Lizzy had found the jewels on her dressing table that afternoon when she went up to change. She gasped when she opened the case and saw the exquisite stones sparkling back up at her. She had never seen finer emeralds, much less imagined wearing them. There was a note with them in Will's hand, explaining that they had been in the family for generations and that tonight, on the first occasion when they would entertain as a married couple, it would give him great pleasure to see Lizzy wearing them.

'I have still not thanked you properly for them.'

'An unpardonable oversight that requires immediate rectification.'

Lizzy slanted him a flirtatious gaze. 'Yes, but how?'

Will laughed. 'Let me refresh your memory.'

He claimed her lips in a deep incendiary kiss that fuelled her hunger and caused a vortex of desire to surge through her. Helpless against the raging force of her need for him, Lizzy responded with passion, conscious of his hands greedily running down the length of her torso, coming to rest in their favourite place on her breasts. Those breasts were very sensitive nowadays, and she flinched when he closed his hands on them. He immediately broke the kiss and looked at her askance.

'Did I hurt you, my love?'

'Not in the least.' The urge to admit her condition was compelling, but now was not the time. He was so protective of her, she wouldn't put it past him to call the entire party off and send Lydia back to Hertfordshire. 'It is just that I forgot for a moment everything you have taught me about being patient.'

He quirked a brow. 'You require another lesson?'

'Apparently so.' She smiled up at him. 'Did Mr Bingley tell you he plans to purchase an estate in this area?'

His hands returned to her breasts, more gently this time. 'Yes, I knew he was considering the possibility. I made some enquiries on his behalf and have pointed him in the direction of a couple that might suit.'

'You didn't mention anything about it.'

'I thought it better not to excite your anticipation until he made up his mind. But it seems he's now quite set on the idea and wants me to look at the places with him.'

'Of course he does!'

Will laughed. 'I know what you're thinking. He *is* capable of making his own decisions, otherwise he would not be married to your sister after all the opposition—'

'Ah, but you withdrew your opposition before he offered for Jane.'

'True enough.' Will had the grace to look embarrassed. 'But anyway, Bingley values my opinion.' One of his hands slid beneath her nightgown. 'You will enjoy having Jane close by.'

'Of course I shall.'

'And Kitty, too? I won't object to her spending time up here with us if her behaviour continues to improve.'

'Jane must take the credit for that. She's even persuaded her to take an interest in sketching again. She and Captain Turner are planning to set up their easels beside the lake tomorrow.'

'Turner's a good man.'

'Yes, I have taken a liking to him too. He's very shy, because of his stutter I suppose, but Kitty has shown great maturity in realising it and drawing him out.' Will's magical hands worked slowly up her thighs, causing Lizzy to throw back her head and moan. 'Will, please!'

'Yes, my dear?' He raised a brow in innocent enquiry. 'Is there something you desire?'

'Actually, now that you mention it, I cannot think of a single thing.'

Will laughed, his eyes alight with wicked humour. 'Then perhaps I should remind you.'

'Perhaps you should. I am clearly not an attentive student.'

Lizzy had no one she could ask – their own mother hadn't said a word to her and Jane on the subject on the eve of their wedding – but she was fairly sure husband and wife did not traditionally enjoy one another's bodies in the nude. But Will would not have it any other way. On their wedding night he had come to her, pulled her into his arms and kissed her with such fiery passion that it had caused her knees to buckle and her head to spin. He had then told her that he wanted to feel her skin against his, warning her that he would never tire of the feeling.

'Whatever happens between a man and his wife in the sanctity of their bedchamber is no one's business but their own,' he had told her. 'And I promise you, my darling Lizzy, I will never harm you, and I will never do anything that repulses you.'

'Am I supposed to enjoy this?' she had asked. 'A woman's marital obligations are to be endured, are they not?'

Will had chuckled, a deep throaty sound she had not heard him utter before, as alien as it was welcome. 'I shall feel like a failure if you take no pleasure from it.' He had wagged a finger at her. 'And don't imagine you can fool me. I shall know if you're cutting a sham.'

Thus far he had kept his word, taking the trouble to explain what he was doing to her every step of the way, encouraging her to respond in accordance with her body's dictates. She shed her inhibitions and did so, and so far he had given her nothing but the most unimaginably exquisite pleasure.

Lizzy wasn't surprised when her nightgown was removed, swiftly followed by her shift. Naked, her hair already slipping from its braid, she sat on the edge of the bed, watching her handsome husband step out of his clothes. Another shiver of anticipation coursed through her as she drank in the sight of his glorious chest adorned with a matt of black curling hair, muscled thighs, and lower – always lower. Hair tumbling across his brow, he cursed beneath his breath when his toe caught in his breeches and caused him to stumble. A kernel of sensation, primitive and acute, gripped her as Will lifted her from the bed and into his arms. She wrapped her legs around his torso and met his lips, melting as his tongue, velvety and sensuous, cut a path through her mouth.

'Has anyone ever told you, Mrs Darcy,' he asked, his voice thick with urgent passion, 'that you are more tempting than you have any right to be? I can't be in the same room as you without anticipating possessing you.'

'I yearn for you.' She breathed in the musky scent of his arousal, closed her eyes and floated on a wave of endless sensation. 'More than you could possibly know.'

'Prove it to me, my love,' he replied, laying her on the bed and covering her body with his much larger one, trailing hot kisses down her belly. 'Never stop proving it to me.'

That, she wanted to tell him, was a given, but she was so taken up with the things he was doing to her that she had no breath available for speech. Perhaps, she thought dreamily, things would work out for the best after all. Even Lydia or Miss Bingley couldn't break the indefinable thing that bound the two of them together more closely than mere wedding vows ever would.

Could they?

* * *

George Wickham died a little inside when his opponent turned over the ace of hearts, but he kept his expression impassive. Of all the damnable luck! He was so sure he had this hand, and he had bet his last sovereign accordingly. The ace was *the* only card that could have defeated him. What were the chances of it being in his adversary's hand? Coulton had to be cheating – no one's luck held the way his had this evening – but Wickham knew better than to accuse him without proof.

'Back luck, Wickham,' Coulton said insincerely, scooping up his substantial winnings – winnings Wickham had been relying on to keep him out of dun territory for several more months. 'Want an opportunity to get your revenge?'

Wickham would have liked nothing better, but he had no funds left to gamble with. 'Another time,' he said as languidly as he could manage around the virulent anger that clogged his vocal chords.

Wickham left the gaming hell and ventured out into the night, resigned to the long walk from Mayfair to Whitechapel, where he was lodging with Mrs Younge. He didn't even have the blunt for a cab. How could he have fallen so far, so fast? It was all Darcy's fault, of course, and Wickham would never forgive the man for cheating him out of the riches that the late, much lamented, senior Mr Darcy had always intended to visit upon Wickham. Just because he had not troubled himself to write those wishes down, his son assumed he could disregard them. Well, he had chosen the wrong man to swindle, and Wickham would find a way to gain his revenge if it was the last thing he ever did.

When he heard Lizzy was to marry Darcy, he tried to suppress his jealousy, consoling himself with the thought that his fortunes would improve in the wake of hers. As he trudged back to Whitechapel, he thought about Elizabeth Bennet, as she'd been when he first met her, and his dire mood lightened. Her lively personality, sparkling wit and outspokenness had drawn Wickham towards her, and he had been as close to actually falling in love with her as he had ever come with any woman before or since. If things had been different... But once again, Darcy had usurped him and married the woman whom Wickham himself would have claimed had it not been necessary to enhance his fortunes through marriage.

Miss King would have suited him perfectly, but her wretched grandfather put paid to his ambitions by spiriting her out of Wickham's reach. How he finished up united with Lydia was still a puzzle to him, but he *was* married to her, and now that her sister was the mistress of Pemberley, it was starting to make sense. The fates had thrown Lydia at him as a means to push for his rights, which was precisely what he intended to do. Wickham flexed his jaw in grim determination. He would use Lydia's connection to Lizzy to get what was rightfully his from Darcy, or die in the attempt.

It ought to have been obvious to anyone who knew him that Wickham was too sensitive for soldiering – he was no strategist and felt nauseous at the sight of blood – so why the devil had Darcy purchased him a commission in the regulars? He had already turned towards the army when Darcy interceded, that much was true, but only as a result of desperation. Darcy had spitefully bestowed the living that had been promised to him elsewhere, and so Wickham had to support himself somehow. A friend had suggested the army, and… well, it had been a huge mistake.

The only alternative left to him now was the law. He would rather enjoy standing up at the Old Bailey, cutting a dashing figure as he used his wits to successfully prosecute villains. And so, he had come to town to make enquiries, but it appeared the crown had no need of green prosecutors, and his only option was to defend. That was all well and good if one's clients had the ability to pay for one's services, but those who could pay could also afford the most experienced. Only the desperate would turn to Wickham in their hour of need, and he was in no mood to work for charity.

None of the gentlemen of his acquaintance offered him any prospect of employment, nor did they seem inclined to invite Wickham and his wife for a prolonged visit. They were however more than willing to relieve him of his blunt at the gaming tables and had lost no time in doing so.

And so another avenue was closed to him, he thought bitterly as he trudged through increasingly narrow, grimy, unsafe streets. He noticed shadows moving, following him. Everyone was on the lookout for easy pickings in this world, Wickham thought bitterly, but they would be ill-advised to attack Wickham in his current frame of mind. As though sensing it, the shadows evaporated, and he returned to Mrs Younge's dingy dwelling without mishap.

'No luck at the tables?' she asked by way of greeting.

'I have not been playing,' he lied.

'Of course you haven't.' Mrs Younge rolled her eyes. 'What will you do with yourself now? You can't stay here indefinitely.'

As if he would wish to remain in this hovel. 'My wife is at Pemberley. I have a fancy to join her there.'

Mrs Younge blew air through her lips. 'You won't get past the gatehouse.'

'No, but I still have friends in Lambton. I shall repair there and make contact with my wife. Then we shall see what we shall see.'

'Don't go up against Darcy again. You had your chance with his sister and made a mull of it. He's got your measure now.'

Perhaps that was true, but Wickham didn't have any alternatives. 'Has Molly returned?'

'Don't go thinking to dip your wick there. If you want her, you pay, just like everyone else.'

Mrs Younge ran a string of girls out of her Whitechapel dwelling, and made a good living from them. Molly was the best of the bunch, and very partial to Wickham's attentions. He had yet to pay for any woman's services and certainly didn't plan to start now. With no other alternative available to him, Wickham retired to his chamber and went to bed, doing his best to block out the sights and sounds of the east end of London. His last conscious thought before drifting into an uneasy sleep was of Lizzy Bennet, and the way she had looked the last time he saw her, shortly before her marriage to Darcy.

It seemed he and Darcy were destined to fight over the same spoils. They had similar tastes in most things, especially in women. As any gambler worth his salt would tell you, no losing streak went on indefinitely. The stakes had never been higher, and it was beyond time that Wickham's bad luck came to an end. He would get the better of Darcy and earn the money and respect that was his by right, even if he had to use Lizzy to do it.

6

Lizzy awoke feeling satiated and rested, albeit slightly nauseous. The only indication that she had spent the night wrapped in Will's arms, using his broad chest as a headrest, was the slight indentation in the pillows next to her and a lingering aroma that was uniquely male. Lizzy stretched and smiled up at the bed's canopy, wondering how she could allow Caroline Bingley, or even Lydia, to discomfort her when she was the most fortunate woman in the world to have such a caring, compassionate, and violently passionate husband.

Not one to linger in bed, unless Will was on hand to keep her there, Lizzy was up before her maid came in to pull back the curtains.

'It's another fine day, ma'am,' Jessie said cheerfully. 'Shall I bring your breakfast tray up immediately?'

'Thank you, Jessie. And I shall wear the pale blue muslin this morning.'

'Oh, but I thought—'

'I am saving the new gowns for when I am more likely to be seen in them.'

Jessie bobbed a curtsey. 'I'm sure you know best.'

Jessie bustled off, leaving Lizzy with a smile on her lips. Jessie seemed scandalised by the fact that on the first full morning of her house party, Mrs Darcy chose to wear a gown that predated her wedding. What her maid couldn't possibly know was that Lizzy's confidence was sorely in need of a boost, a requirement that could best be achieved through the good offices of a well-cut new gown, but there was no point in wearing such a garment when there was no one about to admire it.

'Stop it!' Lizzy said to her reflection, aware that her thoughts had already drifted towards Miss Bingley, who wouldn't dream of putting in an appearance downstairs this early. 'How silly you are being.'

But Lizzy couldn't help herself. She would take luncheon in a favourite old gown that reminded her of how far she had come each time she gazed down at its familiar floral design.

When she ventured downstairs, the gentlemen had already departed on their fishing expedition. Of the ladies there was, as Lizzy had anticipated, no sign. She welcomed the prospect of an hour or two of privacy in which to consult with Mrs Reynolds over the day's menus and to discharge the myriad other duties that fell to her lot.

'Thank you, Mrs Reynolds. Your suggestion of a cheese soufflé at luncheon is inspired. What would I do without you?'

'The old Mrs Darcy adored soufflés, ma'am,' Mrs Reynolds replied with a distant smile. 'It will be quite like old times.'

'I love them too, but are you sure it won't be too much effort for Cook? It will not be easy to cook so many and have them ready all at the same time.'

'I am sure she'll rise to the challenge, ma'am, and I dare say Mr Darcy will appreciate the gesture.'

'Yes, let's hope so, and please express my gratitude to Cook.'

Mrs Reynolds smiled. 'She will appreciate that, ma'am.'

Lizzy enjoyed doing small things at Pemberley to remind Will of his late mother, settling any lingering doubts he might otherwise have had about her ability to run the house efficiently. She had gone out of her way to cultivate Mrs Reynolds' good opinion from the outset, wise enough to know she would not last five minutes without that lady's help. Her efforts appeared to have paid off, and Mrs Reynolds did everything she could to ease Lizzy's path, correcting any small errors she might make with discreet suggestions rather than scornful disdain.

Lizzy cast a final eye over the menus for the entire day and nodded.

'Has a chamber been prepared for Mr and Mrs Gardiner?'

'Yes, ma'am. Everything's in order.'

'In that case, I shall let you get on.'

Mrs Reynolds had only just left her when Lizzy heard footsteps in the hall.

'Lizzy, are you there?'

'In the small parlour, Kitty.' Lizzy looked up from the letter to Charlotte Collins that she had been endeavouring to write for two days and smiled at her sister. Kitty looked fresh and quite pretty in checked pink muslin, a decorated straw bonnet sitting on top of her curls, a sketchpad and charcoals clutched in one hand. If Lizzy wasn't much mistaken, Kitty had gone to considerable trouble to tame those curls that morning. Ah, so her interest in Captain Turner extended beyond sketching. Lizzy had wondered about that. Hopefully her interest was genuine and not pecuniary. Knowing the sheer bliss of loving one's husband and being loved in return, Lizzy wished for similar felicity in marriage for her two unattached sisters. 'Are you ready for your sketching?'

'Yes.' Kitty wrinkled her nose, looking unsure of herself. 'I hope Captain Turner doesn't think me a fraud. Jane would keep telling him at dinner last night that I have talent. Naturally, she's biased, and I'm afraid she has over-emphasised my abilities.'

'Kitty, you know very well you are a competent artist and have nothing to feel ashamed about. It is just that you haven't bothered to employ your skill for a while.' Lizzy laughed. 'Sketching is something one can either instinctively do or one cannot. I don't have an artistic bone in my body, but *you* most assuredly do.'

The conversation put Lizzy in mind of a similar one she had shared with Lady Catherine de Bourgh, Will's aunt, when she had met the formidable lady in Kent the previous year while visiting Charlotte Collins. Lady Catherine had enquired into every aspect of Lizzy's life, and that of her sisters', thinking she had the right to pry. When asked if any of them drew, Lizzy had said they did not. That wasn't precisely true, since Kitty certainly showed great promise as an artist. However, she had stopped drawing, preferring to join Lydia in her pursuit of officers, and Lizzy had no wish to explain any of that to Lady Catherine.

'Oh no, it's easy to learn to draw,' Kitty said. 'There is absolutely nothing remarkable about it.'

'I disagree. Drawing isn't like playing the piano, which anyone can do, albeit badly, with determination and enough practice. Artistic ability is a gift.'

'I don't really know why I stopped drawing when I have always enjoyed it so much. Anyway, I'm glad I have taken it up again and have something to occupy my time with.'

'And what of Captain Turner?'

'He seems very nice. I felt sorry for him when we were first introduced. He seemed so awkward and nervous, and I know how that feels.'

Lizzy quirked a brow. 'You?'

'Yes.' Kitty laughed. 'I know it probably never looked that way, but Lydia always made me feel invisible. She is so lively and forthright—'

'Which is not always such a good thing. Look where it's landed her.'

'What is happening with her and Mr Wickham?' Kitty placed her drawing supplies aside and perched on the edge of a couch. 'I tried to ask her about him when we were alone last night, but I might as well have saved my breath. You know how Lydia can be when she doesn't want to face a subject, and her determination to not talk about her husband worried me.' Kitty shrugged. 'Not so long ago we couldn't stop her rambling endlessly on about his attributes.'

'Lydia has made her bed, Kitty, and she must live with the consequences. Mr Darcy won't allow Wickham to come to Pemberley, and that's an end to it.'

'Why not?' Kitty frowned. 'I have always wondered about the animosity between them.'

'G-good morning, ladies.' Captain Turner entered the room, and it amused Lizzy to see Kitty's face turn pink. 'A f-fine day for sketching, is it not?'

'Indeed it is, Captain Turner,' Lizzy replied. 'I am ashamed to say I cannot draw to save my life, but I do believe the light is exactly right at this time of day for those of you who can. Do you have all the supplies you require?'

'Thank you, yes. I found everything I need waiting for me in the drawing room, just as you told me I would.' The captain picked up Kitty's supplies as well as his own. 'Shall we, Miss Bennet?'

'By all means. I shall see you at luncheon, Lizzy,' Kitty said, walking through the door on the captain's arm.

'Make the most of your morning.'

Lizzy enjoyed another half hour's solitude, actually making some progress with her letter, describing in detail how it felt to be hostess at Pemberley during her first house party. Charlotte was one of the few people with whom she could be completely honest, knowing her friend would respect her confidence.

Miss Bingley treats Mr Darcy just as she did before he married me, stopping just short of outright flirtation. It clearly peeves her to defer to me, and I don't think she has addressed me by my new name above once. She also watches me like a hawk, obviously hoping I will do or say something to anger Mr Darcy. I almost feel sorry for her, but at the same time her attitude worries me. You will think I am being foolish, or insecure, but it is as though she is not yet ready to give up her claims, either on my husband or on Pemberley.

Colonel Fitzwilliam arrived...

'Lizzy.'

Lizzy put aside her pen and smiled. 'Good morning, Jane. Did you sleep well?'

'Thank you, yes. Who could not in such a sumptuous chamber?'

'You look pale.' Lizzy examined her sister's face at close quarters. 'Are you all right?'

'Mornings are difficult for me at present, but I am told it will pass.'

'You feel queasy?'

'Yes, and the only remedy is to eat, but the thought of eating when one's on the point of casting up one's accounts is repellent.'

'Poor Jane.' Lizzy placed a comforting arm around her sister's shoulders. 'Come and sit down, and I shall ring for some tea. Will you be able to manage a cup?'

'Certainly. I feel better already, just at the thought of it.'

The sisters spent an agreeable time together, secure in the

knowledge that it was far too early to be joined by Caroline Bingley or Mrs Hurst. Thankfully, Lydia didn't appear either, and Georgiana was ensconced in the music room with her tutor. They talked of general things – Jane's secret desire for a daughter, even though her husband naturally wished for a son; the improvements in Kitty's behaviour; Mr Bingley's enthusiasm for an estate in Derbyshire – everything except Lydia's predicament, a subject Lizzy was happy to avoid.

Their discourse was brought to an end by the sound of wheels on gravel. The sisters were on the front steps by the time Mr and Mrs Gardiner alighted from their carriage, and they greeted their aunt and uncle with uncontrived pleasure.

'Lizzy!' Mrs Gardiner held her niece at arm's length and subjected her person to a close scrutiny. 'How well you look. And you too, Jane. I think married life must agree with you both.'

'With Pemberley to soothe my jaded spirit, how could it not?' Lizzy replied, eliciting a laugh from her relations.

'How was Scotland?' Jane asked, aware that their uncle and aunt were returning from a journey north of the border.

'Very cold, but interesting,' Mrs Gardiner replied. 'Mr Gardiner was able to carry out his business, but we were subjected to an exhausting round of social niceties too.'

'The hardest part was trying to understand what was being said to us,' Mr Gardiner told them, making everyone laugh.

'You do look tired, Aunt,' Lizzy said sympathetically. 'But you can relax now you are here and need do absolutely nothing, unless you wish to.'

'On the contrary, I want to know everything about this wonderful place,' Mrs Gardiner replied. 'We came here as visitors such a short time ago. Who would have imagined we would return and have our niece as our hostess?'

'Yes,' Lizzy replied, ringing the bell for refreshments. 'Sometimes I think it is all a dream, and I expect to wake up back in my own bed at Longbourn.'

'I think Mr Darcy would have something to say on the subject if you tried to run back there,' Mrs Gardiner replied, smiling.

'I took you seriously when you suggested a pony cart to see the entire estate, Aunt,' Lizzy continued, 'and we shall do precisely that as soon as you have recovered from your journey.'

'Thank you, Lizzy, that is very thoughtful of you.'

They hadn't been seated in the drawing room for more than five minutes before Lydia burst upon them. Lizzy had not had an opportunity to warn her aunt and uncle about her being there. She saw surprise and then concern flit across her aunt's face.

'Are you surprised to see me here, Aunt?' Lydia asked boisterously.

'It is a complete shock,' Mrs Gardiner replied. 'Whatever brings you to Pemberley?'

'I thought it would be such a lark to surprise my sisters, and it worked a treat. They were totally astonished.' Lydia laughed and clapped her hands. 'You should have seen Lizzy's face.'

Mrs Gardiner was too well-manned to grimace. 'I can imagine,' she said, sending Lizzy a sympathetic smile.

'Kitty is here as well,' Lizzy explained. 'She has gone out sketching with one of our guests, Captain Turner.'

'I am glad Kitty's taken up sketching again,' Mrs Gardiner said. 'She has a natural talent for it.'

'I agree,' Lizzy replied. 'And I dare say we shall see the fruits of their labours at luncheon.'

'It is such a shame for Kitty that it should be Captain Turner who enjoys sketching rather than Major Halstead,' Lydia said. 'The captain isn't at all good looking, but Major Halstead most certainly is.'

'You are a married woman, Lydia,' Jane said. 'You should not be making such observations, certainly not out loud.'

Lydia brushed aside Jane's criticism with a careless wave of her hand. 'If I can't speak my mind in front of my family, when can I?'

'Sometimes it is much better to keep one's thoughts to oneself,' Lizzy replied with asperity. Not that she had much expectation of Lydia doing so.

'Where are the gentlemen?' Mr Gardiner asked.

'They are fishing this morning, Uncle, but will return for luncheon. This afternoon I have other activities planned.'

'What activities, Lizzy?' Lydia had been prancing restlessly around the room, picking up objects at random and putting them down again.

'Put that down please, Lydia.' Lizzy winced as Lydia carelessly played with a jade box. 'It is very delicate.'

Lydia abandoned the jade with a casual shrug and took up a seat beside Jane on one of the sumptuous couches. 'My, what a grand place Pemberley is,' she said, as though she had only just noticed. 'Wickham grew up here, you know, but he never explained to me just how rich the estate was.'

'Lydia!' Lizzy and Jane cried in unison.

'Now what have I done wrong?' Lydia asked peevishly.

'We shall be taking tea on the lawns,' Lizzy said in response to Lydia's earlier question. 'We also have targets set up for archery and—'

'Oh, I am sure Major Halstead excels at archery,' Lydia said with enthusiasm. 'I shall ask him to teach me.'

Lizzy rolled her eyes at Jane. 'We also have pale-maille.'

'I have heard the name, Lizzy,' Mrs Gardiner said, 'but I'm not sure I am familiar with the game.'

'Oh, it is very simple.' Lizzy laughed. 'Even I can manage it. One must strike a round box ball with a mallet through a high arch of iron. Whoever manages it with the fewest blows, or at the number of blows agreed upon in advance, is the winner.'

'It sounds like fun,' Jane said. 'And much easier than archery.'

Mrs Reynolds was summoned to show the Gardiners to their room so they could refresh themselves before luncheon. Mrs Hurst and Miss Bingley appeared, but mercifully Lydia took herself off somewhere. It could have been awkward, but with Jane there to keep the conversation flowing, the interlude passed without incident.

The gentlemen returned at about the same time as Kitty and Captain Turner. Lizzy was delighted to see Will welcome the Gardiners with genuine-seeming warmth. He fell into easy conversation with her uncle about Scotland, which in turn led to a discussion about that morning's sport. It seemed the fishing had been a success and the party would enjoy tasting the catch at dinner that evening.

'Nothing like fresh trout to tempt the appetite,' Colonel Fitzwilliam said.

Kitty and Captain Turner's sketches were admired. Lizzy didn't have to pretend to be impressed with Kitty's skill. Will looked over her shoulder and nodded his approval.

'You have the perspective exactly right,' he said, causing Kitty to beam and blush simultaneously.

'Perhaps,' she replied, 'but the lily pads are all out of proportion. They look more like stepping stones than floating pond life. Captain Turner made a much better job of them.'

'N-no, Miss Bennet, a-absolutely not.'

Lizzy left the artists to their amicable squabble as she organised her guests for luncheon. The meal passed without incident, and when it was over Lizzy repaired to her chamber to rest before changing for the afternoon. She felt tired, her courses still had not arrived, and she had an unsettled stomach that allowed for the ingestion of little food.

She lay on her bed, feeling mildly elated at having survived the morning without any major mishaps. Even so, she couldn't seem to shake a feeling of impending doom. Putting her fears into writing in her letter to Charlotte made them so much more real somehow.

She mentally berated herself. Everything here at Pemberley was elegant, peaceful, and meticulously organised. Nothing could possibly happen to spoil it. Will's good opinion was the only thing Lizzy craved, and no matter what stunts Lydia pulled, she knew she had it, even if Will did not make his devotion apparent to all and sundry. And yet, her unsettled feeling endured, making her tense and heralding the return of the previous night's headache.

All the reasoning and self-adjuration in the world, it seemed, couldn't prevent Lizzy from feeling that she was living on borrowed time.

One hour later, she strolled onto the terrace on her husband's arm. Lizzy had selected a new afternoon gown of bronze muslin edged with Flemish lace – a colour Will had once admired on her. He did so again.

'I approve of your gown, Mrs Darcy,' he said as they closed the distance between themselves and their guests assembled beneath the shade of an ancient oak tree, 'but do not think I haven't guessed at your strategy.'

She sent him a sparkling smile. 'And what strategy would that be, sir?'

'You mean to distract me, imagining my mind will be too full of the treasures you've concealed beneath the gown's clinging lines to pay proper attention to the games we are about to play.' He drilled her with an intense gaze. 'Are you so desperate to win, madam?'

'Only your approval.'

He squeezed the fingers that rested on his arm. 'That you are assured of always having. You own my heart, as you very well know, but I will still have to chastise you later for being such a tease.'

Lizzy's own heart soared. 'Your argument defeats itself since you have yet to administer a chastisement that meets with my disapproval.'

'Then I shall just have to be more inventive.'

'Give me a clue as to your intentions,' she said, a warm feeling sweeping through her body when he emitted a decidedly predatory chuckle.

'Where would be the fun in that?'

Absorbed by their cluster of guests, Lizzy and Will were separated. Everyone seemed to be soporific, and little interest was expressed in the games Lizzy had devised. Desultory conversations were conducted in low tones in order not to waken those who chose to doze, principally Mr Hurst. Lizzy was delighted when Colonel Fitzwilliam proffered his arm and invited her to stroll around the lake with him.

'We have not yet had an opportunity to enjoy one another's company,' he said. 'As our hostess, your attention seems permanently engaged.'

'I hope you do not mean that as a criticism, Colonel,' Lizzy replied, placing her hand on his sleeve, having opened her parasol to protect her complexion from the strong afternoon sun.

'Not in the least.'

'I'm relieved to hear you say so. If you want to know the truth, this party has me giddy with apprehension.'

'You?' He stopped walking and looked at her with open surprise. 'Why ever should it? You are very good at what you do, Mrs Darcy. Never doubt it for a moment.'

'I feel as though everyone outside of my immediate family is waiting for me to put a foot wrong, just so they can say they always knew it would happen. I am perfectly sure they think Darcy has made a grave error and are just waiting for a chance to say how sorry they are for him to have been taken in by me.'

Colonel Fitzwilliam laughed aloud. 'I can assure you, no one feels that way. Goodness, even the weather has fallen in with your plans.'

Lizzy glanced around the beautiful grounds, bathed in warm sunshine, and smiled. It was true. The rain that had beset the area for the previous month had disappeared and left crystal clear skies in its wake. The gardens looked at their very best, a quintessentially English scene. Bees lazily pollinated the flowers, the birds chorused their joy, and butterflies chased one another.

'It is kind of you to say so, about people's opinion of me, I mean, but I am not so easily convinced.'

They walked on for a while in companionable silence. 'My cousin is a lucky man,' the colonel said, so quietly Lizzy barely heard him. She was both surprised and embarrassed by the compliment. She and Colonel Fitzwilliam had been attracted to one another when they'd met in Kent, it was true, but she had not realised his admiration endured.

'Thank you.' She smiled up at him. 'But tell me, since we last met, have you had any success in fixing your affections on a suitable lady?'

'Ah, what I would give for a wealthy wife who is fair of face, intelligent of mind, *and* willing to put up with me.'

Lizzy laughed. 'Now who is not looking at himself in a proper light? You don't need me to tell you, Colonel, that any number of ladies would feel privileged to receive your address.'

'Since you raise the subject, there is one who has been encouraged to expect it,' he said with a grim twist to his lips.

'Really?' Lizzy paused, aware there was something not quite right about the colonel's reaction. If he had fixed his interest upon a lady, why was he not more enthusiastic about her? Unless... 'Ah, Miss de Bourgh?'

'Precisely.' The colonel's lips were now pulled into a taut grimace. 'My aunt, being in a high dudgeon with Darcy because he dared to defy her, has decided to make me the favoured nephew.'

'I am sorry to be the cause of your trouble.'

'Think nothing of it. The changes you have wrought in my cousin in six short months are nothing short of remarkable.'

'Can you actually see any changes in him? I can, of course, but in public he appears as severe as ever.'

'Rome wasn't built in a day, Mrs Darcy.' The colonel offered her a distracted smile. 'But alone with me, and men like Bingley with whom he's comfortable, the differences are impossible to miss.'

'I rejoice to hear you say so. My one purpose in life is to make Mr Darcy happy and not have him regret his decision to marry me.'

'That he will never do.'

They had reached the far side of the lake and paused to admire the delightful prospect. The water shimmered in the afternoon sunshine, the occasional dragonfly making barely a ripple as it skimmed its surface. Lizzy gasped with pleasure when a family of ducks made slow, stately progress across the torpid water, feathers shining with iridescent lustre, six babies following their parents in a neat row. One of the bolder ones tried to take the lead and was swiftly pushed back into his place by his siblings.

'They remind me of myself and my sisters leaving church when we were younger,' Lizzy said, laughing. 'There was a strict pecking order, pun intended, and woe betide her who forgot her place.'

The colonel smiled. 'It must be nice to be part of such a large family.'

Lizzy rolled her eyes. 'Only occasionally.'

As though sensing Lizzy's thoughts had stalled on Lydia, the colonel discreetly coughed and said nothing.

'So what of you, sir?' Lizzy asked as they resumed their walk, taking them past the summerhouse. It made Lizzy smile to think of it as such a lowly establishment when it contained several rooms and was larger than many of the cottages in Meryton. There was a walk-around porch with wooden railings painted white and glorious flower beds in full bloom on either side on the entrance steps. A fat robin sat on the railings, singing its heart out, and Lizzy paused to enjoy its song. 'Shall you follow your aunt's dictate and marry her daughter? It will give you financial security for the rest of your days. Rosings is an impressive establishment.'

'Indeed, and I have no objections to marrying Anne, I suppose. She would not necessarily be my first choice,' he said with a pointed glance in Lizzy's direction, 'but beggars cannot be choosers. But... no, I shouldn't say it.'

'Then let me anticipate you. You are thinking that if Lady Catherine would be obliging enough to take herself off to the dower house and leave you to run the Rosings estate as you see fit, the arrangement might work very well.'

'Quite, but the possibility of Lady Catherine ceding control is unimaginable.'

'Hmm, I see your difficulty. My opinion is that Miss de Bourgh could be quite interesting if she was separated from her mama and permitted to think and act for herself.'

'I agree, but as things stand...' He turned his full attention upon Lizzy. 'What would you do in my position, Mrs Darcy?'

What indeed? Lizzy was hardly the right person to ask. She wondered how he would react if he knew she had rejected Mr Collins's proposal because she didn't love or respect him, when by accepting him she would have secured her entire family's future. Selfish or selfless? Lizzy still wasn't sure which. She had then rejected Darcy, and all the advantages that union now afforded her, because she had misjudged his character and neither loved nor admired him in the way she now did.

'It is my opinion that Lady Catherine's bluster covers a raft of insecurities.'

The colonel's eyebrows disappeared beneath his hairline. 'Go on,' he said.

'Stand up to her, let her know you are a man to be reckoned with, and you will enjoy far greater felicity in your union with Miss de Bourgh. But,' she added, 'make sure you stand up to her and state your terms *before* the marriage takes place.'

The colonel smiled. 'You make it all sound so straightforward.'

'That's because I am not personally involved. I used to stand up to Lady Catherine and she hated me as a consequence, so perhaps my advice is not worth listening to.'

'On the contrary. Thank you, you have given me much food for thought.'

They had completed their tour of the lake and were returning to the rest of the party when Lizzy noticed Lydia interrupting Major Halstead's conversation with Georgiana in an effort to persuade him to help her with her archery.

'Oh Lord. Excuse me, Colonel Fitzwilliam, I ought to go and rescue the poor major before my sister disgraces us all.'

7

'Ah, here you are, Caroline. I have been searching all over for you. What on earth are you doing, buried away here? Are you feeling unwell?'

Caroline scowled at her sister for asking such a foolish question. 'Hardly buried,' she replied peevishly. 'I have always enjoyed the peace and quiet in this room.'

Louisa had found Caroline in the small conservatory that faced a pretty courtyard dominated by a fountain, beyond which was Pemberley's formal herb garden. Caroline had come across the room quite by chance the last time she had been at Pemberley. It was late morning on the third day of the house party and she had come here again, deliberately this time, in the hope of finding privacy, the better to indulge her resentful mood and rethink her strategy. Now Louisa had come in search of her and seemed determined to talk.

'The other ladies are in the drawing room. It is not polite to avoid their society.'

'I am not avoiding it.'

Well, that was not precisely true. She certainly had no wish to experience more of Eliza's artless behaviour and had kept out of her way as much as possible. The manner in which she deliberately emphasised her role as hostess when in Caroline's company was abhorrent. Still, what else could she have expected from one so lacking in the social graces? There was an air of desperation about Eliza's conduct, presumably because she knew Darcy's obsession with her was already on the wane. He was formal and assiduously correct in his behaviour towards her, treating her as though she was almost a stranger to him. Presumably Mrs Wickham's presence at Pemberley had reminded him of her lowly connections, if any reminder was necessary.

Caroline was unsure whether she felt sorry for him or took satisfaction from his disappointment. Not that her feelings were of any consequence. It was the reputation of the noble Darcy name that Caroline wasn't prepared to see besmirched, simply because its current guardian had fallen prey to a pair of fine eyes. Oh no, Caroline had strength, determination and common sense on her side, and she would employ those traits to help Darcy help himself. Gentlemen could sometimes be such children. Darcy, with his strong sense of honour, would definitely consider his mistake unfixable. Well, Caroline wasn't about to let him waste his life. If he cast Eliza aside, there would naturally be some scandal, but no one would blame Darcy – not if society understood he was the wronged party.

In order to save him, it would be necessary for Caroline to cultivate Mrs Wickham's friendship. She inwardly sighed, surprised at the lengths she was prepared to go to in her quest for justice. Inexplicably, her efforts with Mrs Wickham had so far met with failure. Well, not so inexplicable, when one thought about it. There were single gentlemen in attendance, and they had so far engaged all of Mrs Wickham's attention. And when the gentlemen were not around, neither was Mrs Wickham.

Caroline felt the full weight of Louisa's steady gaze fixed upon her profile and threw up her hands, ready to tell Louisa what she wished to hear. There would be no getting rid of her unless she did. 'You were right, Louisa. It was a mistake for me to come.'

'I am so sorry, my dear, I can only imagine how you must be suffering. Take my advice and fix your interest elsewhere. You could do a deal worse than Major Halstead.'

'He has his sights set on Georgiana.'

'You could tempt him away. Your fortune is not as great as Georgiana's, but you are more mature—'

'Is that a polite way of saying I am desperate?'

'Not in the least. I merely meant to imply that you've seen more of life than Georgiana, know how to speak intelligently on all the right subjects and... well, I am inordinately fond of Georgiana, but she does not share her brother's fine looks, and—'

'It's all right, Louisa.' Caroline expelled a heavy sigh. 'I know what you are trying to say is that I understand how to attract a gentleman, if I put my mind to it.'

'Precisely.'

'It is of no consequence. I don't want Major Halstead, and I do not think he has any interest in me.'

'Only because you haven't taken the trouble to try and attract him.'

Caroline made an unladylike scoffing noise at the back of her throat. 'My name isn't Lydia Wickham.'

The luncheon gong sounded, bringing their conversation to an end and the ladies to their feet.

'Only another four days to endure,' Louisa said, presumably thinking that would make Caroline feel better.

It had the reverse effect. She had had a violent disagreement with Charles the night before when he blithely informed her that he planned to purchase an estate in this part of the country. Apparently, he would be remaining at Pemberley in order to start his search in earnest when everyone else had left.

'You might have told me before we left Hertfordshire,' Caroline had told him. 'What am I supposed to do?'

'I thought you would be pleased. You've hinted often enough that you don't enjoy the local society in Hertfordshire.'

Being clear of Mrs Bennet's influence would indeed be a blessing, but Caroline was in no mood to admit it. 'I would not have come to this party if I'd known you meant to abandon me at the end of it, Charles.'

'Stop being so dramatic, Caroline.' Charles had had the audacity to laugh at her. 'This is not about you and, anyway, I have no intention of abandoning you. You will return to London with Louisa, and I shall collect you when Jane and I return to Netherfield.'

'You make me sound like an inconvenient parcel.'

Charles ignored her scowl and again laughed, refusing to be riled into arguing with her, damn him. 'Not in the least. Your home is with Jane and me for as long as you wish it to be. But we must first decide upon where that home will be.'

She hated it when her brother was reasonable, and she stormed from the room, slamming the door behind her. She had not seen Charles since then and, as far as she could tell from her subsequent behaviour, Jane knew nothing of the disagreement between them.

'I was thinking, Caroline,' Louisa said as they made their way towards the dining room. 'There is no one worth knowing in London at this time of year. I believe Mr Hurst has a wish to bury himself at his club so you and I might take ourselves off to Brighton. Would that please you?'

Caroline made a huge effort to pull herself together. Louisa was only trying to be supportive, and Caroline's responses had been less than gracious the entire week.

'Yes, perhaps a little sea-bathing would be just the thing,' Caroline replied, trying to sound enthusiastic.

'Excellent. I shall see what arrangements can be made.'

'Ah, now I understand you.' Caroline was furious at the thought of being used for others' convenience. 'Does Mr Henley happen to have a house in Brighton, or do I mistake the matter?'

'Do you know, now you mention it, I believe he does.'

Caroline laughed in spite of herself, and the tension between the sisters eased.

A little later over luncheon, Eliza asked Mrs Gardiner, 'Are you ready for our tour of the park this afternoon, Aunt?'

'I am greatly looking forward to it, Lizzy.'

'What about us?' Mrs Wickham asked in a tone that bordered on petulant. 'What are we all to do?'

Caroline knew her brother and Darcy were planning to look at a nearby estate that afternoon. Colonel Fitzwilliam and Mr Gardiner were going with them. If the place was deemed suitable, Charles would pay a second visit and take Jane with him. Mr Hurst would probably sleep the afternoon away.

'Would anyone care to walk through the woods?' Major Halstead asked. 'Darcy tells me there's a ruined folly a convenient distance away.'

'It is a bit of a climb since it's at the top of a hill,' Darcy said. 'But the view makes the effort to reach it worthwhile.'

Caroline waited for Mrs Wickham to jump at the invitation. To her utter astonishment, she remained silent. Georgiana sent Major Halstead a shy smile and expressed her willingness to form part of the party.

'I would like to see it too,' Jane said.

'Are you sure, my dear?' Charles asked. 'Do not on any account over-exert yourself.'

'I certainly won't do that.'

'A-and you, Miss Bennet?' Turner asked. 'Will you join us?'

Kitty blushed. 'Yes, with pleasure.'

'I plan to spend the afternoon quietly reading,' Louisa said, not being fond of walking.

Reading or pining for Mr Henley's attentions? Caroline wondered, still smarting at being used as an excuse to go to Brighton.

'Lizzy, would it be all right if I went into Kympton?' Mrs Wickham asked. 'Could a carriage be spared?'

'You cannot go alone, Lydia.'

'Why not? It is not as though I'm unmarried like Kitty. Besides, this is the country.'

'Yes, but even so.'

'I would be happy to go with Mrs Wickham,' Caroline said, seizing the opportunity. 'I should enjoy seeing the village. I gather the church is of great historic interest, but I didn't visit it the last time we were here.'

'You?' Eliza couldn't hide her surprise. Nor too could Louisa, whose eyes widened in astonishment. 'Are you quite sure it wouldn't be an inconvenience?'

'Perfectly.'

'There you are, Lizzy.' Mrs Wickham flashed a grateful smile, causing Caroline to wonder if there was more to her urgent desire to go into the village than merely visiting the milliner's establishment. She had heard her pestering her sister on the matter on more than one occasion. 'You can't possibly object now.'

'No, of course not, if you're sure you do not mind, Miss Bingley.'

'It would be my pleasure.'

* * *

Wickham rested his shoulder against the worn squabs, uncomfortably crushed between the window and the flanks of the overweight woman seated beside him. She kept falling asleep, her head lolling onto Wickham's shoulder, and then jolting awake whenever the coach hit a rut in the road. That he was reduced to travelling by public coach caused his anger to erupt. Worse yet, he'd had to beg a loan of the fare from Mrs Younge. The only thought that kept him focused as the coach slowly ate up the miles between London and Derbyshire was revenging himself upon Darcy. His straitened circumstances were entirely that gentleman's fault and Wickham owed it to his late, much respected, godfather to redress the balance.

The only factor that had eased his ire at being forced to endure this humiliating journey was the lady seated opposite, next to her much older husband. Wickham enjoyed a pretty face as much as the next man, and his fair travelling companion was certainly that. People had joined and left the coach at various stages on the road from London, but these two had remained on board the entire time. The husband was fiercely protective of his young wife, scowling at any admiring glances sent her way. Wickham made sure not to give offence, at least until the old man finally fell asleep. As soon as he did so, the flaxen-haired angel at his side threw Wickham openly flirtatious smiles that would have tested the resolve of a man with far greater resistance than Wickham would ever possess. He returned her smile, his gaze lingering on her body as he recklessly blew her a kiss.

The young woman blushed and smothered a giggle, making Wickham's mind up for him. When they stopped for the night – their final stop before Wickham's interminable journey came to an end – he would make an effort to befriend the lady's husband and force him into conversation, if only for the pleasure of learning his wife's name. Mind you, Wickham thought sourly, the way his fortunes were running at present, the couple would probably leave the coach at the next stop. There would then be nothing pleasurable with which to occupy his mind until he reached Lambton, and probably nothing even then.

Lydia would be at Pemberley now, he thought, trying not to resent her presence there without him. It was his birth right to stand in the magnificent drawing room, at Darcy's shoulder, being deferred to by his sycophantic guests. Old Mr Darcy had looked upon him, Wickham, as a second son, and Darcy had absolutely no right to deprive him of that honorary position.

Lydia had gone to Pemberley because he had told her to, but not until two weeks after he himself had left Newcastle for London. The expense of hiring a carriage to take her there was one Wickham could have done without, but there was no help for that. Even he would not expect his wife to travel alone on the sort of conveyance Wickham was currently being forced to endure. If Lydia had arrived at Pemberley before her sister was preoccupied with the arrangements for her house party, she would have asked too many probing questions regarding their enforced departure from Newcastle. And even if she didn't ask, with no other diversions available to her, Lydia would have blurted out unnecessary information. Discretion was not one of his wife's strengths.

As if not being at Pemberley himself was hard enough to endure, the thought of Lizzy now being its hostess filled him with regret. He did not resent Lizzy her good fortune, even if it did mean her opinion of him could no longer be favourable. Darcy would have told her half-truths about their history and poisoned her mind against him. Wickham was surprised at the strength of his regret in that regard. Darcy had clearly seen in Lizzy Bennet whatever it was that had attracted Wickham to her, highlighting the similarity in their characters. Wickham had been shocked and surprised when he had heard of their betrothal, not because Darcy admired her, but because of the strength of that admiration. If it was sufficient to overcome his pride and disappoint his relations, then his passions must run deep. Wickham seethed with this additional cause for resentment. Had Darcy treated him fairly, then he would by now be established as the gentleman he had been educated to become and would have been in a position to offer for Lizzy himself.

Wickham knew in his heart of hearts that Lizzy had always preferred him above any other man, including Darcy. They had conducted several frank conversations regarding that gentleman's character, and Lizzy had openly admitted to actively disliking him. But it seemed even she could put her prejudices aside in favour of riches and a position of consequence as Pemberley's mistress.

Damn it, she ought to have been his!

Finally, the coach rattled into the mews at the Boar's Head, and its weary occupants stirred themselves. Wickham alighted, stretched, and then held out a hand to help the large woman from the conveyance. She offered him grudging thanks, pulled her weird assortment of shawls more closely about her shoulders, and waddled off. Presumably this was her destination. It was the most natural thing in the world for Wickham to leave his hand extended and help the pretty wife from the coach, also. He dropped her hand immediately and inclined his head respectfully in her husband's direction, noticing he walked with a pronounced limp and leaned heavily on a cane.

'We've been on the road for two days together,' he said, 'and have yet to exchange names.'

'Porter,' the man replied shortly. 'And Mrs Porter.'

'George Wickham, at your service.'

Porter threw back his head and sniffed the air. 'There's rain on the way,' he said. 'I can smell it. I'm never wrong about these things.'

All Wickham could smell was hot horseflesh and unwashed

bodies, but he bowed to the older man's supposed knowledge. 'Do you, like me, finish your journey in Derby tomorrow, sir?' he asked.

'Indeed, and I shan't be the slightest bit sorry to say goodbye to this rattletrap, I don't mind telling you.'

They entered the inn together and waited while the landlord sorted out accommodation for them all.

'Damnation, this won't do!' Porter thundered.

Wickham thought so too, at first. Not for the first time on this journey, there were not enough chambers available. Only one small single room remained unoccupied.

'My wife had better take that,' Porter said in a disgruntled tone. 'I shall bunk in with you, Wickham, and that other gentleman.' He pointed at one of their fellow travellers, affording Wickham the opportunity to exchange a quick smile with Mrs. Porter.

'By all means,' he said.

The lure of the crowded tap room was compelling, but Wickham's sixth sense told him there would be profit in befriending Porter, to say nothing of his badly neglected wife.

'You live in Derby, Mr Porter?' he asked politely.

'No, sir. We live in Denton.'

'Denton? How extraordinary. That's less than ten miles from where I grew up at Pemberley.'

'Well, I'll be damned.' Porter's surly and suspicious attitude gave way to a broad smile as he slapped Wickham's back, hard. 'Wickham. I knew I recognised the name. Your father was estate manager at Pemberley?'

'Yes, he was. Did you know him?'

'Indeed I did, and a better man never drew breath.'

'You're in the right of it.' Wickham spared a brief glance for Porter's wife, all thoughts of flirtation fleeing his head. Something told him that Porter was in a position to be of service to him, which was far more important than the diversion of a brief flirtation. 'How did you know my father, sir?'

'All in good time, Wickham, all in good time. I've a need to rest. Dine with Alice and me tonight, and you'll hear it all.'

'It would be my pleasure.'

Wickham extracted his last clean shirt from his valise and took especial care with his toilette before joining the Porters at the appropriate hour. Wickham had supposed Porter would reserve a private dining room to save his wife from exposure to the crowded tap room. He hadn't done so, and Wickham could see Mrs Porter was uncomfortable with the amount of attention she was receiving. Porter's glares did little to deter the gawkers, but when Wickham, elegant in his gentlemanly attire, joined their party, it had the desired effect and the ruffians turned away.

Wickham made polite conversation, using his charm and wits to put Porter at his ease. Only when they had steaming plates of mutton stew in front of them did Wickham raise the subject that had been plaguing his mind.

'You were going to tell me how you came to know my esteemed father, sir.'

'Nothing could be more easily explained. I have had the honour of being the estate manager at Campton Park these past thirty years.'

'Ah yes. I believe I recall my father mentioning your name,' Wickham lied. 'He spoke highly of you.'

'Alice's pa runs the tavern in Denton village,' Porter said. 'That's where I first saw her, serving tankards of ale and having to endure all manner of indignities.'

That explained their unlikely marriage. Being manager of a large estate was the closest thing to being a gentleman and, his age notwithstanding, marriage to Porter was a big step up the social ladder for Alice.

'A tavern is no place for such beauty,' Wickham said gallantly.

'My thoughts precisely,' Porter replied. 'Couldn't leave her to the not-so-tender mercies of the coves who frequented that place.'

'I give daily thanks for that,' Alice said, speaking for the first time.

Porter patted her hand. 'There, there, my dear.' He returned his attention to his food, then to Wickham. 'Are you on your way to Pemberley now?'

'Indeed.' It wasn't precisely a lie. 'The new Mrs Darcy is giving her first house party. My wife is her sister and so, naturally, she is there.'

'You're responsible for Darcy getting leg-shackled then?'

'In a manner of speaking.' It didn't seem to occur to Porter to wonder why someone in Wickham's position was travelling by public coach. 'What business took you to London, sir, if it's not an indelicate question?'

'My damned gout.' Ah, that explained the limp, and the cane. 'It's got so I can't stand the weight of my own body. Went to see a fancy doctor in London, but there's nothing he can do for me.' Porter sniffed. 'Just as well the estate's being sold.'

'The Harringtons have quit Campton Park?'

'Yes, the old earl died last year and his heirs have no use for the place, being already established elsewhere. But they do need the money the sale will bring.'

'I had no idea. I'm out of touch with local events, having been in the army, doing my duty for King and country.'

'Yes, well, the Harringtons did the right thing by me. I've served them well, and they've shown proper respect for my faithful service.'

'I would expect no less of such a well-established family.'

'They gave me the choice of staying on as estate manager or taking a rich reward for quitting the place.' Porter sighed. 'Well, that old sawbones in London has made the decision for me. I'll be no good to anyone with this damned leg. It's time to retire.'

'So the estate manager's position at Campton Park is vacant?'

Wickham's mind whirled with previously unthought of possibilities. Darcy was too mean spirited to recommend him for another living, even if one within his gift became vacant. He had outlived his usefulness in the army, and the law was a closed door to him. Estate management would be a step down from his expectations, but at the same time a man had to grasp the opportunities that came his way. His father had enjoyed occupation of a large establishment in the grounds of Pemberley, the respect that went with it, and had complete autonomy over the estate during Darcy's frequent absences. Wickham could do a lot worse.

'Unless the purchasers bring their own person with them, which don't seem likely.'

'Has a sale been agreed?'

'Not yet.' Porter ordered more ale for himself and Wickham. 'You sound like you're interested in the vacancy.'

'I might well be.'

'Hmm, might be a step down for you. The place ain't half the size of Pemberley and... well, if you're now related to the Darcys by marriage as well as history—'

'I don't like to be idle, sir. I have just finished in the army and am looking for a suitable occupation. This could be just the thing.'

'Your qualifications speak for themselves. Not only are you the son of one of the best estate managers ever to draw breath but, unless I mistake the matter, you also enjoyed a good education and are quick on the uptake.'

Wickham inclined his head. 'Thank you. I flatter myself that you speak the truth.'

'Well then, get yourself a letter of recommendation from the current Mr Darcy and send it to me at Campton Park. I'll see what I can arrange for you. I don't like to leave the place unattended and see all my hard work over the years fall apart. You could be just the man I've been looking for, Wickham. It was a happy day when we boarded the same damned coach.'

Indeed it was, Wickham thought bleakly, except Darcy writing a recommendation for Wickham was about as likely as snow in August. Especially since Wickham didn't have the first idea about estate management. He'd been brought up to think himself better than that and had never imagined he would have a use for such knowledge.

8

Everyone appeared satisfied with the arrangements for the afternoon's entertainments and went their separate ways as soon as luncheon was over. A half-hour later, Caroline and Mrs Wickham were driven along Pemberley's magnificent and very long driveway at a brisk trot in one of Darcy's curricles.

'This is really most obliging of you, Miss Bingley,' Mrs Wickham said. 'Lizzy has been very mean, not allowing me to set foot off the estate once before now. Anyone would think I was still a green girl with no knowledge of the world, rather than a respectably married woman used to running her own household.'

'From my observations, your sister *is* being a little over-protective, but I am sure she only has your best interests at heart.'

'And I am not sure of any such thing.' Mrs Wickham's face came alight with indignation. 'Really, I wouldn't say anything if you had not raised the matter, but I hardly know Lizzy any more. Marriage has changed her. Just because Mr Darcy is such an influential gentleman, she... well, excuse me, perhaps I have said too much.' Mrs Wickham clapped a hand over her mouth, as though trying to hold back a giggle. It escaped anyway. 'Sometimes my tongue runs away with me.'

'It is perfectly all right,' Caroline forced herself to say. 'After all, we are practically family now, what with Jane being married to my brother. You may rest assured that anything you say to me will remain a secret between us.'

'Marriage hasn't changed Jane in the least, but it has given Lizzy the most infuriating airs and graces.'

There was nothing Caroline could possibly say to that, other than to agree. That wouldn't be wise, and so she changed the subject. 'Is Mr Wickham planning to join us?' she asked.

Mrs Wickham's expression darkened. 'No,' she said shortly.

'Oh, excuse me, but I thought he grew up on the estate.'

'He did. He is old Mr Darcy's godson, you know.'

'Actually, I did not know that, but it is obviously a delicate subject. Besides, it is really none of my business.' *But I plan to make it so.* 'Let us speak of something else.'

'I am glad you suggested it. I am not supposed to talk about Wickham's rift with Mr Darcy, you see. I promised my sister most particularly.'

'There is a rift?' Caroline forced a surprised expression. 'I thought there was some slight unpleasantness when the gentlemen met in Hertfordshire, but I assumed it was just a misunderstanding.'

Mrs Wickham shook her head. 'I wish there really was nothing more to it than that. Really, it is *so* unfair. I don't mean to speak ill of my sister's husband, but he has treated Wickham in an infamous manner.'

Caroline glanced out the window, affecting a casual attitude when every nerve in her body was on edge. 'Is that so?'

'Old Mr Darcy promised Wickham the living in Kympton.' Mrs

Wickham's bosom swelled at the apparent injustice of unfulfilled pledges. 'But when it fell vacant, do you know what he did?'

'I have absolutely no idea.'

'Well, unfortunately the old Mr Darcy had passed away by then. Wickham just assumed the current Mr Darcy would honour his father's wishes, but instead he blithely gave the living to someone else.' Mrs Wickham scowled. 'There, what do you say to that?'

'How extraordinary.' Caroline decided to elevate one brow, hoping the gesture would convey the impression of both surprise and sympathy, neither of which she actually felt. 'Whatever made him do such a thing?'

'Wickham has no idea. In spite of the differences in their situations, Wickham and Darcy were the best of friends as boys, and then at Cambridge. But then something happened.' Her scowl intensified. 'I have no idea what, Wickham won't say. And if Lizzy knows, she is not saying either.'

'And so your husband was forced into a career in the army. That's very different to being a clergyman.'

'Yes, and it does not suit his sensitive temperament.'

'I wonder what caused Mr Darcy to banish your husband from the estate.'

'Rich men can do as they please.' Mrs Wickham shrugged. 'My opinion, for what it's worth, is that he resented his father's high opinion of Wickham. My husband has such natural charm and easy manners, but Mr Darcy is not similarly blessed. He is always so stiff and formal. He likes to scowl at the world as though he disapproves of everything and everyone in it. I wonder Lizzy can stand it. Anyway, he pretended not to mind, about Wickham that is, while old Mr Darcy was alive, but he took his revenge as soon as he was in his grave.'

'How extraordinary.'

'Wickham feels it dreadfully.'

'Did I hear it said somewhere that Mrs Darcy and Mr Wickham once enjoyed a close friendship?'

'Hardly that.' Mrs Wickham flashed a condescending smile. 'I believe Lizzy liked him, but her regard wasn't returned.' She straightened her shoulders and flashed a triumphant smile. 'Wickham much preferred me.'

Caroline very much doubted that. There had been something rushed about Wickham's marriage to the then Lydia Bennet. Caroline had quizzed both Charles and Jane on the subject, but no useful information had been forthcoming. Even so, Caroline remained convinced Wickham had been somehow coerced into the union. He thought far too well of himself to marry a young girl with no money and nothing to recommend her and had probably hoped to win a wife with fortune enough to secure his future.

'Where is your husband now?'

'He's gone to London. He thinks of a career in the law and has friends there willing to give him a helping hand.'

'I am sure he will make a most dashing advocate.'

Mrs Wickham beamed. 'That is what I think, too.'

'But what of his commitment to the army?'

'Oh, that's all done with.' Mrs Wickham flapped a hand and spoke with casual disdain. 'Soldiering does not suit Wickham's personality.'

Caroline struggled to keep her lips straight in the face of Mrs Wickham's firm belief that the entire world was to blame for her husband's lack of commitment to his profession. Still, at least she had confirmed Caroline's suspicions. Wickham had done something to earn Darcy's displeasure. Caroline had no difficulty in believing Wickham was at fault. A gentleman with Darcy's strong principles would never go against his father's wishes, no matter how great the provocation.

She had also confirmed Wickham had been attracted to Eliza.

Caroline swallowed down her annoyance, wondering what all these gentlemen saw in her, apart from her fine eyes, of course. Caroline conceded that Eliza was loyal to her family and would probably be tolerant of Wickham's plight, if only for her sister's sake. There had to be something she could do to exploit that situation to her advantage, but for the fact that Wickham was in London.

'Where shall you live when your husband embarks upon his new career, Mrs Wickham?'

'Oh, in London, I shouldn't wonder. I shall like that above anything. The theatres, the parties, and... well, everything. I so like to be in the centre of things, you know.'

Caroline did know and turned away so Mrs Wickham would not see her roll her eyes. 'When do you plan to travel to London and be reunited with your husband? You must miss his society.'

'Oh no, I'm quite used to Wickham being away. His duties in the army often kept us apart.'

'Presumably you will remain at Pemberley until he sends for you?'

Mrs Wickham frowned. 'I don't precisely know about that. Wickham won't send word to me there. He so dislikes Mr Darcy, he cannot even bring himself to write Pemberley's direction.'

'That is extraordinary.' *And there has to be more to it than that.*

'He does not trust Mr Darcy not to open a letter with Wickham's handwriting on it, you see, even if it isn't addressed to him.'

Caroline wanted to laugh. Darcy was a gentleman. He would *never* interfere with correspondence between husband and wife. 'Then when will you know to leave?'

'Oh, Wickham still has people whom he can depend upon in the district.' Mrs Wickham lowered her voice to a conspiratorial whisper. 'That is why I was so keen to visit the village. He will send word to me here.'

'Already? Forgive me, but I thought you had only just arrived at Pemberley. Your husband cannot have reached London and sent a letter to you already.'

'Oh no, he went several weeks before me. I... er, had to close up our lodgings in Newcastle before I could come here.'

'I see.'

And Caroline did see, all too clearly. She understood that Wickham had left a string of debts behind him in Hertfordshire. Presumably history had repeated itself.

'Ah, here we are.'

The curricle turned into the mews at the inn in Lambton. Mrs Wickham alighted before the driver could come to her assistance. Caroline displayed more patience and waited for the man to come to her aid.

'We shall return in an hour or so,' Mrs Wickham said to the driver, not bothering to thank him. 'Do you wish to visit the shops, Miss Bingley? I myself have somewhere I must be.'

'I'm perfectly at your disposal, Mrs Wickham, if you will accept my company.'

'With the greatest of pleasure.' The impertinent child linked her arm through Caroline's. 'I'm so glad we have become friends. Do you know, I always thought you were aloof. How wrong I was.'

'Where are we going?'

'To Mr Long's cottage. He was one of the keepers at Pemberley when Wickham's father had management of the estate. He's quite old now and lives in the village with his widowed daughter who cares for him. Wickham stays with them if he has business in Lambton and—'

'And writes to you there?'

'Precisely. Oh, and you mustn't mind Mrs Allwood. That's Mr Long's daughter. Her manner with me is rather reserved but, like her father, she supports Wickham's cause, which is all that really signifies.'

Mrs Wickham's chatter brought them to a well-kept cottage set a little apart from its fellows on a small street. Mrs Wickham's knock was answered by a good-looking woman whom Caroline judged to be in her late twenties.

'Oh, it's you,' she said, looking beyond Lydia Wickham and sizing Caroline up with one sweep of her suspicious eyes.

'Good afternoon, Mrs Allwood. Is there any word from my husband?'

'You'd best come in,' Mrs Allwood said ungraciously, stepping back.

Once inside a small, cramped living room, Mrs Allwood snatched up a letter and handed it to Mrs Wickham.

'Oh good!'

Mrs Wickham removed herself as far away from Mrs Allwood and Caroline as the confines of the small room permitted and greedily read her letter.

'Oh dear, Wickham's expectations did not bear fruit.' Mrs Wickham pouted. 'He is on his way back here. This was written two days ago, so he should arrive by tomorrow or the day after.'

Mrs Wickham was occupied with re-reading her letter and so, unlike Caroline, she probably didn't notice the animation this intelligence brought to Mrs Allwood's attractive features.

* * *

Will handed Mrs Gardiner into the pony trap, and then helped Lizzy into the driving seat before passing her the ribbons.

'Are you sure you will be all right?' he asked for the third time. 'I could have a groom drive you in a curricle.'

'Do stop fussing,' Lizzy scolded. 'I have practised driving this thing many times at your insistence. Besides, this pony is the most docile creature on God's earth, which is precisely why you trust me with her.'

'Even so, I would not have you become distracted and overset the conveyance.'

'Thank you for the vote of confidence.'

'Lizzy!'

'Just go off and look at Campton Park with Mr Bingley and leave us ladies to our own business.'

'Well, I know when I'm not wanted,' he replied with a wry twist to his lips, touching her gloved hand briefly.

Lizzy couldn't help smiling at Will's over-protective manner and the fact that he was willing to display it in front of her relations. 'Right, are you ready, Aunt?'

'Perfectly, and I have complete faith in your driving abilities.'

'Thank you. I shall endeavour not to disappoint.'

Lizzy slapped the reins against the pony's rump and breathed an audible sigh of relief as they moved off. The prospect of spending the afternoon alone with her aunt, with no responsibilities for anyone's welfare other than their own, filled her with a renewed energy that made her headache fade away.

'It is a perfect afternoon for this excursion, Lizzy, and I'm sure the park never looked better. I have been long anticipating it.'

'As have I, Aunt. I have so much to be thankful for and so I hope you won't think me boastful if I show off the place and revel in my good fortune.'

Mrs Gardiner laughed. 'No one can blame you for wanting to share this wonderful estate. You have certainly come a long way since we were last here together as mere visitors.'

'Speaking of which, there's something you should know about that.'

Lizzy briefly explained how she had rejected Will when he first proposed to her in Kent. Her aunt gasped and clapped a hand over her mouth.

'Oh, poor Lizzy! No wonder you were so embarrassed when I suggested visiting Pemberley. You should have said something.'

'How could I?'

'Yes, I suppose it put you in an awkward position. Still, it all worked out in the end.'

'Yes, thanks to you insisting upon coming here.' Lizzy concentrated on driving along the pristine gravel driveway that led to the park. 'It's strange how things transpired.' She laughed. 'Can you imagine how Mama would have reacted had she known about the original proposal? It was bad enough when I rejected Mr Collins.'

Mrs Gardiner laughed as well. 'It is definitely as well that she never knew.'

Lizzy's smile endured. 'Then we are agreed on that score.'

'Are you entirely happy, Lizzy? Well, that's a ridiculous question.' Mrs Gardiner flapped a dismissive hand before Lizzy could respond. 'I can see you and Darcy enjoy a harmonious relationship.'

'You can? I thought he remained quite severe in company, although he is very different when we don't have visitors.'

'Yes, he does have a serious mien, it's true, but I can see through that. He looks at you when you are probably not aware of it with such deep admiration in his eye.'

'He's probably checking that I don't do or say something out of place. You know how outspoken I can be.'

'I know you are very anxious about this party, but there's absolutely no need for you to be.'

Lizzy sent her aunt a sideways glance. 'That's easy for you to say. I feel like I'm on public display.'

'Why? No one here wishes you anything other than the very best of good fortune.'

'Including Miss Bingley?'

'Well...'

'It is bad enough having that lady's constant disapproval to manage without having Lydia foisted upon me as well.'

Lizzy halted the trap so her aunt could admire the prospect of the lake with the summerhouse in the distance. Once again, bright sunshine reflected on the glassy surface of the water, but Lizzy's family of ducks was nowhere in sight. 'Oh, that's delightful! So peaceful, so inspiring. Just the thing to restore a jaded spirit.'

'Are you feeling jaded, Aunt?'

'Not in the least. I was speaking figuratively. You really are very lucky, Lizzy.'

'Yes, I know that,' she said, driving on at a walk.

'I don't say that because you are mistress of such an extensive estate. I hope I'm not that mercenary. I said it because you're obviously so very happy with Mr Darcy.'

Lizzy nodded. 'Yes, I am.'

'Not all ladies are so fortunate, you know.'

'Nor would I have been, had I given in to Mama's pressure and accepted Mr Collins.'

'Thankfully you had more sense than that. But, where were we? Oh yes, Miss Bingley. My advice would be not to worry about her, and to forgive me for feeling triumphant at her expense. After all, she did try and keep Jane and Bingley apart, so I cannot help it. I saw how much Jane suffered while she was with us in London, trying to remain cheerful and pretend she didn't feel Bingley's desertion, when all the time it was that wicked woman's interference that caused the problems.'

'Certainly you are forgiven.'

'Miss Bingley wanted Darcy for herself and hasn't yet recovered from her disappointment. She hates to see you here in the role she always imagined filling herself, and so rather than worrying about her, you should enjoy your moment of triumph.'

'No amount of time will make her like me, or me her. Just having her here makes me uneasy, although I can't precisely say why.'

'Forget Miss Bingley and concentrate your worries where they belong, if you must worry at all.'

'You refer to Lydia, I collect.'

'Yes, she *is* a cause for concern.'

Lizzy managed a humourless laugh. 'She certainly hasn't changed in that respect.'

'What's happening with her, Lizzy?'

Lizzy shrugged. 'I wish I knew. She turned up quite unexpectedly, and I had no choice but to let her stay. And now, every time Darcy looks at her, it cannot fail to remind him of Wickham. It must be torture for him. He probably feels Pemberley will never be free of the man's shadow, and yet he tolerates her for my sake.'

'Which shows just how much he wishes to please you. That, at least, is cause for celebration.'

'The problem is that Wickham's unlikely to find an opening in the law. When he's exhausted that possibility, I expect he will call upon Darcy for yet more help, which puts me in an awkward position.'

'Yes, I can quite see that.' Mrs Gardiner shook her head. 'Lydia is very silly and immature, but she *is* your sister, and you can hardly see her starve.'

'I also have some sympathy for Wickham's situation. Not that I would tell my husband so, of course, but you must bear in mind he enjoyed the same education as Darcy. A gentleman's education. In fact, he was led to believe he was Darcy's equal in all respects, which of course he is not. I blame old Mr Darcy for that—'

'And for misjudging Wickham's character. Wickham knew very

well he would be expected to earn his own living when he finished university and was given every financial encouragement to do so. Don't waste your pity on a lost cause, Lizzy.'

'Oh, Aunt,' Lizzy cried with feeling. 'How I have missed your sound common sense. I feel better already for having shared my concerns with you.'

'You're entirely welcome.' Mrs Gardiner returned her attention to the view. 'Now, where are we?'

'We have circled the woods where Jane and the others are walking.' Lizzy removed one hand from the reins and pointed. 'That is the folly they're aiming to walk to.'

'It's a very long trek. I hope Jane doesn't tire herself.'

Lizzy smiled. 'Ah, so you know.'

Mrs Gardiner laughed. 'Mr and Mrs Bingley are far too transparent to keep secrets. Not that they told me precisely but, observing their manner, it was easy enough to guess.'

'Well, I hope when they finally make their announcement the Hursts will take Miss Bingley under their wing for a while and give Jane and Bingley time alone to enjoy their new family.' Lizzy shook her head. 'Sometimes I wonder if Mr Hurst actually does own a house of his own, he spends so much time under Bingley's roof.'

'And Mr Bingley is far too good-natured to suggest they leave.'

'Quite. Anyway, we're at the furthest point on the estate now.' Lizzy pointed again. 'All those fields are part of the estate, but it's not safe to drive along the lanes in this trap. I promised Mr Darcy I would stick to the gravel drives.'

'Quite right, too.' Mrs Gardiner settled herself into a more comfortable position on the cushioned seat. 'Now, tell me about Kitty and her Captain Turner. Do I detect more than a passing fancy there?'

Lizzy took a moment to consider the question. 'They certainly appear to enjoy one another's company, and I think the attraction is genuine rather than Kitty having set her cap at him because he is not a pauper.'

'I am glad to hear you say so. He's not the sort of man I would have expected Kitty to form an attachment to, which shows maturity on her part. His attractions don't run to the physical, and you know how she and Lydia used to be, chasing after the most attractive officers all the time.'

'Kitty isn't stupid. I think she has seen for herself the reality of Lydia's marriage and wants better for herself. Since she's been removed from Lydia's influence and has spent so much time with Jane, Kitty has improved beyond my wildest expectations.' Lizzy paused. 'Do you know, she told me the other day that she sympathised with Captain Turner. Apparently his stammer is a result of being the youngest of four boys. He was bullied by his father because he suffered from childhood illnesses, for which his father appeared to hold him responsible. He took his belt to him to try and beat the weakness out of him.'

'I have heard about men of that ilk.' Mrs Gardiner looked off into the distance, a disdainful expression on her face. 'All his sons must be rumbustious or it reflects poorly upon him as their father. Remarkable.'

'His father sounds very disagreeable. No wonder Captain Turner wants little to do with him. Kitty says their paths seldom cross.'

'And it probably explains why he enlisted. He's out to prove something to his father as well as to himself.'

'I hadn't considered the matter in that light before, but you could well be right. I believe the captain is moderately wealthy in his own right. He could, I suppose, have settled down to a quiet life as a country gentlemen but chose an alternative path, perhaps for the reasons you suggest.'

'I was already inclined to like the young man. Now, I can also admire his strength of character.'

'Yes, indeed.' Lizzy paused to reflect. 'Do you know, Kitty tells me she felt invisible growing up and so understands how it must have been for the captain.'

Mrs Gardiner elevated both brows. 'Kitty said that?'

'Yes. She said she always felt inferior, as though she was somehow to blame when compared to Jane's beauty and found wanting.'

'Your mother did constantly hold up Jane as an example to all of you.' Mrs Gardiner shook her head. 'As though you wouldn't all have chosen to look as angelic as Jane, if you possibly could have.'

'It's not just Jane's beauty we failed to emulate, but her sweet nature, too.' Lizzy laughed. 'I could never look at the world as optimistically as Jane still does.'

'Not many people could, except Mr Bingley, perhaps.'

Lizzy laughed. 'Which is one of the many reasons why they are so well suited. My father is convinced their servants will take advantage of their collective good nature and rob them blind.'

'Then let us hope that doesn't happen. But we were talking of Kitty, and her insights are most illuminating. I had no idea she was such a deep thinker. What else did she reveal?'

'Well, Lydia's liveliness caused her to feel inferior, as did Mary's intellectual opinions, and my outspokenness.'

'How extraordinary.'

'I was astonished at first too, but I've had time to reflect, and I believe I understand what she means. She felt she had no identity of her own because Lydia, being younger than Kitty, ought to have followed Kitty's lead, but Lydia was the one to develop faster.'

'She is paying for that trait now in no uncertain terms.'

'Yes, and Kitty is learning from her sister's mistakes, which is something.' Lizzy guided the trap onto the main driveway, the house visible in the far distance. 'Come along, Aunt. If you've seen enough we shall return to the house and enjoy some tea before the others return.'

'That would be most welcome.' Mrs Gardiner patted Lizzy's shoulder. 'This has been delightful, thank you, Lizzy. But I dare say you have a programme of events arranged for this evening that will wear us all out, and so one would be wise to keep a little energy in reserve.'

'If I keep you all occupied then no one will have the time or inclination to talk about anything serious. That way we will all remain the best of friends.'

'Oh, Lizzy!' Mrs Gardiner laughed and then sighed. 'When will you understand how anxious everyone is to remain on the best of terms with the new Mrs Darcy?'

The walking party returned to Pemberley about half an hour after Lizzy and Mrs Gardiner and joined them in the drawing room.

'Did you have an enjoyable walk?' Lizzy asked.

'It was a long way, and far steeper than I had anticipated,' Jane replied, looking rather red in the face. 'But you were right about the view. It certainly made the effort worthwhile.'

'I did try to warn you.' Lizzy sent her sister a concerned glance. 'Will you take tea, or would you prefer to rest straight away?'

'I think I shall rest until dinner time. Being a chaperone is harder work than I imagined it would be.' She laughed self-consciously. 'All that responsibility.'

'I hope your charges gave you no trouble.'

'Not in the least. It was a charming afternoon, albeit a little too warm for me.'

'Take care, Jane,' Lizzy said anxiously. She should have known the climb would be too much for Jane, and she felt guilty for letting her go ahead with it. 'Mr Bingley will never forgive me if you overexert yourself.'

'Oh, there is no danger of that.'

The others remained with Lizzy and more refreshments were ordered.

'What plans do you have for us this evening, Lizzy?' Kitty asked.

'It's such a fine evening that I thought we would dine al fresco on the terrace.'

'Oh, I wondered what all the activity outside was about,' Georgiana said. 'What a charming idea, Lizzy. I have always wanted to dine beneath the stars.'

'Let's h-hope it doesn't rain, Mrs Darcy,' Captain Turner said. 'I t-thought I smelt a change of weather in t-the air.'

'The elements would not dare to disrupt my plans,' Lizzy replied, making everyone laugh. 'And if the weather cooperates, Lydia will be pleased to learn I have engaged a fiddle player, and we shall have some impromptu dancing after dinner.'

'What was that I just overheard?' Lizzy rolled her eyes when Lydia and Miss Bingley stepped into the room. 'Did someone mention dancing?'

'How was your excursion?' Lizzy asked.

'Oh, quite agreeable,' Lydia replied. 'Miss Bingley and I are now such friends.'

Lizzy swallowed down a feeling of unease at this unlikely alliance and told her sister about her plans for the evening.

'But I have nothing to wear,' Lydia wailed. 'I keep telling you, Lizzy, I have no clothes with me. You must lend me something.'

Oh, must I?

'I hope our walk has left you with enough energy for dancing, Miss Bennet,' Captain Turner said, not once stammering.

Kitty shared a shy smile with him. Significantly, Lizzy happened to notice a lingering exchange of glances between Major Halstead and Georgiana also take place. Lizzy had been so taken up with the transformation in Kitty and her developing *tendre* for Captain Turner, she hadn't paid proper attention to Georgiana and

Halstead. She must find a moment to have a quiet word with Georgiana and see if the attraction she clearly felt towards Major Halstead was anything more than a passing fancy.

She examined Georgiana now as she conversed with Kitty and the two gentlemen. Her cheeks turned pink in response to something Halstead said to her. It appeared to Lizzy as though her manner wasn't quite so reserved when she was in that gentleman's company. How would Will react if he thought his sister's affections were engaged? If they were, and Lizzy satisfied herself that Halstead's interest in Georgiana went beyond her fortune, then Lizzy would fight for Georgiana to have her way. And she would need to fight. Will thought highly of Halstead, but something told Lizzy no one would be good enough for his beloved sister.

'If there's to be dancing,' Major Halstead said, 'I should like to claim your hand for the first, Miss Darcy.'

'You're very precipitate, Major,' Georgiana replied, her blush deepening.

The major laughed. 'A good soldier always plans his strategy several moves in advance.'

'I'm hardly one of your soldiers, sir.'

'Well said, Miss D-Darcy.' Captain Turner applauded Georgiana. 'But for once, Halstead has come up with a sound idea. So, M-Miss Bennet, will you stand up with me?'

'With the greatest of pleasure,' Kitty replied.

Lizzy felt positively ancient, watching the young people's verbal exchanges, fascinated almost as much by what they didn't say as by the formal words that slipped past their lips. Lydia looked angry to be excluded but, at a warning glance from Lizzy, refrained from putting herself forward.

They were interrupted by the return of the gentlemen.

'How was Campton Park, Mr Bingley?' Lizzy asked. 'Did it meet your expectations?'

'Indeed. It was very interesting. Is Jane about? She will want to hear all about it.'

'She's gone to rest. The walk tired her.'

Mr Bingley frowned. 'I say, is she all right?'

'She's perfectly fine,' Lizzy replied with a reassuring smile. 'She suffers from nothing more taxing than slight fatigue following an excess of fresh air. I'm sure she will be pleased to see you.'

'Then, if you will excuse me, Mrs Darcy, I shall go and tell her all about the house. It has the most impressive drawing room. Nothing on a scale to Pemberley, of course, but then what is?'

The others drifted away in Mr Bingley's wake, and Lizzy was left alone with Will. His stern demeanour gave way to a meltingly gentle smile as he took the seat beside her and claimed her hand.

'How was the ride around the estate?' he asked.

'My aunt enjoyed herself, and you will be pleased to hear that I managed to keep the trap on its wheels for the entire time.'

He laughed. 'You must forgive me if I seem over-protective, my love, but I refuse to apologise for it. The thought of any harm coming to you is beyond unendurable. It took considerable trouble to win your regard, and I don't plan to part with you now that I actually have you at my side.'

'There is no danger of that. You ought to know by now that I'm indestructible.'

'And also tired.' He examined her face closely, frowning as he stood up and, still holding her hand, pulled her to her feet with him. 'Everyone else has gone to rest. We could do worse than follow their example.'

'Don't think to fool me,' she replied, her heart quickening as they headed for the stairs. 'Resting is the last thing you have on your mind.'

He quirked a brow. 'Already you know me so well. Just as a matter of interest, what gave me away?'

'Oh, that is easily explained. Your eyes darken and take on a hot sheen, a muscle leaps in your jaw and, well...' She glanced down at his groin as they climbed the stairs together. 'The evidence is rather difficult to conceal in those tight-fitting inexpressibles.'

'I'm sorry, Lizzy. Whatever must you think of me?' Will looked both confused and chastened. 'I confess I had no idea I could be so demanding in the bedroom, but you must shoulder part of the blame for that. You compel me in ways I was unaware were possible for a man as reserved as I am by nature.'

Lizzy bit her lip, overwhelmed by the passion behind his words. 'I would not have it any other way. What you have taught me, the pleasure you have given me these months, has been both a revelation and a joy.'

'I am glad to hear you say so, but I don't mean to force myself upon you again so soon if you would prefer to rest.'

'Fitzwilliam Darcy, now is not the time to become considerate!'

He affected a surprised expression that made her smile. 'I am inconsiderate of your feelings?'

'I fail to see how you can ever achieve that ambition. My feelings always seem to mirror your own, you see, for which I hold you entirely responsible. I am sure it's not at all seemly for a husband and wife to be always... well, you know what I mean.'

'You are charming when you blush.'

'You give me much to blush about.'

'For which you must again take part of the blame. I have obviously married a shameless wanton.'

'Perhaps you have, but you must make the best of it because it is too late to send me back now.'

'Yes.' He sighed. 'I suppose that's true.'

'As long as you continue to satisfy my desires, I shall have no complaints.'

'I shall do my humble best.'

Lizzy harrumphed. 'There is absolutely nothing humble about you.'

'Well, they do say that humility should be reserved for those with something to be humble about.'

Lizzy playfully punched his arm. 'I shall pretend you didn't say that.'

He opened the door to their adjoining chambers, laughing as he did so. 'Everything downstairs is in order, Mrs Darcy. We are not needed there and will only be in the way if we go down too early. What shall we do instead?'

She plucked at her lower lip, as though seeking inspiration. 'I have absolutely no idea,' she said, smiling as she shook her head.

Will shrugged out of his coat and threw it casually aside. He then swept her from the floor and carried her to her bed. Lizzy leaned her head against his muscular chest, almost ashamed of the way in which she responded with such indecent haste to his flirtatious challenges. She really ought to put up more of a fight, just to add a salacious edge to their games. Not that her pretence would ever succeed in fooling Will, but still...

She lay where he placed her, not caring that her gown would become impossibly creased, and watched her handsome husband as he shed his clothes with apparent disregard for their welfare.

'May I undress you, Mrs Darcy?' he asked so politely that she laughed aloud.

'I shall feel very badly done by if you do not.'

'Then please sit up and allow me to play the part of lady's maid.'

He started with her hair, just as she'd known he would. He had been fascinated by it from the first, and that enchantment showed no signs of abating. He removed the pins slowly, running his fingers repeatedly through the tresses as they fell free. Those fingers made deliberate contact with her nape and the sensitive areas below her ears, sending spirals of readiness coursing through her as he skilfully heightened the physical alchemy that had existed between them since the first.

When her hair was completely loose, Will wound it around one hand and tugged gently, forcing her head backwards so he could claim her lips in a deep, sensual kiss. Her scalp prickled, and she found having her hair pulled to be surprisingly erotic. She returned his kiss with fervour, their tongues tangling in an exotic dance that left her panting with expectation when Will finally broke it.

'You like me pulling your hair?'

'I find it stimulating, and exciting.' Lizzy's expression probably mirrored her surprise. 'Who would have thought it?'

'Good.' He trailed a line of kisses down the length of her neck. 'That was the general idea. I know how responsive you are, but if I ever do anything that hurts you, if I get too carried away in my desire to love you, you must promise to tell me so.'

'Let's put that theory to the test, Mr Darcy. What do you plan to do to me next?'

'Well, now you look overdressed.'

'How strange. The same thought just occurred to me.'

Will surprised her when, instead of loosening her bodice, he laid her back on the bed and targeted her feet. He removed her slippers and threw them aside. Then he lifted her skirts and trailed his fingers seductively up the insides of her legs – legs which instinctively fell open for him. Her impatience earned an amused chuckle from her husband, nothing more. His questing fingers halted their journey far sooner than she would have wished, stopping when they reached her garters. Slowly he rolled her stockings down her legs. When he'd removed the second one, he retained possession of her foot and sucked her toes into his mouth, one at a time. Lizzy gasped as a vortex of desire tangled with feelings of inexorable need deep within her core.

'Will, what are you doing?' she asked, thrashing her head from side to side, since bearing this torture passively would have been beyond her.

'Testing your limits,' he replied calmly, lifting his head and flashing a wicked grin.

'I think you have already reached them,' she admitted grudgingly, her voice sounding as fractured as her breathing. 'I hate allowing you to win, but you're more experienced at this sort of thing than I am, so it's not an equal contest.'

'Well, in that case, we had best try something else.'

He pulled her into a sitting position and finally released her bodice. Lizzy lifted her bottom so he could pull her gown away. It was carelessly thrown on the floor to join his own discarded clothing. Jessie would have a fit when she saw the state of it. Will lost no time in dealing with her chemise and petticoats, and she was now wearing nothing except a thin lawn shift. Will's eyes darkened with need as he looked at her, causing excitement to riot through her insides. That she could have such a profound effect upon a gentleman of Will's ilk both astonished and empowered her.

Slowly and expertly, Will agitated her passions until she was panting with need.

'You are my life, Lizzy Darcy. I hope you know that by now. Without you, I was only ever a shell of a man. What I saw in you... when I saw you first... I think I knew, on some level, you were capable of unimaginable passion, and that you were the woman I had been waiting to find.'

'No one but you could have awoken the beast inside me. I yearn for you, Will. Fill me, my love. Never stop filling me with your desire.'

'Damn it, Lizzy, look in the mirror. Look at your eyes. Look at mine.'

Lizzy turned her head sideways, caught sight of them both in the full-length glass, and gasped. Will's eyes were black with passion. She had seen them that way many times since their marriage, but she had never examined her own expression before. Her brown eyes glowed with a licentious need that was both shocking and exciting. She barely recognised the person she had become beneath Will's expert tutelage, and said as much.

'This is who you were born to be, Lizzy. Never feel the need to apologise to me because of it or pretend otherwise.'

'You should know enough of my frankness by now to be aware that I never pretend.'

'Good.' He skewered her with his desire, breathing heavily. 'That is definitely good.'

Will made a low, animalistic sound at the back of his throat as intoxicating friction, a product of his desperate need, communicated itself to Lizzy. He lowered his head and bit at her shoulder, the hardness of his body a thrilling contrast to her own softer form as he took her to the brink, and then teased her by holding back.

'Will, I need to—'

'I know you do, and we will do this together.'

And then they did. Lizzy cried out, not caring if the entire household heard her, as her limbs trembled and the flickering heat deep inside turned into a raging inferno.

They were both still breathing hard long after the trembling ceased. Lizzy felt as though every bone in her body had been liquefied, but she somehow found the energy to lift one hand and trail her fingers gently down Will's face.

'You never cease to amaze me,' she said.

'I can't take the credit for that, Mrs Darcy. You're just a naturally sensual woman with a body that plays by its own rules.'

He pulled the covers back, deposited Lizzy in bed and climbed in with her, pulling the blankets back up to their chins. One of his arms circled her shoulders, and she snuggled up to her husband, tired yet euphoric, wondering if this was the moment to tell him she was almost convinced she carried his child.

No, not yet. Don't spoil the glow. Will seldom made love to her in the afternoon and, if he did, he never joined her in bed again afterwards. Besides, if he thought there was even the remotest chance that she was increasing, he'd probably refuse to continue with her erotic education for fear of harming her or the child. That was a risk Lizzy simply wasn't prepared to take.

'What's more,' Will added, 'I'm willing to wager that we have barely scratched the surface of your sensuality. There's a lot more we can do, if you're willing.'

'I enjoyed watching you in the mirror just now.' She smiled. 'When I remembered to keep my eyes open, that is. When passion explodes I tend to close them, I find.'

'Voyeurism has been used as a means of stimulation throughout the ages. I'm not surprised you took to it so readily. Now close those lovely eyes again and get some rest.'

'Don't leave me.'

'I wasn't planning to. I shall be here to wake you when it's time.'

He did wake her, an hour later, with a kiss. That kiss became passionate and charged. Lizzy didn't know what had changed between them. They'd been inclined to make love once a day since their marriage. Now that they had a houseful of guests and Lizzy had all sorts of additional responsibilities, Will didn't seem able to restrain his impulses. She asked him about it afterwards.

'I have no explanation for it,' he said. 'I hope you're not objecting.'

'Not in the least, but I think I know what has happened.'

Will elevated a brow. 'You do?'

'Certainly. When we are here alone you can visit me at any time you wish. When we have guests, it's a different matter. Any competent student of human nature will tell you it's natural to crave what one cannot have.'

'Well, just so that you know, I haven't finished with you yet, Mrs Darcy. I intend to have you again when the evening's entertainments are over with.'

'I shall consider it as a fixed engagement.'

'As well you should.'

'Tell me about Campton Park. Do you think it will be suitable for Jane and Mr Bingley?'

'It certainly has possibilities, and the owners are very keen to sell. He ought to be able to negotiate a good price.'

'It would be lovely to have her so close.'

'Yes, I think that's one of the factors influencing Bingley.'

'You sound as though you are condemning him for wishing to be near you, his closest friend, and for Jane to be near me.'

'Not in the least. I shall enjoy Bingley's society, as long as it doesn't mean a prolonged visit from your mother.'

Lizzy laughed. 'Don't worry. She does not care to travel too far from Longbourn.'

'There are other estates to see still, but none of them are quite so close. They will require a couple of days away from here once the party is over with so we can view them all at once.'

'Of course.' Lizzy paused, wondering how best to phrase what needed to be said. In the end she just came right out and said it. 'Major Halstead and Georgiana seem to be getting along well.'

As she had known would be the case, Will scowled. 'Don't go reading too much into that. Georgiana has seen little of society. It's only natural she feels flattered by the attentions of a handsome gentleman. We will remove to London for the season where she will have a wider choice of beaux.'

'You still plan to go ahead with that scheme?'

'Of course.' Will looked at her askance. 'Why would I not?'

'Perhaps it isn't what Georgiana wishes.' *And I might well not be in a condition to be seen in public by then.* 'Have you asked her about it?'

'Well, no, I just assumed.'

'Georgiana is shy. She admitted to me quite recently that the thought of appearing in London's salons terrifies her.'

Will's surprised expression intensified. 'She will change her mind. She has already matured a lot since you've been here to guide her, and the attention she receives from Halstead will give her more confidence still.'

'I think she really likes him.'

Will's lips tightened. 'Halstead's a fortune hunter.'

'So will be most of the gentlemen who take an interest in your sister.' Lizzy paused, tracing idle patterns on Will's chest with her forefinger. 'That is what most people probably accuse me of.'

Will chuckled. 'That's because most people don't know you rejected my first proposal.'

'Yes, but even so.'

'I shall keep a closer eye on Halstead for the rest of the week. I know nothing to his detriment, but I am not convinced he's the right man for my sister.'

Lizzy rolled her eyes. 'I doubt there's a man on the planet who would meet your exacting standards.'

10

Caroline delayed her appearance on the terrace until the last possible moment. She had a stunning new gown to show off, and she planned to make a grand entrance wearing the violet silk creation that had cost her a small fortune. Eliza had demonstrated a marked lack of style this entire week, which was hardly to be wondered at, given her unprepossessing background. What passed for fashion in rural Hertfordshire was unlikely to make any sort of impression against Pemberley's majestic backdrop.

Now was the right time to remind Mr Darcy who could have been sitting at the opposite end of his table, enhancing Pemberley's standing with her elegant taste and sense of refinement, had he been more successful in curbing his momentary lust. Caroline took a deep breath. The time had come. She placed one delicately slippered foot on the paving stones of the terrace, but conversations continued as though nothing remarkable had happened, and no admiring glances were directed her way. Undeterred, she moved the second foot to join the first, ensuring her skirts made an exaggerated whooshing sound as she did so.

Still nothing.

'Ah, there you are.' Caroline sensed a presence behind her and recognised her sister's perfume. 'I was about to come in search of you.'

'You're too kind,' Caroline said acerbically.

Louisa sent Caroline a quizzical glance but made no comment about her gown or the additional effort she had taken with her preparations. This was not an auspicious start, but Caroline reminded herself Louisa had preoccupations of her own to wrestle with. She happened to know that she had received a letter from her paramour in the morning post, which had upset Louisa in some way. Louisa had refused to say why, and Caroline was insufficiently interested to pursue the matter.

Mr Darcy was in deep conversation with Major Halstead and Georgiana at the other end of the terrace, which would explain why he hadn't noticed her yet. Pride salvaged, Caroline pushed her irritation to one side. Mr Darcy was deeply protective of his sister – an admirable trait – and appeared to have become even more concerned with her affairs since making such an unfortunate marriage himself. Presumably, he did not wish his wife to unduly influence Georgiana with her outspoken ways and tendency to voice her opinions far too freely.

'Ah, Miss Bingley.'

Damnation, it was Eliza, and she looked radiant in a crimson gown of the very latest fashion. The bodice, beaded with exquisite jet, was a perfect fit. The hem and her décolletage were trimmed with beautiful black lace, which infuriated Caroline. As a single lady she couldn't have worn such a risqué garment without causing a scandal. Caroline suspected Eliza's gown was a deliberate taunt aimed at her, emphasising her status as Mr Darcy's legal wife and the freedom it afforded her to dress as she pleased. Caroline refrained from sneering. Eliza was no better than a common slut and clearly felt threatened by Caroline's presence, as well she might.

Enjoy your triumph while you can.

Annoyingly, even Caroline had to admit Eliza carried the gown off with a rather contrived elegance. There was something about her complexion too – a glow that made her skin seem translucent and that caused her damned eyes to sparkle. Caroline felt disadvantaged by her adversary's tactics, which was unthinkable. She was considerably more elegant than Eliza and absolutely refused to be intimidated. She squared her shoulders, aware that decision time was neigh, and reluctantly gave Eliza her attention.

'Good evening,' she said, her tone bordering on the uncivil. 'I trust I didn't keep you waiting.'

'Not at all. We're very informal this evening, as you can see.' Eliza cleared her throat. 'I have been waiting for you because I wanted most particularly to thank you for spending the afternoon with my sister. It was most kind of you.'

'It was a pleasure.' Caroline stubbornly refused to address this usurper as *Mrs Darcy*, not caring if she appeared impolite. 'Your sister was engaging company.'

Eliza widened her eyes. 'I'm very pleased to hear you say so. Lydia sometimes allows her tongue to run away with her, but she has a good heart.'

Caroline beckoned to her brother, who happened to approach them at that moment. 'Charles, you have yet to tell me about the estate you viewed today. I am most anxious to hear all the particulars.'

'And I have been equally anxious to tell you, but I was unable to find you.'

'Well, I'm here now.'

'I believe we are ready to go to the table, Miss Bingley,' Eliza said, 'so I'm afraid it will have to wait a little longer. You are seated beside my husband tonight.'

'Thank you.' Eliza had spitefully avoided seating her beside Darcy before tonight, clearly worried about where that might lead. 'Mr Darcy and I are old intimates and take pleasure in one another's society.'

Now why had she said that? Instead of making Eliza uneasy, Caroline's declaration appeared to startle and then amuse her adversary. Mr Darcy approached them at that moment and proffered his arm to Caroline, sending his wife a speaking look that contained little warmth.

'I believe I am to have the pleasure of your company at dinner, Miss Bingley,' he said.

'So I understand, sir.'

She walked away on Darcy's arm, following his example, and not bothering to excuse herself from Eliza. Darcy helped her with her chair, waiting for Turner to settle Mrs Gardiner on his opposite side before he took his own seat.

'Did you enjoy your tour of the park, Mrs Gardiner?' Darcy asked her.

'Very much so. I had no idea it was quite so extensive.'

'And yet you spent much of your youth in the locality.'

'In the village, Mr Darcy. I did visit Pemberley on a couple of occasions, but I have never seen much of the park before today.'

And nor will you again, Caroline thought malevolently, *if I have any say in the matter.* Darcy had chosen to address Mrs Gardiner, the more senior of his dinner companions, first, as politeness dictated. Caroline was ready to wait her turn, secure in the knowledge that their discourse would be far livelier and more agreeable because they would have so much to say to one another.

Mr Hurst was seated on her other side. Caroline made brief responses to his equally brief conversation. At the same time she allowed her mind to wander, thinking over the afternoon's excursion and all she'd learned from Lydia Wickham. That lady was an enigma. It was obvious she had deep feelings for her husband and erroneously considered he had been wronged by Darcy. Naturally, she took her husband's part, but Caroline knew she must have got it wrong because Mr Darcy was incapable of behaving dishonourably. There had to be more to it than that. She watched Lydia now, flirting rather desperately with Major Halstead, and wondered how she could behave in such a fashion if her attachment to Wickham ran so deep.

Caroline had to admit that Wickham cut a dashing figure. Even she had looked twice on the first occasion when they had met. He had exquisite manners and compelling charm to add to his extreme good looks, and Caroline could appreciate a handsome face as well as the next woman. But even if Wickham had not proven to be Darcy's enemy, she would never have developed a *tendre* for him or any other man because, of course, it could only be a matter of time before Darcy proposed to her.

She glowed down the length of the table at Eliza, wishing her all manner of ill-will.

Wickham clearly played fast and loose with his wife's affections, Caroline thought. She didn't have to look any further than Louisa to know it was common for married people to live in such a fashion. But Wickham ought to remember his priorities and secure his future before he turned his attention to pleasures of the flesh – something he appeared singularly disinclined to do. Lydia had been unable to hide her disappointment when she read Wickham's letter and learned he had failed to secure a position within legal circles. Why he was returning to Derbyshire was less clear, but it could only be bad news for Darcy.

Caroline, on the other hand, was encouraged to learn of his plans. She glanced at Mr Darcy, still deep in conversation with Mrs

Gardiner, mesmerised by his long, elegant fingers as they played absently with the stem of his wine glass. His noble profile, cast into light and shadow by the flickering flambeaux lighting the terrace, made her pulse quicken and her heart rate accelerate. She could tell he was deeply unhappy. Not many others would be able to detect the signs, because he was so adept at hiding his feelings. But Caroline had spent much time in his company prior to his infamous marriage and had studied his every mood, his every nuance, until she understood him better than he understood himself.

The plain fact of the matter was that he was too proud to admit he had made a disastrous mistake. But for all that, for the first time she had doubts about the extreme action she intended to take to save him and Pemberley from his momentary lapse of judgement. Then he turned to face her and his lips quirked, almost as though he could read her thoughts and was giving her permission to act out her half-formed plans for his salvation and their happiness. It was the sign she had been waiting for, and Caroline's lingering doubts evaporated. Provided Wickham arrived before the party came to an end, she would find a way to use his desperation and Lizzy's loyalty to her family to orchestrate her downfall. She chanced another glance at Darcy's dear profile, relaxed and smiling at something Mrs Gardiner had just said to him, and became absolutely determined. She would use her wits and guile to save this gentleman from his own folly if it was the last thing she ever did.

'Tell me of your plans when you leave here, Miss Bingley,' Darcy said to her with an arch smile, now focusing his full attention upon her.

Ah, so he was interested enough in her movements to want to know the particulars. That was excellent. With a charming smile, she told him about Louisa's plans to remove to Brighton.

'The prospect of sea-bathing pleases you?'

Caroline was unsure if she ought to admit to it. Perhaps Darcy thought it was a little vulgar. 'I am not entirely sure about that,' she said evasively. 'I have never tried it.'

'Oh, but you must. I can highly recommend the pleasure. It is most invigorating, and very beneficial for one's health, apparently.'

'Well, if you think so. I shall as always be swayed by your advice.'

'It would be a pity to spend time in Brighton and not take a dip.'

'We are to have dancing this evening, I understand.' Caroline thought it was rather common to have a fiddler playing on the terrace when there was a full-sized ballroom in the house that would much better suit their purpose. Not that there were enough of them to fill the ballroom, but still, these things ought to be done properly or not at all.

'The idea was mine,' Darcy replied. 'There is something coercive about impromptu dancing beneath the stars on a fine summer's evening. Would you not agree?'

'Oh, absolutely.'

* * *

Wickham waited until Porter was snoring in harmony with his other roommate and then slipped quietly from the cramped chamber the three men occupied. He lifted the latch, relieved when it failed to squeak, and walked in stockinged feet down the corridor. This was extreme folly, and he repeatedly asked himself what he thought he was doing. If he was caught then Porter would have every right to feel aggrieved. A man of his age and sickly constitution could hardly call Wickham out, but he could most certainly withdraw his recommendation that Wickham take on the estate management at Campton Park. That would be a shame, because it was a situation he had already persuaded himself would suit him perfectly. The fact that it was so close to Pemberley, and he would become a permanent thorn in Darcy's side, was an added attraction. Derbyshire was every bit as much Wickham's home as it was Darcy's. He had connections in the locality and saw no reason why he should be driven from the county just because Darcy was jealous of him.

In spite of the voice of reason, there was something about the delightful Mrs Porter that overcame his reservations. She had signalled her availability during supper by repeatedly brushing her thigh against his beneath the table. Wickham was powerless to resist such a brazen invitation. He had been feeling badly treated and out of charity with the world in general since his ill-fated visit to London. Alice Porter was just the person to restore his wounded pride.

Her room was at the end of the corridor. Little bigger than a cupboard, it had a steeply sloping ceiling and just about enough room for a cot. Wickham presumed that Alice would be expecting him, and he slid quietly into the room without first knocking. To his astonishment, she appeared to be sound asleep. Bent double to prevent bashing his head on the ceiling, he moved to the bed and touched her arm. She made a startled sound that was far too loud, sat up and blinked.

'Horatio, what is it? Are you unwell, my dear?'

'It's me,' Wickham said in a soft whisper. 'Keep your voice low. These walls are thin.'

'You!' Her surprise appeared genuine, her expression not particularly welcoming. She hugged her knees to her chest and pulled the covers up to her chin. 'What are you doing in here?' she hissed. 'If Horatio finds you he—'

'Shush, it's all right. Your husband is sound asleep.'

'Even so, you shouldn't be here.'

No, but he was, and he hadn't risked his all just to be rejected. 'I thought you were expecting me,' he said, perching one buttock on the edge of her bed and sending her his most winsome smile. 'Your invitation *was* rather direct.'

'Oh, that was just me having fun.' She sent him a considering look. 'It didn't mean anything.'

Wickham lifted one hand and gently traced the curve of her lovely face with the tips of his fingers. So, the little vixen planned to lead him a merry dance, did she? So much the better. Wickham disliked an easy victory. Encouraged when she didn't flinch from the touch of his fingers, he lunged for her and pulled her into his embrace. She giggled and made a half-hearted attempt to push him off.

'Oh no you don't,' he whispered. 'You asked for this.'

'There's no space,' she replied, abandoning all pretence with a speed that implied no real conviction.

'Then we shall just have to be inventive.'

He bent to kiss her as he edged into bed beside her, pulling her up and forcing her to sit on his thighs. With one hand, he unfastened his breeches.

'See what I have for you, my dear. It's a crime that your charms are wasted on that old man.'

She giggled. 'That old man has been good to me, in his way.'

'But he can't give you anything like this.'

Wickham moved her aside and allowed her a good view of what he was offering her. Her gaze was fixed on his manhood as the tip of her tongue moistened her lower lip. She reminded him of Lizzy in some respects, which only served to fire his lust. There was something about her eyes that made him think of the woman who ought to have been his wife, had there been any justice in this world.

'No, he certainly doesn't have anything like that,' Alice agreed, biting her lip now as though trying to contain a giggle.

'Then what shall we do with it?'

Wickham didn't waste any more time. The slightest noise out of place could awaken the entire inn so they needed to get this done quickly. Leaning his torso against the wall, he encouraged Alice to straddle him. As soon as she did so, he grabbed her hips and sank into her. She groaned, but if he was hurting her she didn't seem to mind it, and her eyes now sparkled with desire.

'What would your wife say?' Alice asked with a mischievous smile.

'Let's not talk about her.'

'But I—'

'Shush, come on, stay with me.'

Alice rode him like a seasoned professional, hair tumbling around her shoulders as she rotated her head and threw it backwards, urging him on with throaty little moans. She was a little too good at this for it to be the first time she had deceived her husband, Wickham thought. Someone had taught her well. She stifled a cry as they reached their pinnacle together. Wickham watched her expression, eyes closed, head still flung backwards as she gave herself over to pleasure. As always in such situations, he wondered what Lizzy's reaction would be like if it was her with his cock buried deep inside her.

Dear God, what he would give to find out. Just once.

Wickham rose from the bed to fasten his breeches. She moved into the space he vacated and sent him a satiated smile.

'I shall enjoy having you at Campton Park,' she said. 'It's a very short distance from the cottage we will be living in.'

'Then you must make sure your husband recommends me for the position.'

'Oh, he will, never fear. But you, in return, must ensure I am not neglected.'

'That would be unpardonable.'

'You have just discovered how much I enjoy... well, what we just did. But I think, in the right place and circumstances, we can do a lot better than that by one another.'

Wickham felt a moment's unease. She was beautiful and comely, but she also knew her worth and would be demanding. She could ruin things for him in the blink of an eye if she felt ignored, and she was already making sure he knew it. Still, Wickham could handle lovely little Alice, and he leaned in for another brief kiss, sealing their agreement.

'I believe we understand one another perfectly, Mrs Porter.'

She sent him a devilish smile. 'I believe we do, Mr Wickham.'

Wickham let himself quietly back into the room he was sharing with Alice's husband, feeling a whole lot better about life in general. Both of his roommates were still sound asleep, and he had got away with his nocturnal activities. At last, matters were going his way. Even Darcy could not object to writing him a character for a position to which he was so well suited, he decided, amending his original opinion about that gentleman's willingness to do so. Estate management – deciding what needed to be done and making sure others carried out the actual work – would be an ideal career. Wickham was surprised he hadn't thought to follow his father's example before now.

He climbed into his narrow cot, his head bursting with plans. No, Darcy would definitely do him this small service and recommend him to the new owners of Campton Park. It wouldn't cost him anything in terms of money and might actually ease his conscience for having treated him so shabbily. If Lydia got bored she could pay long visits at Pemberley. That would leave Wickham at leisure to attend to his other duties, such as Alice Porter and faithful Maria Allwood, patiently awaiting his return in Lambton.

11

Lizzy sat beside Jane, smiling as they watched the younger set dancing an energetic country dance.

'Did we used to have that much vigour?' Jane asked.

'Lydia and Kitty still do, but then neither of them is in your condition.' Lizzy shuddered. 'Well, I sincerely hope Lydia is not. She has more than enough problems to be going on with.'

'Even if she is, there's no reason for her not to dance. I would be dancing myself, but for the fact that Charles is more ferocious than a seasoned gaoler.' Jane's fond smile neutralised the rebuke in her words. 'Anyone would think I was the first woman in the world to be expecting a child.'

'You are fortunate he cares so deeply.'

'Oh yes, I know I am. I did not mean to complain.'

'I know you didn't.' Lizzy smiled at her sister. 'Now, tell me all about Campton Park. Was Mr Bingley pleased with what he saw?'

'Very much so. He plans to take me to visit the place next week. It's about the same size as Longbourn apparently, with very pretty rooms and lovely gardens, which would give me great pleasure.

There is also a well-managed farm and, best of all, the situation is very convenient.'

'Especially for Pemberley. It would be lovely to have you so close by.'

'Yes, that's one of the attractions.'

Their aunt joined them and the conversation turned to more general subjects. The dance came to an end, and those who had taken part in it took a moment to regain their breath. Then the fiddler struck up a cotillion and Lizzy looked up to find Will approaching.

'May I have the pleasure, Mrs Darcy?' he asked with a theatrical bow, sending her a wink only she could see as he lifted his head.

'Certainly you may.'

'You are to be congratulated upon another successful evening,' he told her as he led her into the dance.

'At the expense of barely seeing you at all.' Lizzy wrinkled her nose, wishing he would smile and at least look as though he was enjoying himself. 'I am not sure the reward is worth the sacrifice.'

'Not even if I promise to make it up to you later?'

She shook her head decisively. 'Not even then.'

'Not being in your company has not prevented me from thinking about you,' he said in an undertone. 'That gown has a lot to answer for.'

Lizzy affected surprise. 'You don't like it?'

'On the contrary, it reminds me a little too graphically for my comfort what you conceal beneath it.'

'My, sir, what a very short memory you have,' she said as they separated.

'My memory is in perfect working order,' he told her when the dance brought them back together again. 'Would you like to know what I have planned for you later on?'

Lizzy moistened her lips. They suddenly felt inexplicably dry. Will might be looking as remote and severe as always, but the salacious nature of his discourse told a very different story. 'By all means. Although it *will* rather spoil the surprise.'

He whispered in her ear, causing her to blush scarlet.

'That is not physically possible, surely.'

Will chuckled but somehow kept his lips set in a straight line as he did so. Lizzy noticed that Miss Bingley, dancing with Colonel Fitzwilliam, was watching them with an expression of malicious glee. Why, oh why, did she make Lizzy feel so uneasy? She reminded herself for the thousandth time that she was secure in Will's affection for her. There was absolutely nothing Miss Bingley could do to come between them.

Even so, her disquiet persevered.

'If I didn't know better, Mrs Darcy, I would say you were challenging me.'

'Then it's a very good thing you know better,' she replied, twirling away from him and smiling at Colonel Fitzwilliam as they came together.

'Miss Bingley hasn't stopped looking at you all evening,' Lizzy told Will when they again joined hands.

'You are mistaken.'

'Us ladies never mistake such matters. We have a sixth sense that tells us who is interested in whom. You look so stern she probably thinks you regret marrying me.'

'I can't help the way I look,' he replied, sounding a little insulted.

'Perhaps not, but you might pretend you enjoy dancing with me.'

'I enjoy what I have in mind for later considerably more.'

'Then smile at me.'

'Gentlemen don't smile in public, especially not at their wives. It is not done.'

She could tell he believed it was true. Lizzy would have to work on him and get him to see the error of his ways. 'Would you oblige me then by admitting to your plans for later in Miss Bingley's hearing?'

'Lizzy, what is it?' He frowned at her, looking more severe than ever. 'It's not like you to feel insecure, especially when you have no need to, and well you know it.'

'Oh, don't worry about me. I am still getting accustomed to being your wife and all the responsibilities that position entails.'

'Are you sure you're all right?' He canted his head and examined her face. 'You look a little pale.'

'Take no notice of me. I shall get used to other women coveting my husband in due time, I'm sure, and I might even learn not to mind about it.'

'Especially since there is absolutely nothing for you to mind. Do you really think me as inconstant as all that?'

'No, of course not.'

'Halstead cornered me earlier and asked for a private interview in the morning,' Will said in an abrupt change of subject.

'So soon?' Lizzy's brows rose. 'What shall you tell him?'

'That rather depends upon Georgiana's feelings. Will you have a word with her in the morning, before I see Halstead?'

'Of course, if you would like me to.'

'She is more likely to talk freely to you about her feelings.' They moved away from one another and seamlessly continued their conversation when they came together again. 'Whatever Georgiana's feelings, I will not permit Halstead to offer for her. It's too soon and she is too young to know her own mind. However, if his duties permit it, and if she desires it, I will allow him to call upon her here at Pemberley.'

That was a greater concession than Lizzy had expected him to make. 'I think you are being very reasonable.'

'Georgiana can count herself fortunate that my mind is constantly occupied with one subject, and one subject only nowadays, otherwise my reaction might be very different.'

'Really, sir?' Lizzy joined in the applause at the end of the dance, treating her husband to a glance of innocent enquiry. 'Whatever subject can that be, I wonder.'

He leaned his lips close to her ear and spoke in a barely audible whisper. 'You look at me in public that way again and you won't be able to sit down for a week.'

He sauntered away, hands clasped behind his back, leaving Lizzy gaping at his retreating form. The desire to smile at his outrageous comment rapidly receded when she felt Miss Bingley's intense gaze once again fixed upon her, a self-satisfied smile playing about her lips. She had obviously witnessed Lizzy's exchange with Will and assumed Lizzy had displeased him in some way. Regardless of Will's assurances to the contrary, Lizzy just *knew* Miss Bingley was out to cause trouble here at Pemberley.

And she had already gone a fair way to succeeding because Lizzy would not know a moment's peace until the wretched woman left them again.

* * *

Wickham enjoyed the final day's journey on the public coach that took them into Derby. Sitting opposite Alice, he was able to enjoy her smiles while her husband dosed on and off for the entire trip. Better yet, upon arrival at their destination, Porter offered him a seat in the carriage that had been sent from Campton Park to collect him, delivering Wickham right to the door of Long's cottage in Lambton.

'I shall expect to hear from you soon then, Wickham,' Porter said when they arrived at that location. 'Don't waste any time getting Darcy to write that character. As soon as I tell the owners I plan to retire, they will need to decide whether or not to appoint anyone else. They will ask my opinion, and I'd like to be able to recommend you. It would please me to know the work I've done there over the years has been passed into capable hands.' Porter wagged a finger at him. 'Don't let me down now.'

'I won't, sir, and thank you so very much for thinking of me.'

'No thanks are necessary. I like to help young men who have the desire to get on in life and ain't afraid of a little hard work.'

'I am certainly very desirous of this position,' Wickham replied, sending Alice a wink when Porter's attention was briefly diverted.

'We'll be hearing from you then,' Porter said, telling the coachman to drive on.

Maria Allwood opened the door of the cottage to Wickham, full of smiles and ready to feed him a wholesome meal.

'Your wife called yesterday,' she said, pulling a face as she sat across from him in the cramped kitchen and watched him eat. 'Had some fine lady with her, so she did.'

'Really?' Wickham's heart beat a little faster. Surely Lizzy hadn't come here? Damn it, he had to stop obsessing over her. 'Did the lady give her name?'

'Aye, Miss Bingley.'

'Bingley?' Wickham put his fork aside and stared at Maria. 'Are you absolutely sure about that?'

'Course I'm sure. Thick as thieves they were, her and your wife. Didn't stop chattering the whole time they were here.'

This was remarkable. What the devil did Lydia think she was up to? Wickham had told her to make herself agreeable while at Pemberley. To her credit, she found it easy to make friends, simply because she didn't think too deeply. Well, she didn't think at all, but that was beside the point. Caroline Bingley had a very high opinion of herself and was the last person he would have expected to enjoy his wife's society. Wickham shrugged. Perhaps Jane now being a Bingley explained it. Not that it really mattered how the unlikely friendship had come about. The more people Wickham had in his corner, the better it would be for everyone. For once, Lydia had exceeded his expectations.

He leaned back in his chair, unable to eat another bite. His appetites took another direction the moment his glance landed on Maria's ample bosom. Maria grinned at him and leaned further across the table, affording him an even better view when she crossed her arms and squeezed her breasts together. She was a good, obliging sort of girl who had kept him periodically entertained for several years before his marriage. Wickham had seen no reason to bring that arrangement to an end once he'd taken a wife. Besides, he needed eyes and ears in Lambton so he could keep abreast of activities at Pemberley, and that was another service Maria was happy to provide.

'Can I get you anything else?' Maria asked, her meaning unmistakable.

'That would be charming, but first I need to send word to my wife. Do you have pen and ink?'

Maria pouted but produced writing materials. 'Don't know why you are so keen to see her when you have me here, ready and willing.'

'It's purely business, my dear.' Wickham patted her rear. 'You know that very well.'

'Do I?'

Wickham scribbled two lines, summoning Lydia to Lambton immediately. 'Can your son pass this on?' he asked.

'Aye, tomorrow morning he should be able to manage it.'

'Excellent.' Maria's son was an under-gardener on the estate. He was very good at making himself invisible and cheeky enough to appear in places he had no reason to be, receiving no more than a clip around the ear if he was caught. 'Now then, what shall we do to pass the time?'

Wickham tapped his lap and Maria fell heavily onto it, slipping her arms around his neck and offering him a saucy smile. His hands lost no time in ridding her of her bodice.

'We'll have to be quick,' she said. 'Mr Long will be home directly.'

* * *

Lizzy planned to be about early the following day in order to have a private talk with Georgiana. Instead she overslept, for which she held Will entirely responsible. His demands became nightly more... well, demanding, but she had no complaints to make about his passionate inventiveness. She stretched and wiggled her toes, feeling smug and totally content, all thoughts of Miss Bingley's antipathy briefly eradicated.

She hadn't had it confirmed, but Lizzy was no longer in any doubt about her condition. Just the thought of eating breakfast caused her stomach to rebel, she was sure the sensitivity in her breasts had nothing to do with the prolonged attention they received from Will and, most significantly, her courses still had not arrived. She was now four weeks overdue. Lizzy had cross-questioned Jane on her symptoms the evening before, being careful to make her enquires sound more like expressions of sympathy. Everything Jane had said coincided with the way Lizzy felt. A broad smile invaded her features as she anticipated imparting the glad tidings to Will, even though she would delay doing so until the party was over. Selfishly, she wanted his complete attention when the time came and was in no mood to share the precious moment while Miss Bingley was still under their roof.

Foregoing breakfast, Lizzy was dressed half an hour later and went in search of Georgiana. As expected, she found her in the music room, idly running her fingers across the keys of the pianoforte but not actually playing anything. Lizzy guessed from her distracted expression that she was thinking about her handsome major.

'Good morning,' Lizzy said. 'I thought I would find you here.'

Georgiana smiled. 'How well you know me.'

'I *am* surprised to find you up so early. You did a lot of dancing last night, and it was very late when we all went to bed. Are you not still tired? I don't want you making yourself unwell. If that happens your brother will blame me.'

Georgiana removed one hand from the keys and waved it in the air. 'As you can see, I am wide awake and perfectly well. It was fun, Lizzy. I was unsure about the idea at first.' Georgiana flashed an apologetic smile. 'Dancing outside seemed rather... well, not quite the thing, especially here at Pemberley. You know how formal Fitzwilliam can be.'

Lizzy rolled her eyes, thinking again about how severe he had looked the entire evening, simply because that was how he thought he ought to behave. 'Yes, but it *was* his suggestion.'

'Really? Well, it was a good one, and it proved to be refreshing. One gets so warm dancing, but the fresh air kept us all vitalised.'

'I am glad to hear you say so.' Lizzy paused, wondering how to raise the subject uppermost in her mind without appearing to pry. Did Georgiana even know Major Halstead had asked to speak with Will? 'Tell me about Major Halstead,' she invited, deciding upon the direct approach. 'You appear to enjoy his society.'

Georgiana's face lit up but her eyes remained wary. 'I do. He has seen and done so much, and his conversation is lively and interesting. He behaves like a perfect gentleman and puts me at my ease.'

'Well, of course he does. Colonel Fitzwilliam would have him up on a charge if he did not.'

Georgiana laughed. 'I expect my brother thinks he's a fortune hunter.'

'What do *you* think?'

'Well, I know he doesn't have much money of his own, so I suppose it is not unreasonable that he would like me for my fortune.'

'Oh, Georgiana!' Lizzy impulsively hugged the younger woman. 'It never occurred to me until now how difficult it must be to grow up as an heiress.' She made a wry face. 'It is not a difficulty I ever had to wrangle with, you see.'

'Well...' Georgiana coloured. 'You know my history. Once bitten—'

'Don't tar all young men with the same brush, Georgie. The major and Wickham are two very different propositions. Yes, the naked truth is that Major Halstead must marry for money, but that does not mean he can't also fall in love with an heiress.'

Georgiana shook her head, setting her curls dancing. 'Major Halstead is not in love with me, Lizzy.'

'Perhaps not yet, but the admiration I see in his expression whenever he looks at you has nothing to do with avarice.'

Georgiana's wariness gave way to a cautious smile. 'Do you really think so?'

'I am absolutely certain of it.'

'Well, even if you happen to be right, it doesn't signify since my brother is quite determined I will go to London next season. He won't allow me to enter into any commitments until I have at least sampled the supposed delights of the good society. Not that I wish to, precisely,' she added hastily, 'but still, I—'

'Major Halstead has asked to speak with Will this morning.'

Georgiana's eyes widened. 'He has? I had no idea. Still, I don't suppose it has anything to do with me.'

Lizzy smiled as she patted Georgiana's hand. 'And I believe it has everything to do with you. Will asked me to talk to you about the major. You are right to say he thinks it too soon for you to enter into a binding commitment, but if you like the major's society—'

'Oh, I do, very much.'

'Well then, your brother will make no objection to his calling upon you here at Pemberley, provided you are properly chaperoned, of course.'

'Oh, Lizzy!' Animated, Georgiana jumped up and threw her arms around Lizzy. 'This is your doing, I just know it is. Fitzwilliam would never have listened to my opinion. Thank you.'

'You are entirely welcome. I like Major Halstead and understand your disinclination to go to London.' Lizzy stood up and smiled. 'But who knows what might happen between then and now.' Lizzy resisted the urge to pat her stomach. 'You never know. It might not actually happen.'

As Lizzy left the music room, she saved herself a long walk by cutting down a back corridor with a view over the kitchen garden. The wagon that went regularly into the village to collect supplies was just moving off. Lizzy barely spared it a glance at first, but she noticed something strange about it and took a closer look. A young woman was seated beside the liveried driver. A young woman who was very familiar to Lizzy.

'Lydia,' she said aloud, frowning. 'What the devil are you doing?'

Lizzy walked slowly towards her favourite parlour, wondering at Lydia even being up so early, much less dressed and heading for the village. Some of the ladies were planning an excursion into Lambton later in the morning. Lydia must have heard it discussed last night. If she was so desperate to go there herself, what could be so urgent that she couldn't wait and go with them?

The feeling of unease Lizzy felt when contemplating Miss Bingley's machinations applied equally when her thoughts turned to Lydia. She felt quite weak at the knees and hastened to take a chair, wondering what on earth her sister was up to this time.

12

Wickham was alone in the cottage when Lydia arrived, squealed at the sight of him, and hurled herself into his arms. Suppressing a sigh, Wickham gave her a dutiful peck on the cheek.

'It is such a shame you didn't make any progress in London!' she cried indignantly. 'Your friends ought to be ashamed of themselves. They promised you so faithfully.'

Actually they had made no such promises, but Lydia didn't need to know that. 'Yes, well, these are difficult times, but they did what they could.'

'Which wasn't nearly enough. A man of your abilities ought to be snapped up. Sometimes I think the entire world has turned against us.'

'I shall find something else.' He removed her arms from around his neck. 'Tell me how things are at Pemberley. More to the point, how did you come to call here in Miss Bingley's company?'

'I had no idea Pemberley was quite *so* grand.'

'It ought to be my home,' Wickham muttered malevolently.

'I can easily imagine you living there. Indeed, it would be so much jollier if you were the master of Pemberley. At least you wouldn't frown if you thought anyone had spoken out of turn.'

'Yes, but—'

'You wanted to know about Miss Bingley. Well, that is easily explained. She offered to come into Lambton with me because Lizzy is being very mean and wouldn't permit me to come alone.' Lydia puffed out her cheeks. 'I am not important enough to put the coachman to the trouble of driving the short distance, you see. Really, Lizzy has a very high opinion of herself now she's married to Mr Darcy. Still, at least Miss Bingley and I are such friends now, and she agrees with me. Not that she actually said so, of course. Well, she couldn't, I suppose, not with Lizzy being my sister, but I could feel her sympathy, which was really very kind of her.'

Yes, Wickham thought, *I'm sure you could*. Miss Bingley had her sights set on Darcy. She thought far too well of herself to take kindly to having him spirited away from beneath her very nose.

'And what of Darcy himself?' he asked.

'Oh, he is as aloof as ever.' Lydia waved the question aside. 'He hardly ever speaks to me, but whenever he looks at me he sees something to make him frown.'

'Who else is there?'

'My Aunt and Uncle Gardiner, the Bingleys and Hursts and Colonel Fitzwilliam and two other officers. One of them is Major Halstead and he seems very keen on Miss Darcy.'

'The devil he does!' Wickham cursed softly beneath his breath when he recalled how close he had come to cooking that particular goose, revenging himself on Darcy and securing his own future comfort into the bargain.

'And Captain Turner is there, too. He and Kitty appear close, but I think Kitty only likes him because he is related to an earl. I can't quite remember how close the connection is.' Lydia shrugged. 'Still, that must be the attraction because he isn't at all handsome and speaks with an unfortunate stammer.' Lydia shrugged. 'I had no idea Kitty could be quite so shallow.'

Wickham's cursing became more colourful. He was acquainted with Turner, and not in a good way. He owed him money for losses at cards. Unlike other dues, debts of honour could not be ignored indefinitely. Hopefully, Turner had forgotten about the wager or hadn't made the connection between Lydia and himself.

'Has it occurred to you that Kitty might actually *like* the captain?' Wickham asked, hoping to promote the match. If Wickham and Turner became related by marriage, Turner couldn't possibly press Wickham for payment.

'I fail to see how.' Lydia wrinkled her nose. 'The man has absolutely nothing to recommend him, apart from money and good connections.'

Which, Wickham knew very well, was the only requirement.

Lydia chatted away about Pemberley and the activities taking place there. Wickham listened with half an ear, pretending an interest he no longer felt when it became apparent she had nothing more of consequence to impart.

'What shall you do now?' she asked. 'Shall you ask Mr Darcy for his help?'

'No, not Darcy.'

Wickham told his wife about the opening at Campton Park for an estate manager. Lydia seemed less than enamoured by the idea.

'An estate manager?' She blinked repeatedly, reminding Wickham of an outraged owl. 'But you deserve better than that. Your talents would be wasted in such a position. Besides, I don't think I should like it very much, being stuck in some out-of-the-way place and never seeing anyone for days at a time.'

'Then what would you have me do?' Wickham held on to his temper with difficulty. Sometimes his wife was so impractical he wanted to shake her. 'You know how badly I've been treated by those who ought to know better. If I am to support you in the style you have every right to expect, I must grasp whatever opportunities come my way.'

'Oh, my love, I didn't mean to criticise *you*. I know none of this is your fault, but it is so unfair. I had quite set my heart on being in London.'

'And so you shall be, in due course. But first I need you to do something for me.'

'Anything.'

'Talk to Lizzy. Explain the situation and tell her that I require Darcy to do me a small service and write me a character.'

'Oh, is that all? Why don't I tell Mr Darcy directly?'

'No, it wouldn't be right for you to approach him on matters of business, but it's natural for you to talk to your sister about my circumstances. She will persuade him to do the right thing.'

'It infuriates me that he requires any persuading, especially when it won't cost him anything more than a few minutes of his time.'

'Quite so, but that's the way of the world when gentlemen who think too well of themselves are involved.' Wickham sighed, anxious for Lydia to be on her way back to Pemberley. 'How shall you get back?'

'Some of the ladies were coming into the village this morning. I shall find them and go back with them. I came ahead because I was anxious to see you. I thought it might give us more time together.'

'Perhaps you ought to go and look for them now. It wouldn't do for you to miss them and have to walk.'

'Yes, all right. But once Mr Darcy has written your character, can I come and live here with you, until you get your new position? I miss you so much.'

Wickham could imagine what Maria Allwood would have to say about that suggestion. 'I am too embarrassed to show you the miserable space I'm reduced to sleeping in, my dear. I couldn't possibly ask you to share it with me. Besides, there is insufficient room for us both.'

'You are such a caring husband!' she cried passionately.

'Here, I have written down the name of the gentleman who owns the estate and the name of the estate itself for you to pass on to your sister.'

'Just as well,' Lydia said with a careless laugh, 'since I have forgotten it already.'

There was a knock at the door. Wickham wasn't expecting callers and was never more surprised when he saw who their visitor was.

'Miss Bingley!' Wickham turned on a charming smile, took her outstretched hand and bowed over it. 'What a delightful surprise. Please come in.'

'I don't mean to intrude, Mr Wickham, but I have been charged with seeking out your wife. She was nowhere to be found when we left Pemberley, and so I promised Jane I would look for her.'

'And here she is.'

Wickham stood back, observing Miss Bingley as she greeted Lydia with enthusiasm that didn't come close to matching his wife's uncontrived pleasure at seeing her new 'friend'. What was she doing here in this damp cottage, deliberately seeking out Lydia's society? The fine walking gown she wore and the equally fine opinion of herself she failed to adequately conceal from Wickham's perusal were completely out of place in this hovel. He couldn't begin to decide what it was she needed from Lydia, and so he stored Miss Bingley's strange behaviour away for later consideration.

'I don't mean to rush you, Mrs Wickham, but if you are to return to Pemberley for luncheon with the rest of us then I must urge you to make haste. The carriage will leave the inn in less than ten minutes.'

Lydia collected up the letter Wickham had written for Darcy. 'I shall return tomorrow, having accomplished the task you've set me, my dear, never doubt it.'

Lydia stood on her toes and kissed Wickham's cheek. He glanced over her head as she did so and caught Miss Bingley in the process of wrinkling her nose. She saw him watching her too late to wipe the disdainful expression from her face.

* * *

Lizzy was alone in the small salon immediately after luncheon when Lydia came bursting in. It was raining hard outside, which put a damper on Lizzy's planned outdoor activities. Most of the gentlemen were in the billiards room, except Major Halstead, who had offered to read aloud to the ladies in the drawing room. She would wager that Captain Turner had eschewed billiards and accompanied his friend. In both their cases, literature was definitely not the attraction.

'Ah, Lizzy, I'm glad to find you alone.' Lydia sat down beside Lizzy, her face wreathed in smiles. 'I have a small favour to ask of you.'

Lizzy flinched. Lydia's favours were never small. 'Do you not wish to listen to Major Halstead?'

'No, I have something important to talk to you about that cannot wait.'

'If you are going to ask me again if you can borrow any of my clothes, the answer is still *no*. You are taller than me so they wouldn't fit you anyway.'

'Oh no, it's nothing like that.'

'All right. But first, tell me what took you off to the village in such a tearing hurry this morning. You shouldn't have gone without telling anyone.'

Lydia blinked. 'Why ever not? I wasn't likely to be missed.'

'You are quite wrong about that.' Lizzy suppressed a sigh. As usual Lydia had behaved with total disregard for anyone's convenience other than her own. Jane had been in such a tizzy about Lydia's absence that servants had been sent all over the house to look for her. When Lizzy heard of it, she was able to set Jane's mind at rest, but by then the entire house was in an uproar. 'Besides, you would have been more comfortable if you'd waited for the other ladies and gone in the carriage with them.'

'Oh, Wickham has returned from London, and I was too anxious to see him to wait for the others to be ready.'

Lizzy gasped. 'Wickham is in Lambton?'

'Why should he not be?' Lydia bridled. 'Mr Darcy doesn't own the entire village, you know, and Wickham still has friends here willing to lend him their support.'

'How did you know he had returned?' As far as Lizzy was aware, Lydia had received no letters since arriving at Pemberley.

'He sent a message through one of the boys who lives in the village and works here in the gardens. A housemaid delivered it to my room this morning.'

'I see.' But why the need for such a convoluted method of communication? Even Will couldn't object to Wickham writing to his wife while she was at Pemberley. 'Was he successful in finding employment in London?'

'No, unfortunately there was nothing available, but another possibility has arisen. And that is why I need a favour.'

Lizzy pushed both her hands, palms outward, towards Lydia. 'Don't ask me to approach Mr Darcy on your husband's behalf again. I would be wasting my breath.'

'We are not asking for any of your precious money, if that's what

concerns you.' Lydia tossed her head, her eyes flashing with indignation. 'And there is no occasion to be so defensive just because I
dared to mention Wickham's name in your hearing. The ceilings
won't come tumbling down, you know.'

'It is good that you don't require money,' Lizzy replied calmly,
'because you have already wasted more than you were entitled to
expect.'

'Oh, I knew you would be like this! I'm sure Wickham's done
nothing to deserve *your* censure.'

Oh, Lydia, if only you knew!

'Anyway, I came to you in the spirit of sisterly affection, and I
have no wish to fight with you over the past.'

Lizzy closed her eyes for an expressive moment, willing herself
to exercise patience. Lydia was very good at making her feel guilty,
and torn, when she had nothing to be guilty about, and her loyalties ought to have been straightforward. She patted her sister's
hand, once again fighting nausea and the ever-present headache.
'And I have no wish to fight with you. I am however very tired, so
please, just tell me what you require of me and be done with it.'

'Wickham feels wretched because he doesn't think he looks
after me as well as he ought, and so he is forced to consider
employment that is beneath him. A position has arisen for an
estate manager and—'

'But that's how Wickham's father was employed here at Pemberley. Does Wickham know anything about managing estates
himself?'

Lydia shrugged, as though she had not even considered the
question, which she almost certainly had not. 'What is there for
him to know?'

A very great deal, Lizzy suspected, but it would be a waste of
energy to say so.

'He is well educated and intelligent, which are all the qualifications he requires. All he needs to secure the position is a character from Mr Darcy.'

Lizzy's heart sank. Will was far too honourable to recommend Wickham for a position he was ill-qualified to fill. 'Where is the estate located that requires a manager?' Lizzy asked, hoping it would be a long distance from Pemberley.

'Oh, it is not at all far from here, which is why Wickham is bound to get the position. The current manager remembers his father, you see. Anyway, Wickham wrote all the particulars down because he thought I might forget.' She giggled. 'He was right, of course, because I already have.'

Lizzy took the paper from Lydia's fingers and unfolded it slowly, smothering a gasp when she read the words written there: *Campton Park*. Dear God, wasn't that the estate Mr Bingley was considering?

13

Lydia tried wheedling, cajoling and then flattering Lizzy into giving her word. When all her stratagems failed she turned on the tears and did her best to make Lizzy feel guilty by pointing out the huge divide between their individual situations. Lizzy had endured sixteen years of Lydia's theatrics and had become immune to her manipulative ways. She remained calm in the face of her sister's growing hysteria, telling her she would think about her request without making any promises. In the end, Lydia left the room, muttering under her breath about sisters who feathered their own nests and then seemed to forget the duty they owed to their own flesh and blood.

Left alone, Lydia's shill voice no longer bouncing off the walls and drilling into her aching head, Lizzy allowed the quiet to wash over her. She closed her eyes and massaged her pounding temple with the tips of her fingers. What the devil was she supposed to do about Lydia's request? She dreaded telling Will, but knew she would have to, even though she also knew he wouldn't help Wickham again. For her sake, he had already behaved handsomely towards a man he had every reason to despise. Having anything at all to do with him still must stir up the most unpalatable memories. Wickham certainly didn't deserve Will's largesse, nor did he appear to appreciate it, and she instinctively knew this latest demand would be the final straw.

The door opened again and, assuming it was Lydia returning with more to say for herself, Lizzy's heart sank. But it wasn't Lydia. Instead Kitty walked in, looking fresh and pretty in a pale blue muslin gown Lizzy had not seen her wear before. Thankful for the diversion, Lizzy glanced at her sister's face. She expected to see her features glowing, as only those in the face of a young lady enjoying the attentions of an eligible gentleman for the first time ever can. Instead she was confronted by a downturned mouth and glum expression.

'Whatever is the matter, Kitty?'

'Am I disturbing you?'

'Not at all. I shall be glad of your company,' Lizzy lied. 'Are you tired of listening to Major Halstead's reading?'

'I was listening, but—'

Lizzy smiled. 'Let me guess – Captain Turner was required to make up the numbers in the billiards room, and when he left, Major Halstead's reading lost its appeal.'

Kitty blushed. 'Is it that obvious?'

'It is certainly evident that you and the captain enjoy one another's company.'

'Oh, I do enjoy being with him. Very much. I find him easy to talk to. He is one of those rare gentlemen who listens to what a lady has to say and takes an interest in her opinions. Lydia says I only like him because he has private means, and because his father is Lord Turner.' Kitty's eyes briefly lost their dull expression. 'Only imagine that.'

'You are a gentleman's daughter, and worthy of Captain Turner's attentions in every respect.' Lizzy patted her sister's shoulder. 'Never lose sight of that fact.'

'Lydia is quite wrong. It doesn't matter to me who his relations are, or that Captain Turner is not very handsome. There is more to life than appearances.'

When did Kitty become so wise? 'Certainly there is.'

'Mr Wickham might be handsome and full of charm, but he doesn't seem to look after Lydia very well.'

'No, he does not.' *And, regardless of her opinion of Captain Turner, Lydia would be the first to beat a path to your door, begging bowl in hand, were the two of you to marry.* 'We have established that you enjoy Captain Turner's society, Kitty, and neither Jane nor I can see any harm in it, so why the glum expression?'

'Georgiana is in fine spirits because Mr Darcy has given Major Halstead his permission to call at Pemberley and, well—'

'Ah, now I understand.' Lizzy nodded. 'The major and the captain are in the same regiment, quartered less than half a day's ride from here, and you are remaining at Pemberley for the rest of the summer.'

'Yes, but they might as well be on the other side of the country for all the difference it will make to me. Captain Turner will not be returning after this party.'

Kitty's anguished expression caused Lizzy to feel deeply for her. She had met a gentleman who truly excited her passions, but she obviously thought her feelings were not returned.

'Good gracious, whatever makes you say that?'

'I overheard him in conversation with Major Halstead earlier. I wasn't deliberately eavesdropping, but I happened to be on the stairs and heard them speaking quietly outside the billiards room. I heard my name mentioned, so naturally—'

'I would have listened too,' Lizzy assured her sister. 'It is said eavesdroppers never hear good of themselves, but I cannot persuade myself that Captain Turner would say anything to your detriment.'

'Oh no, he didn't. Major Halstead was telling the captain about his interview with Mr Darcy. He was in alt because he had been given permission to call here and visit Georgiana. He asked Captain Turner if he would seek permission to call upon me, but he said there was no point.'

'No point?' Lizzy probably looked as dumfounded as she felt. 'I thought him more constant than that.'

'He said nothing would give him greater pleasure, that he enjoyed my society, but his father had plans for him and that was that.'

Lizzy frowned. 'You mean his father wants him to marry someone else.'

'Yes, it seems that way.' Kitty looked close to tears. 'Everything Captain Turner has done in his adult life has been in an effort to obtain his father's respect, you see.'

'Because his father bullied him when he was a child, implying he would never become much of a man.' Lizzy seethed. 'Naturally, the captain wishes to prove him wrong.'

'Yes, I suppose he does.'

'Well, I applaud his character. A lesser man would sink beneath the disapproval of such a tyrannical parent, especially one like Captain Turner, who has the financial means to go his own way.'

'I could wish his standards were a little less rigid,' Kitty replied, brushing a non-existent crease from her skirts.

'As would I in your position.' Lizzy paused, wondering if there was anything she could do to help her sister. 'The captain obviously likes you very much.'

'Which makes everything ten times worse,' Kitty said, looking close to tears.

'My advice is that you continue to enjoy Captain Turner's smiles and leave the rest to me. I shall have a discreet word with him and see if I can find out anything about his intentions.'

'Thank you, but what can you possibly say that would make any difference?'

'Oh, I am sure I shall think of something. You know how inventive I can be when the occasion calls for a little guile.'

Kitty actually managed a brief smile. 'You *did* stand up to Mama when you declined Mr Collins's proposal of marriage. I have always admired you for that. I would have caved beneath the pressure long since.'

'Well, there you are then.' Lizzy patted Kitty's shoulder. 'Your captain stands no chance.'

Kitty looked warily optimistic. 'I'm probably being fanciful, and nothing will come of it anyway, but... oh, I don't know, I like him so very much.' She closed her eyes and hugged her arms around her torso. 'I can't seem to think about anything else. But if he is able to regard our separation with apparent indifference, perhaps I am deceiving myself into believing there is more between us than actually exists, simply because I wish it to be so. After all, he has not actually declared himself.'

'Go back to the drawing room.' Lizzy shooed Kitty away with her hands. 'I am sure the captain will rejoin the other ladies as soon as he can and will wonder where you are. I will let you know when I have spoken to him.'

'Very well.' Kitty stood up and then leaned down to kiss Lizzy's brow. 'Thank you,' she said softly.

'You are entirely welcome.'

Lizzy watched her go, feeling the full burden of the responsibility she now bore for her sisters. First Lydia, now Kitty. Just as well Mary wasn't here, too.

'Oh, hello, Aunt.'

'You look exhausted, Lizzy.' Mrs Gardiner took the seat Kitty had just vacated and sent Lizzy a probing glance. 'Are you all right?'

'Just a little tired.'

'You're doing too much. My advice is to allow your guests to entertain themselves this afternoon. You don't need to be checking up on them every two minutes.' Her aunt sent her another considering look, as though she had guessed at Lizzy's real reason for feeling so tired. 'You are not needed here at the moment. Everyone is gainfully occupied, and the unmarried members of the party are suitably chaperoned. Take yourself off and have a good, long rest.'

'Well, that idea does have appeal. If you're absolutely sure I can be spared. Perhaps—'

'Just go.' Mrs Gardiner spoke adamantly. 'I'm here if anyone needs anything.'

'Thank you, Aunt.' Lizzy covered her mouth to stifle a yawn. 'I shall not be absent for long.'

'Take all the time you need.'

Lizzy headed for her chamber, in urgent need of the guarantee of solitude in order to consider all Lydia had told her and decide how best to handle the situation. Kitty's predicament would have to wait. For once she was glad Lydia paid so little attention to what others said, unless it impeded directly upon her own comforts. Mr Bingley wasn't talking openly about his intention of purchasing an estate in the locality, but he wasn't exactly keeping it a secret either. She had heard Campton Park spoken of openly on several occasions since her brother-in-law visited the estate, but thankfully Lydia had failed to make the connection. If she did, she would badger Jane mercilessly until her husband agreed to employ Wickham as his estate manager. Wickham would then take shameless advantage of Mr Bingley's good nature, spoiling Jane's pleasure in her new home, to say nothing of her peace of mind.

That absolutely could not be allowed to happen, and it fell to

Lizzy's lot to ensure that it did not. She wouldn't risk compromising Jane's happiness for the sake of her selfish youngest sister's comfort, and that was an end to the matter. Lydia had made her choices and must live with the consequences.

Lizzy's head was pounding, and she threw herself, fully clothed, on her bed. What to do? Was there a way in which she could help Lydia and Wickham without Will's knowledge, on condition they took themselves a long way away from Pemberley, of course? Even if there was, dare she risk doing something so diametrically opposed to her husband's wishes? Besides, there was no guarantee they would *stay* far away.

Lizzy was motivated by the desire to protect Jane and save Will from the trouble of having to deal with Wickham. A full year had not yet elapsed since he had last helped his nemesis. Wickham, on the other hand, was not so highly principled. If he discovered that she had defied Will, he would not scruple to use that knowledge against her if he thought he could somehow profit from it. Besides, if Will found out she had acted without his knowledge, it would drive an unbridgeable gap between them.

She wasn't prepared to take that risk. Lydia and Wickham had already shown just how careless they were of any help directed their way, and so her kindness would be bound to come back to haunt her.

There had to be another way.

She must have dozed – how, when her head was spinning with unpalatable possibilities, she could not have said. A noise woke her and she sat up abruptly, disorientated, just in time to observe Will creeping out of her room. She rubbed sleep from her eyes and called his name.

'I'm sorry, my dear. Did I wake you?'

'No, and I am quite out of character with you for that precise reason.'

'You looked so exhausted that I couldn't bear to disturb you.' He sat on the edge of her bed and brushed the hair away from her brow. 'This party is too much for you. You have put too much effort into it, which is what I feared might happen. It's simply not in your character to do anything half-heartedly.'

'Nonsense, I am as strong as an ox.'

He smiled. 'Oxen don't sleep soundly in the middle of the day.'

'If you were to cuddle me, I'm sure it would restore the strength you appear to think I lack.'

Deep, rich masculine laughter filled the room. 'If I were to cuddle you, matters wouldn't rest there.'

She sent him a dazzling smile. 'Precisely!'

He shook his head. 'Sometimes I despair of you.'

'How can I be to blame for my enthusiasm? It was you who awoke my passions in the first place and so you ought to finish what you started. I am sure there is still a very great deal more that you can teach me.'

His expression softened as his lips brushed lightly across her forehead. 'Well, I suppose the responsibility does rest with me.'

Already in shirtsleeves and bare-footed, he lay down beside her and pulled her into his arms. Now, she thought, would be the ideal time to tell him about Lydia, while he was relaxed and in a good mood. *I should not delay, not even another moment. There should be no secrets between us.*

She would have told him, too, had he not kissed her with such burning passion that she could think of nothing but responding with an urgency to match his own. His hands were as crushing as his lips, threatening to rip her bodice apart in his desire to reach her breasts. Lizzy found the ties that held her gown in place and loosened them before he actually damaged the expensive garment. Normally, Will had infuriating patience in the bedchamber and gloried in making her beg him for release. This afternoon desperation appeared to have won out over finesse. His mood was infectious, and her own desire blossomed on the back of his.

'Will,' she said breathlessly. 'There is something we need to talk about.'

He rolled his eyes and laughed. 'Now she wishes to talk.'

His hands continued to work their magic. Lizzy melted beneath them and soon had trouble recalling what she wished to talk about or why it was so important.

'Well, perhaps not immediately,' she conceded.

'Let's get you out of this pretty gown, Mrs Darcy, before it becomes impossibly creased.'

She lifted her hips and surrendered to her husband's skilful care, temporarily pushing her worries to the back of her mind. She drifted on a wave of anticipation as her petticoats were also whisked down her legs. She reached for Will and found his chest bare. Briefly opening one eye, she discovered the rest of him was, too. She was absolutely sure he'd had *some* clothes on just a moment or two ago, and she idly wondered how he could have shed them without her knowledge. There was a rough urgency about his actions today, as though he had demons to exorcise. *And I'm about to add to them by telling him of Wickham's latest scheme.*

'Is it terribly unfashionable for a man to tell his wife that he loves her?' he asked, his voice heavy with passion. 'I believe admitting to loving one's wife is not at all the done thing.'

Her heart soared. For such a reserved man as Will to so readily admit to his love for her was no mean achievement. How different he was to the proud, austere gentleman she had so disliked when they had first met in Hertfordshire, even if those differences weren't readily apparent when they were in public.

'I have been told more than once that my sense of fashion is behind the times.'

'In that case you might as well know that you are my life, Lizzy

Darcy, and I love you to distraction. Everything I do in this world is done with thoughts of your happiness in mind.'

One look at the desperate passion in his eye and liquid heat coursed through Lizzy's bloodstream, depriving her of the breath necessary to tell him how much he was loved in return. Well, actions spoke louder than words, and Lizzy was perfectly ready to match Will's frantic urgency. She put her heart and soul into following wherever he led, keener than ever to please him because she knew how angry he would be when he learned of Wickham's bald request.

Her heart went out to her husband as she thought about all he had suffered for her sake, and still suffered. He had thought Wickham was gone from his life forever but now, every time he observed Lydia's abandoned behaviour here at Pemberley, he would be reminded of him. Lydia was as silly and selfish as always, flirted almost as much as she had before she married, and appeared to think her family owed her a living.

'Oh my goodness!'

Lizzy gasped as Will released a white hot explosion of energy, transporting her to a place where exquisite shards of intense sensation ripped through her as they tumbled together over the abyss.

'I'm sorry, my dear,' Will said as soon as he recovered his breath. 'I should have taken more time and not been so rough.'

Lizzy smiled at him, wonderfully comfortable cuddled against the solidity of his body, head resting on his chest. 'I enjoy your inventiveness. You never seem to do the same thing in the same way twice in succession.'

'Even so, I was selfish.'

'Never!'

'What were you so anxious to talk about?' he asked, lying flat on his back and staring up at the canopy. 'Has something happened?'

Lizzy sighed. 'Wickham is back in Lambton.'

She felt his body tense. 'He was unsuccessful in finding a new career in London, I assume.'

'Yes.'

'I knew that would be the case, but still I had hoped perhaps this time...' His satiated expression was replaced by a fixed, unreadable mask. 'Did Lydia tell you where he is staying?'

'At a cottage that belongs to someone named Long.'

'Long was a keeper here during Wickham's father's time. Long and Wickham's father were good friends.'

'And I'm sure Wickham would not hesitate to trade upon that friendship and Mr Long's good nature.'

'All right, Lizzy.' Will sounded impossibly weary. 'What does Wickham require of me this time?'

'Lydia tells me he has decided to follow in his father's footsteps.'

'Estate management?' Will raised a brow. 'I recall his father trying to get him to take an interest in running this estate. That would have been a natural succession, but Wickham sneered at the suggestion, thinking himself above such a career.'

'Are you surprised? Your father did provide him with a gentleman's education.'

Lizzy wished the words back when a scowl invaded Will's features. 'You throw your support behind Wickham's cause?' he asked coldly.

'Not in the least, but I do understand something of his character.' Oh lord, she was making matters worse, but she couldn't seem to stop herself from trying to explain how the situation appeared to her. 'I can understand why your father's attentions affected such a vain and weak-willed man in ways Mr Darcy had not intended them to, that's all.'

'A timely lesson in the folly of misguided kindness. It is a mistake I shall never make.' Will's jaw clenched, square and unmoving. 'Wickham has been a thorn in my side for quite long enough and has had all he will ever get from me, which is a great deal more than he deserves. If he supposes his marriage to your sister will soften my stance, then he has gravely miscalculated.'

Lizzy quaked at Will's glacial tone. She had never seen him quite this angry before. She sensed some of that anger was directed at her for giving the impression she had sympathy for Wickham.

'I know,' she said, 'and I understand.'

'So I should hope.'

'Really, you have done more than anyone else in your position would have done. My only fear is that Wickham, in his desperation, will work on Mr Bingley, exploiting his affection for Jane. Mr Bingley doesn't know the particulars of your rift with Wickham and might not see any harm in helping Lydia's husband.'

'I will speak with Bingley.' Will paused. 'What estate does Wickham hope to manage?'

'That's another problem.' When Lizzy failed to suppress a shudder, she saw a flicker of concern break through Will's cold expression.

'What is it?' he asked.

'Someone in a position of authority somewhere is obviously out to test your patience. You see, a position has fallen vacant at Campton Park.'

Will smothered an oath, focusing his malevolent scowl on the opposite wall. 'I know of the man who has held it for years. He was a friend of Wickham's father, too.'

'Apparently Wickham travelled back here on the same public coach as Porter.'

'I suppose Wickham has the nerve to presume I will write him a character.'

'Yes, but I told Lydia you would not do it.'

'Then she will have recovered from her disappointment by now.'

'I'm concerned Lydia will make the connection between that estate and Mr Bingley's interest in it. If she does, my earlier fears will be realised. She *will* most certainly hound Jane, and Mr Bingley will probably appoint Wickham to the position just to keep the peace.'

'I will make sure that doesn't happen.' The vertical lines etched in Will's forehead suddenly seemed a lot deeper. 'Somehow.'

'Perhaps Mr Bingley will decide against Campton Park.'

'I fail to see why my friend should forego an estate that would suit him perfectly just to avoid Wickham.'

'That is not what I mean and you know it.'

His forbidding expression twisted and tore at her insides. 'Do I? Sometimes I'm not sure I know you at all.'

'That's not fair!'

'Is it not?' Will's anger didn't entirely disguise his inner-turmoil, and Lizzy longed to throw herself into his arms and comfort him. She refrained because she knew the gesture would not be welcomed in his current frame of mind. 'You desire to see your sister comfortable does you credit, but you seem to forget that *I* am now your family. All I require is your loyalty. Is that so very much to ask?'

'You have my undivided loyalty, Will. Never doubt it for a moment.'

'Then leave Wickham to me.'

If only it were that easy. Lizzy could think of only one solution that would keep everyone happy, but it required a good deal of courage before she could bring herself to voice it.

'Would it be so very bad to recommend Wickham?' she asked tentatively.

The look Will sent her was one of shock, quickly followed by concentrated fury. 'If that is your solution then you understand even less about these matters than he does.' His tone was silk on steel, and she could see he was holding on to his temper by the sheer force of his will. 'He would be required to know the intricacies of crop rotation, animal husbandry, management of woodland, supervision of workers... shall I go on?'

'I do know what's involved, but it seems to me that Wickham must have learned more than he realised, if his father was so very good at his job.'

'Wickham spent as little time as possible at his father's side. He was always up here at the house.'

Which rather supported Lizzy's argument that Wickham's unrealistic ambitions had been fostered by old Mr Darcy. One glance at the rigid set to Will's features and she knew better than to say so.

'I'm frightened, Will, and worried that something bad will happen. Wickham is desperate, and he has convinced himself he's been treated unjustly. I know better, of course, but I still can't help feeling that if he doesn't get his way, he will do something to hurt us.'

Will openly scoffed. 'So you would give in to him?'

'No, not at all, I—'

'I know he was once a favourite of yours, Lizzy, but you chose to marry me, so you will just have to make the best of a bad job.'

Will got up from the bed, his face white with rage, and gathered up his discarded clothing. Lizzy was speechless with shock. Did he really imagine she harboured secret longings for Wickham?

'I did not mean to imply a partiality for Wickham, and well you know it,' she said, her own temper rising.

'Excuse me, madam. I have business to attend to.'

And, just like that, he left her without a backward glance. Lizzy fell against the pillows, her headache worse than ever, wondering how she could have handled him so ineptly. Tears welled but she was too exhausted, too distraught, and too angry to let them fall.

14

The tension Caroline sensed the moment she entered the drawing room that evening afforded her considerable satisfaction. Either the rain that still poured down outside had cast a pall over the party, or something had happened to displease her host and hostess. She glanced at Mr Darcy as he stood in front of the fire in deep, muted conversation with Charles. Impeccably attired as always, she could see at once that he was seriously displeased about something – or with someone. A lock of his thick hair fell across his dark eyes and she was filled with an impulsive desire to rush up to him and push it aside.

Soon, she reminded herself. Soon, if she carried through with her plan, she would have earned the right to perform that small service for him.

Caroline smothered a smile. She had learned from Mrs Wickham all about her husband's need for a character reference from Darcy. Mrs Wickham appeared to think Darcy would provide it without hesitation, but Caroline suspected the rift between the two men would cause Darcy to refuse. He was far too honourable to recommend a man whom he did not esteem. She would give much to know what had caused that rift, although the blame must lay entirely with Wickham. For all his good looks and charm, he really was a loathsome creature, and Caroline disliked him intently. At the same time, she admired his ruthlessness, his willingness to use anything and anyone to his own advantage – a trait she recognised in herself in situations such as the one she found herself in now – and she fully intended to exploit it to the maximum.

Presumably, Eliza knew why Wickham had been expelled from Pemberley, but had passed on her sister's request anyway, driving a deeper wedge between herself and Darcy than had already existed. Caroline had been depending upon Eliza's loyalty to her ungrateful family to make her behave rashly, and she did not appear to have disappointed. Already the edifice of her infamous marriage was starting to crumble, and she only had herself to blame. She glanced at Eliza, her complexion pale, eyes dull. She was seated with Mrs Gardiner but appeared to have little to say for herself. Darcy was standing just about as far away from his wife as the proportions of the room permitted and never once looked in her direction.

'How did you get on with your sister?' Caroline asked, walking up to Mrs Wickham and forcing herself to smile. 'Presumably she was able to gain her husband's assistance for Mr Wickham.'

'She said she would speak to Mr Darcy, but it was obvious that she would prefer not to. It makes me so angry that she is unprepared to make that small effort.' Mrs Wickham's eyes radiated anger, which was unusual. She was normally indefatigably cheerful. 'Really, it would not surprise me if she didn't even bother.'

'You could always ask him yourself.'

Mrs Wickham chewed her lower lip. 'I could, but Wickham particularly told me not to approach him.'

'Only because he assumed your sister would support your cause.'

'Perhaps you are right, but I shall give Lizzy a little longer before I try anything else. I don't think Mr Darcy likes me very much.'

'Oh, I am sure he does.'

'He is so severe. How can Lizzy be comfortable with him?'

How indeed? 'Well, if there is anything I can do, you have but to say the word.'

'Thank you, Miss Bingley. It is very comforting to know someone in this house cares about my welfare.'

'What are friends for?'

Mrs Wickham wandered away and, predictably, attached herself to Major Halstead. Before Caroline could talk to anyone else, Louisa joined her.

'What are you thinking of, encouraging Mrs Wickham's friendship? Have you lost your senses?'

Caroline lifted one shoulder. 'She is harmless enough and seems a little out of her depth here at Pemberley. I was merely being kind.'

'That is not what you said about her in Hertfordshire when she behaved so badly, and I cannot see that she has improved much. Her flirtatious manner is revolting.'

'She is a married woman, Louisa. It's permitted for her to flirt. You of all people ought to know that.'

'There is no need to take your bad temper out on me,' Louisa replied mildly.

'Sorry, pay me no heed.'

'What is wrong?' Louisa narrowed her eyes. 'What are you up to, Caroline?'

Caroline lifted one shoulder, attempting to emulate Louisa's languid attitude. 'Why should I be up to anything?'

'I know you too well to be deceived. I can always tell when you're scheming.'

'It's the weather. It must be affecting us all.'

'If you're tired of being here, we can always leave early on some pretext or other. I know how hard it is for you.'

'I would not hear of it. I'm having a delightful time.'

Louisa laughed. 'Then try to look as though you are.'

Caroline was grateful when Simpson announced that dinner was served. The sisters were forced to separate and Louisa's interrogation of her came to an end.

It seemed to Caroline as though there was a forced gaiety about the dinner table conversation that evening. The tension between host and hostess had obviously communicated itself to the rest of the party. Caroline wasn't seated anywhere near Darcy, but that did not prevent her from stealing frequent glances in his direction. A near perpetual glower marred his handsome features, even when engaging his dinner companions in conversation. Eliza, for her part, still looked pale and appeared to eat little.

Caroline congratulated herself on a plan well hatched. If she had harboured any doubts about what she intended to do, the tension between Darcy and his unsuitable wife convinced her that she was right to act. There wasn't much time left, just two more days to see the plan through. Darcy was angry with his wife, but that did not mean he wouldn't eventually oblige Wickham by giving him the recommendation he required, if only to keep the peace. Recommendations were easily given and cost nothing. She simply could not allow that to happen. Her entire plot revolved around Wickham's increasing desperation.

When the gentlemen rejoined the ladies, Georgiana took up a place at the pianoforte, and Major Halstead, who possessed a fine baritone voice, sang for the company. For the first time that evening, Caroline noticed Darcy's fierce expression soften as he listened to his sister's elegant performance. Eliza didn't follow Georgiana at the instrument, and Darcy did not suggest that she should. Excellent!

'Come, Louisa,' Caroline said. 'It's our turn.'

The sisters shared the stool, playing and singing together. Caroline chose a duet about doomed love and second chances, singing directly to Mr Darcy. He led the applause at the end of their performance, she caught his eye and their gazes held for a protracted moment.

It's as though he's giving me his approval.

Moving away from the instrument, she seized the opportunity and went to join her host.

'You look distracted this evening, Mr Darcy,' she said.

'Not so distracted that I didn't enjoy your performance, Miss Bingley.'

'Oh that, it was nothing. Louisa and I learned that song years ago.' When he said nothing, she searched her mind for an intelligent comment that would fill the silence. 'Shall we have a fine day again tomorrow, do you suppose?' *Yea gods, is that the best I can do?*

'Let us hope so.'

'I'm glad of this opportunity to have this private word with you, sir.'

'Indeed?' He elevated a brow in a gesture of polite enquiry.

'This is rather delicate and... well, I wouldn't want to speak out of turn.' She could see she had his complete attention and forged ahead before anyone interrupted them. 'I enjoyed my visit to Lambton this morning, but while I was there I overheard something that I found rather disturbing.'

He sent her a sharp glance. 'Overheard? Overheard where?'

'We had just left your carriage in the mews attached to the inn. I realised I had left my reticule behind and returned to fetch it. As I did so, I overheard two men talking, and the mention of your name caught my interest.'

'My name is often mentioned hereabouts.' He relaxed his shoulders. 'It would not necessarily mean anything.'

'Even if the speaker was Mr Wickham?'

Mr Darcy inhaled sharply. 'Are you sure?'

'Oh yes. I recognised him at once. I know you and he are not on the best of terms. That is why his talking about you piqued my interest.'

'Tell me what you heard.'

'I actually saw him pay money to the man he was talking with. He thanked him for telling him about the... what was the word he used?' Caroline wrinkled her brow. 'Ah, yes, the position. I believe that was it. I heard it quite distinctly. He then said he was assured of securing it now, thanks to your wife's intervention.' Caroline canted her head. 'I am not sure what he was referring to, but the man Wickham was speaking to did not look respectable. Perhaps an estate worker, judging by his attire.'

'Go on, Miss Bingley.' Darcy ground his jaw. 'What else did you hear?'

'Let me see if I can remember.' She knew she must be careful not to overplay her hand. 'Ah, yes, I believe the other man said something about a mutually beneficial arrangement, and then took himself off.' She affected an innocent expression. 'Does that mean anything to you?'

'A very great deal. Thank you, Miss Bingley.'

'My pleasure.'

Satisfied that Wickham would not get his character now, she drifted away, conceding to herself that perhaps she had been over-attentive to Darcy in the past and had clung too fiercely. That had taught her a valuable lesson, and she wouldn't make the same mistake again. No gentleman, it seemed, desired a lady who made herself too available. She would definitely be there to catch the man she loved when his world fell apart, but the rest would be up to him.

* * *

Was Lizzy the only person in the room who could detect the tension between herself and Will? With the possible exception of her aunt and, of course, Miss Bingley, who appeared to take great pleasure from it, she suspected that was the case. Her other guests were occupied with their own personal dramas, oblivious to the fact Lizzy had seriously displeased her husband and was now suffering the consequences.

She listened to Georgiana playing the piano like an angel, while her major sang with a combination of gaiety and passion. The music failed to move Lizzy as it normally would, and a deep depression wrapped itself around her like a shroud. She and Will had not exchanged a single word, in private or in public, since their earlier conversation in her chamber, and she had no idea how to right that situation.

Lizzy amended her earlier opinion about her husband's failure to show her any affection in public. She now realised he had fallen into the habit of glancing at her frequently, even if his expression didn't give away his feelings to anyone other than her. The darkening of his eyes as his gaze had rested upon her, every night except this one, melted her insides because she had known precisely what he was thinking. What she would give to receive just one of those unyielding looks now.

Instead, he treated her as though she didn't exist, causing her heart to slowly fragment. How could he possibly suppose she would take Wickham's part against his? Surely all they had been to one another these past months told a very different story. Lizzy was protective of her family, it was true, and would help them if she could, but her first loyalty lay with Will.

The music came to an end, and Lizzy saw Miss Bingley bearing down on her husband. Unwilling to watch her nemesis taking advantage of their rift, and unequal to making polite conversation with anyone, Lizzy headed for the doors to the terrace. The rain had stopped, and she stepped outside, breathing in the fresh scent of damp grass, the heady perfume of summer flowers in full bloom, and listened to the crickets chirping. It wasn't yet full dark, but the sky was completely clear again, and the stars were starting to put on a show. Lizzy leaned on the balustrade and looked up at them, still inhaling deeply, allowing the serenity of Pemberley to wash over her and soothe her troubled spirit, cursing the fate that had brought George Wickham into their lives.

She sensed a presence behind her but knew without looking around that it was not Will. She stifled her disappointment and smiled when Captain Turner joined her.

'I h-hope I'm not disturbing you, ma'am.'

'Not in the least. Are you in need of fresh air too, Captain?'

'A-actually, I s-saw you come this way and was h-hoping for a private word with you.'

'By all means.' Lizzy suspected she knew what he wanted, and she owed it to Kitty to do her best for her. 'How can I help you?'

They began walking, away from some of the others who now spilled out onto the terrace. 'I h-hardly know where to begin.' He clasped his hands behind his back, his posture upright and militarily correct. 'This has been a prodigiously fine p-party.'

'It's been a pleasure having you here, Captain Turner, and I must thank you for taking the trouble to entertain my sister.'

He flashed a smile that seemed genuine. 'That has been entirely my pleasure.'

Lizzy noticed he managed the entire sentence without stuttering, which was probably significant. 'And do you now return to your regiment, Captain?'

'N-no, not immediately. I must report to my f-father. He has summoned me, you see.'

'Oh, that sounds serious.'

'It i-is.' He paused, but Lizzy saw no reason to fill the ensuing silence and waited him out. 'M-may I speak frankly, Mrs Darcy?'

'I usually find that best,' she replied, sending him a reassuring smile.

'W-well, the thing is, I think I know why the pater w-wishes to see me. The f-fact is, he wants me to... t-to marry Lord Markham's daughter.'

'Oh, I see.' What Lizzy actually observed was that the captain's stammer became more marked when he was agitated. And the thought of marriage to Miss Markham clearly agitated him greatly. 'Since you raised the subject, I hope I'm not being indelicate when I ask how you feel about that arrangement.'

'I-I'm torn, if you w-want to know the truth. Have to please the pater, b-but I'm not sure Miss Markham and I would s-suit.'

'Many marriages have flourished following less promising starts.'

'T-true.' Their conversation took them to the end of the terrace, and they turned to retrace their steps. The captain politely placed a hand on Lizzy's elbow as they climbed three steps, then removed it again. 'I w-would have obliged before, but...'

'Shall I let you into a confidence, Captain?'

'I wish you w-would, if you think it would help m-me.'

'Mr Darcy has a very powerful and influential relation.'

'L-lady Catherine. I've heard Colonel Fitzwilliam speak of h-her.'

'Precisely. And Lady Catherine is gifted with very decided views about how people should behave. She and I did not get along when I was introduced to her in Kent last year. That's before Mr Darcy and I were married, of course.' Lizzy smiled. 'I was far too opinionated for her tastes, you see, and she took me in extreme dislike.'

'I find that very h-hard to believe.'

'Oh, unfortunately it is perfectly true, and so you can imagine how agitated she became when she heard that Mr Darcy and I were engaged. She did everything in her considerable power to prevent the marriage from taking place.'

'And yet, Mr Darcy stood h-his ground.' The captain nodded. 'G-good for him. He is his own m-man and refused to be intimidated.'

'Quite so.' *But he probably regrets his decision now.*

They walked on in silence, and Lizzy could sense the young man digesting all she had just told him.

'I-I don't often spend t-time in the company of ladies, Mrs Darcy, but this week h-has opened my eyes.'

'Really? And what has it taught you?'

'A very g-great deal about the felicity of the m-married state. I have only seen my own p-parents' and siblings' rather cold examples of matrimony before now and c-considered that was h-how it was for everyone. But one only h-has to look at you, ma'am, and at Mrs Bingley, to realise it d-doesn't have to be t-that way if one has the courage of one's c-convictions.'

'Then if Jane and I have taught you something, I'm sure we're both very happy to have been of service.'

'Y-you certainly have, ma'am. You h-have given me m-much food for thought, and I t-thank you for it.'

When they parted at the doors to the drawing room, Lizzy was satisfied she'd done all she could to influence Captain Turner's decision. If he was a man of conscience and determination then he would stand up to his father, to whom he appeared to owe little, and follow his heart. If he did not, then Kitty would get over her disappointment and be better off without him.

If only her own falling out with Will could be so easily resolved, she thought with a wistful sigh.

Lizzy re-entered the drawing room and somehow got through

the rest of the evening. By the time she retired, Will still had not spoken a word to her, or sent her a single look – damning or otherwise. She dismissed Jessie and climbed into bed, waiting for Will to visit her, just as he had done every single night since they were married.

An hour later, when he still hadn't come, she blew out her candle and gave way to tears.

15

Caroline slept badly and was up and about much earlier than her usual hour the following day. Just when things had started to go her way, she had received discouraging news from her brother.

'Caroline, there you are.' He had sought her out after the musical recital broke up the previous evening. 'I owe you an apology. Things have been so hectic, I haven't yet had an opportunity to tell you about the estate I visited.'

'Indeed not.' Caroline linked her arm through his. 'And I am most anxious to hear about it. Were you pleased with what you saw?'

'Very much indeed.'

'I am delighted to hear you say so.' It would be pleasant to have her brother so close to Pemberley when she finally took up her rightful position beside Mr Darcy. 'Tell me everything.'

'Well, Campton Park is the most—'

'Campton Park?' Caroline froze. 'Excuse me, Charles, but did you say Campton Park?'

'Yes.' Her brother frowned. 'Do you know something to its detriment?'

'No, not at all, but the name sounds familiar. I must have heard it mentioned somewhere.' She smiled at her brother and made a huge effort to appear normal. 'Pray continue.'

Caroline walked away from the rest of the party, compelling Charles to do the same as he chatted enthusiastically about the property. When Charles finally ran out of words, Caroline was left alone to quietly seethe. Of all the damnable luck! If Mrs Wickham learned about Charles's interest in Campton Park, she would petition Jane mercilessly until she agreed to appoint Wickham to the vacant position. Jane was too soft-hearted for her own good and would never withstand one of Lydia Wickham's determined campaigns. To ensure she was not subjected to one, Caroline had been obliged to attach herself to Mrs Wickham for the remainder of the evening, steering her well clear of anyone likely to give the game away.

Caroline only hoped Mr Darcy would appreciate the measures she had taken to protect him from the parasites who surrounded him at every turn. She glanced in his direction, observing the rigid set to his features, and her heart softened when it occurred to her just how greatly he must be suffering, the poor darling. *Have courage, my love*, she thought. The Darcy name and Pemberley estate would soon be restored to their rightful positions, revered and respected by all.

Now morning was here, and it was time for action. She walked past the small sitting room Eliza favoured and heard a raised voice coming from within – Lydia Wickham's raised voice. Caroline positioned herself out of sight of anyone who might come down the stairs and tried to hear what was being said.

'Lizzy, you are so incredibly mean.'

Eliza's response was pitched too low for Caroline to hear what she said, but it didn't matter. Clearly she had failed to persuade Mr Darcy to support Wickham's search for gainful employment. When the door opened and Lydia stormed from the room, Caroline just happened to be in the entrance vestibule, adjusting her bonnet and pulling on her gloves.

'Good morning, Mrs Wickham,' she said.

'Oh, Miss Bingley.' Lydia rubbed her eyes rather inelegantly with the back of one hand. 'How are you?'

'Considerably better than you, I venture to suggest.' Caroline forced a note of sympathy into her tone. 'Presumably, Mrs Darcy was unable to help your husband.'

Lydia blew air through her lips. 'In all honesty, I don't believe she even took the trouble to try. And now I must go into the village and admit to Wickham that I failed him.' Fresh tears welled. 'He will be furious with me. He had quite set his heart upon that position, and in truth I was warming to the idea myself.'

'Well, at least I can help you in one small respect. I am about to go to the village myself and would be happy to take you along.'

'Oh, are you heading that way?' Fortunately she was too preoccupied to ask Caroline what business could possibly take her there twice in two days. 'Thank you. I shall certainly bear you company.'

'Then let's not waste any more time.'

Lydia spent the entire journey railing against her sister, not seeming to care that Caroline wasn't, strictly speaking, a member of her family.

'I am sure your sister is not to blame, Mrs Wickham,' Caroline said. 'I overheard Mr Darcy speaking with my brother yesterday evening. He mentioned something about your husband's situation and said he was not prepared to help him in any way, no matter what.'

'He said that?' Lydia opened her eyes very wide. 'Then Lizzy must have tried? Otherwise, how would Mr Darcy have known he was here and needed help? Oh dear, I think I owe Lizzy an apology.'

'I got the impression Mr Darcy disliked disappointing his wife, and it had made him unhappy to do so,' Caroline forced herself to say.

'Then I definitely owe Lizzy an apology.'

'You can't apologise without revealing my overheard conversation.' Caroline fixed her with a steady gaze. 'Ladies never admit to eavesdropping, Mrs Wickham.'

'Of course they don't, although everyone knows they do it, otherwise we would have no idea what was going on in society.' She seemed to cheer up a little. 'But don't worry, I won't say a word to Lizzy. I dare say she didn't try too hard to convince Mr Darcy anyway.'

'Possibly not.'

Darcy's carriage deposited them at the inn, and Caroline told the driver to expect them back again in an hour or so. He saluted her with his whip, then turned his attention to the needs of his horse.

'Don't let me detain you, Miss Bingley.' Lydia smoothed wrinkles from her gloves. 'You presumably have something to do here in Lambton. I shall face Wickham, and see you here again later.'

'If you would like me to come with you, I shall be happy to lend you my support. I don't have anything particular to do. If you want to know the truth, I only came into the village to escape the rest of the party for a few hours. I am the most unsocial creature on God's earth, and if I spend too much time cooped up with the same people I become quite querulous.'

'Oh well, in that case.' Lydia's expression was pathetically grateful. 'Wickham so hates to be disappointed, especially when he has his heart set on something, but he can hardly ring a peel over me if you are there too.'

'I am sure he wouldn't do that anyway. He seems to be very fond of you.'

'Oh, he probably would, but he doesn't mean anything by his little temper attacks. Besides, he is always sorry afterwards.'

Caroline tried not to flinch when her new 'friend' had the temerity to link her arm through hers as they made their way to Long's cottage. Wickham himself opened the door to them.

'Miss Bingley.' Annoyance flitted across his countenance, quickly replaced by a charming smile. 'What an unexpected pleasure.'

'Miss Bingley was kind enough to come with me, my dear.' Lydia pushed past her husband and entered the cottage.

'You have me at a disadvantage, ladies,' Wickham said with an apologetic shrug. 'I wasn't expecting visitors so early in the day, and so I have nothing to offer you by way of refreshment.'

'I had to come at once,' Lydia said heatedly. 'You see, Lizzy couldn't persuade Mr Darcy to help you. I am so very sorry.'

'We have company, Lydia. Now is not the time—'

'Oh, it's all right. Miss Bingley knows all about it.'

Wickham sent Caroline a considering glance. 'Does she indeed.' He paused. 'Did Darcy give a reason for his refusal?'

'He said you know nothing about estate management and so it would not be honourable to say that you do.' Lydia's bosom swelled with indignation. 'Honestly, how could he say such a thing when your father served his family faithfully for so many years?'

'Well, that's rich men for you,' Wickham replied, shrugging. 'They play by their own rules.'

'What shall we do now?' Lydia asked.

'I'm not sure.' Wickham furled his brows. 'I need time to consider. I was so convinced Darcy would do this for me, you see, and so I had not thought beyond it.'

Caroline could see how disappointed Wickham was by his wife's failure. It was time for action.

'If I could make a suggestion,' she said.

'You?' Wickham's head shot up. 'Forgive me, Miss Bingley, but I fail to see what business it is of yours, or why you would want to help me either, for that matter. It is no secret that Darcy and I are not on the best of terms, and yet you are one of his intimate circle.'

'I have here something that will explain... Oh bother, I must have left my reticule in the carriage.' And this time she really had – quite deliberately. 'Mrs Wickham, would you do me a small kindness and pop back to fetch it for me?'

Lydia looked less than thrilled to be asked, but nodded anyway. 'Yes, with pleasure. I will be but a moment.'

The cottage was silent when Lydia left it. It was scrupulously clean, Caroline noticed, and larger than average when compared to the rest of the dwellings in the village. Presumably it belonged to Darcy, and he had gifted it to Long for his lifetime in recognition of services rendered. That was so typical of the man Caroline adored.

Caroline's attention returned to Wickham when she realised he was scrutinising her closely, his expression stripped of all pretence.

'You have gone to considerable trouble to speak with me alone,' he said in a deep, arresting tone. 'And I can't help wondering why you are taking such a close interest in my affairs.'

'I have my reasons,' she replied, seating herself in the chair Wickham held out for her.

'Life has taught me not to be as trusting as Lydia, who doesn't seem to find anything unusual in your sudden desire to befriend her. Forgive the bluntness, but I have had to live by my wits for many years now, thanks to Darcy's unwillingness to comply with his father's wishes regarding my wellbeing. Our situations are diametrically opposed, yours and mine, and we would make the most unlikely of bedfellows.'

'We don't have a lot of time,' Caroline replied, trying not to shudder at his typically crude innuendo. 'Your wife will return directly, and so I shall get straight down to business. It would be better if she did not hear what I have to say.'

'Probably.' Wickham rotated his neck, failing to hide his curiosity behind a languid expression. 'Discretion is not one of Lydia's strong points.'

'Are you able to get on to the Pemberley estate undetected, Mr Wickham?'

'Without any difficulty, but if I wander too close to the house I might be observed.' He flexed his jaw. 'I have every right in the world to be there, but I won't risk being detected and give Darcy the satisfaction of having me forcibly evicted.'

'It won't come to that.' Caroline paused to regard him closely. 'Tell me, Mr Wickham, if you had an opportunity to speak with Mrs Darcy alone, would you be able to persuade her to your point of view?'

When a brief expression of longing flitted across his features, Caroline knew she had read him right. His first choice had been Eliza, and he still desired her.

'I am unsure. Darcy will have poisoned her mind against me by now. Besides, she has too much to lose to risk being seen with me.'

'But if I could arrange it?'

'That depends.' Wickham abandoned his casual attitude, sat forward and fixed Caroline with a steely gaze. 'Oblige me by telling me precisely what you have in mind, then I will give you an answer.'

Caroline did so, quickly and succinctly. When she ran out of words, Wickham was smiling broadly. 'You are as devious as you are attractive,' he said.

'Save the flattery. This is a business arrangement between the two of us. I assume you understand now why your wife must know nothing about it.'

'Yes, but what I don't understand is why you are so keen to

make trouble for Darcy.' When she remained silent, his eyes suddenly came alight with comprehension. 'Ah, now I think I see. It is not Darcy whom you wish to discompose.'

'My reasons are my own, but our goals are similar. What do you say?'

'I say it would be a waste of my effort. I very much doubt that Lizzy will be able to change Darcy's mind, no matter how honed her feminine wiles have become. If your plan works, *you* will get what you want out of it, but I will be worse off.'

'I am not without funds of my own, Mr Wickham. If you fail to get what you need from Mr Darcy then I will recompense you.'

'How much?'

'Two hundred guineas.'

Wickham had the nerve to laugh in her face. 'Not nearly enough.'

'But it's a fortune.'

'You want Darcy for yourself too badly to care about the price. Being mistress of Pemberley has to be worth more than two hundred.'

'Three then.'

'I'll do it for five.'

In spite of his disrespect, Caroline found herself grinning. They understood one another perfectly. Caroline was reduced to dealing with a gamester and a womaniser in order to save Darcy from his own stupidity. Wickham only cared about himself, but that was of no consequence. Caroline would make a deal with the devil himself if it got her what she wanted. What she had always wanted. What would, by now, have been hers, were it not for the wretched Bennet family.

'Agreed,' she said, offering him her hand.

'I don't mean any offence, Miss Bingley, but I need more than just your word and a handshake to seal the deal. I have been disappointed too often in the past to take risks of that nature.'

Caroline had expected as much. 'Do you have writing materials?'

Wickham fetched pen and paper and Caroline quickly wrote a promissory note, briefly outlining their agreement and the sum of money involved.

'If you have no objection, I shall call Mrs Allwood to witness our signatures.'

Caroline's head shot up. 'Someone else is in the cottage? Why did you not say? We might have been overheard.'

'Your fears are unfounded. Maria is entirely dependable.'

Wickham called up the narrow staircase and a comely young woman clumped down the wooden steps, sending Wickham a look of such total adoration when she entered the room that Caroline's fears receded. How Wickham would keep her a secret from his wife if he settled in the area was anyone's guess. It was no concern of Caroline's; and anyway, she didn't much care.

'Don't worry about Maria.' Wickham patted the woman's rear. 'She is entirely trustworthy.'

Caroline hoped Wickham would have the good sense to keep her sweet, at least for the next few days. By then their plan would have been put into action and there was nothing Maria Attwood could say or do to make trouble.

The note was signed, witnessed, and disappeared into Wickham's pocket seconds before his wife returned and Maria disappeared upstairs again.

'Here you are, Miss Bingley,' Lydia said, looking warm and out of breath.

'Thank you, Mrs Wickham. But now, if you will excuse me, I will leave you alone with your husband and await your return at the inn. I am sure you have things to say to one another in private.'

Wickham shot her a condemning glance, clearly not enjoying the prospect of having his wife and mistress beneath the same roof. 'Go with Miss Bingley, my dear,' he said.

'Oh, but I thought—'

'I need to decide what to do about this situation. I shall send word when I have made up my mind.'

'You will need to be quick. I don't think Lizzy wants me to stay once her house party is over. Besides, I have no wish to be there unless you are too.'

'I will arrange something,' Wickham replied, leading them the short distance to the door and opening it.

'Just so long as you are not angry with me. I did try very hard, you know.'

'Yes, I am sure you did.' Wickham turned to Caroline and offered her the ghost of a wink, the impertinent upstart! 'It's been a pleasure, Miss Bingley, and I look forward to seeing you again very soon.'

* * *

The situation was exasperating. Lizzy's nerves were stretched to breaking point and she was not prepared to tolerate the situation. Will had not only ignored her last night, but had continued to do so this morning. Lydia was furious with her, blaming her because Will refused to help her ungrateful husband, and Kitty was still walking around, looking as though the world had come to an end.

Lizzy herself had slept badly, still felt nauseous all the time and had a near permanent headache. Patience not being one of her virtues, decisive action was called for. At first, she had been mortified to have visited Wickham's name upon Darcy, knowing how hard it was for him to hear it. Now she felt angry at him for imagining she could ever take Wickham's side against him.

She tapped on the closed door to his library and entered without waiting to be invited. Lizzy knew he would be there and hoped to catch him at a time when no one was with him. That proved to be the case. He looked up when she walked in and set his pen aside. Nothing in his expression changed and he didn't smile. Lizzy had not imagined he would and refused to be deterred.

'Good morning,' he said with icy politeness, standing until she took the seat on the opposite side of his desk and then resuming his own chair.

Well, at least his manners endured. She looked at him more closely and noticed dark circles beneath his eyes. It gave her no pleasure to realise he had probably slept no better than she had. The remedy to his insomnia had lain tossing and turning on the other side of one thin door that separated their chambers, jumping expectantly at every creak the old house made in the hope that it heralded the approach of its owner.

She inverted her chin but said nothing, perfectly prepared to sit there all day until he treated her as something other than a stranger. Angry words, false accusations, anything would be better than cold contempt. She felt the dull ache of loneliness wash through her as all her old insecurities about her ability to measure up as his wife reasserted themselves, and the brutal, remorseless reality of her situation struck home. Being the mistress of this fine estate would never be enough for Lizzy if she had already lost Will's love and respect. She sighed, accepting that was likely all she had left because something had changed inside her husband. Perhaps mixing with his elegant friends this week had brought home to him the extent of the sacrifice he had made in marrying her.

She had to somehow cross a divide that could not be breached with mere words. So what could she do to convince Will that he was the centre of her universe and without his love the sun would never shine for Lizzy ever again?

'Is there something I can do for you?' he asked in a politely distant voice when the silence was in danger of becoming embarrassing.

'What have I done?' she asked plaintively. 'What has changed between us, and what can I do to make things right?'

He regarded her in silence, causing her nerves to jangle as he dragged the moment out to its lengthiest extreme. He rested one elbow on his desk, rubbed his chin between his thumb and forefinger, but still did not speak. Oh, this was ridiculous! Lizzy could take no more and spoke again.

'I am very sorry if I have somehow disappointed you, Will, but if you seriously imagine that my loyalties lie anywhere, other than with you, especially... well, especially after all we've been to one another.' Her blush could leave him in no doubt what thoughts occupied her brain. 'Well then, I might as well save my breath because I don't suppose there is anything I can say or do to convince you otherwise.'

'You know what that man did to me.' The liquid venom is Will's tone, the burning anger in his eyes, truly frightened her. She had never seen him like this before and had no idea what to say. 'I still have nightmares whenever I think how close he came to defiling Georgiana. It was pure good fortune I stopped him in time and I—'

'And you had to deal with him again, for my sake.' Lizzy shook her head. 'Don't think I am not aware how hard that must have been for you.'

'Then why did you even suggest I write a character for the man? I allowed your sister to stay here this week, knowing what it would do to Georgiana every time she heard her addressed as "Mrs Wickham".'

'Georgiana has been preoccupied with Major Halstead's attentions—'

'Attentions Lydia has done her best to divert in her direction. Georgiana is delicate, she feels things—'

'Yes.' Lizzy lowered her eyes, feeling her anger draining away, to be replaced with guilt. 'I am well aware of that.'

'Is it too much to ask that occasionally, just occasionally, you put the interests of my family ahead of your own?'

'I had to tell you he was back in Lambton,' Lizzy replied, her anger reigniting. This was not her fault and yet Will appeared to be placing the blame for his presence at her door. 'And I told Lydia you wouldn't write him a character.'

'But you still tried to persuade me. That is what I find so hard to forgive.'

'I was merely trying to think of a solution that would rid us of Wickham, that's all.'

Will curled his upper lip. 'For how long? Even if he was qualified to fill the position, he would squander the opportunity, just as he has squandered all the other chances he's been given.'

'Yes, I know. But what of Mr Bingley? If he purchases Campton Park—'

'I have spoken with him and made it very plain he shouldn't consider Wickham for the position, if that situation arises.'

Lizzy shook her head. 'I hope he heeds your advice. Lydia can be very persuasive.'

'And as you pointed out, Wickham has received the benefit of a gentleman's education. There are many occupations available to him as a consequence, if he would lower his expectations and take responsibility for himself. The time has come for him to stand on his own two feet. He will receive nothing more from me.'

'Yes.' The spectre of Lydia loomed large in Lizzy's mind's eye, but she pushed it aside. 'You are quite right about that.'

'You must excuse me, Elizabeth,' Will said, standing. 'My steward awaits me in the estate office.'

Elizabeth? He never used her full name, which told Lizzy it would be pointless trying to prolong the conversation. They would just have to endure the final two days of this wretched party, somehow. Then they would be at leisure to examine the damage she had done to their relationship with a few careless words, spoken with the best of intentions.

With a heavy sigh, she returned to the small salon, aware that Mrs Reynolds would be waiting to discuss the day's menus with her.

16

Lizzy got through the rest of the day, and then the interminable evening, somehow. She felt tired and listless, her condition not improved by the fact her heart was smashed to smithereens. No one appeared to notice her lethargy, or the coolness between herself and Will, with the exception of Miss Bingley. Her nemesis looked radiant, floating around the drawing room as though *she* was the mistress of Pemberley. Lizzy couldn't summon sufficient effort to care.

The following morning, Major Halstead and Captain Turner took punts out on the lake, showing off their prowess as oarsmen to their willing passengers, Georgiana and Kitty. Miss Bingley and Mrs Hurst remained in the house, expressing no interest in taking to the water. Jane and Mrs Gardiner sat with Lizzy on the terrace, watching the activities from dry land. For the first in what felt like forever, Lizzy was able to summon a smile as she observed Kitty. She was dressed in pale muslin, a large straw bonnet covering her curls, and was sat in the bow of Captain Turner's punt, trailing her fingers lazily through the water. At least Kitty was enjoying herself.

'Where has Lydia got to?' Jane asked. 'I should have thought she would have been hungry for her share of punting.'

Lizzy rolled her eyes. 'We had a disagreement and she is now sulking.'

'Oh, I'm sorry. What unreasonable demands did she make this time?'

'Nothing out of the ordinary.' Lizzy avoided meeting Jane's eye. 'She claims she has nothing fit to be seen in and can't understand why I refuse to throw my wardrobe open to her.' Well, it was true, even if it was not the reason why Lydia was so out of charity with her.

'It will take her a while to realise her sulking won't have people dancing to her tune, as it always did with your mother,' Mrs Gardiner remarked.

'Yes, it's time Lydia grew up,' Lizzy agreed.

'Are you feeling quite well, Lizzy?' Jane asked, frowning. 'You are very pale.'

Mrs Gardiner nodded. 'I was about to ask the same question.'

'Oh, I'm perfectly well, thank you,' Lizzy replied. 'Just a little tired. I so wanted this week to be a success, you see, and arguing with Lydia has spoiled my pleasure in it.'

'It has been a huge success,' Jane assured her, giving her hand a squeeze. 'Don't allow Lydia to ruin things.'

'I'm glad you think so, but you can hardly claim to be unbiased.'

'No, it's true. Everyone says as much.'

'Dear Jane!' Lizzy gave her sister a brief hug.

'And tonight you have a big party of neighbours joining us. No wonder you're so exhausted.'

'Yes, but it's all arranged. There's nothing left for me to do.'

Except to wonder what had possessed her to suggest such a gathering. The prospect of standing beside Will as the new Mrs

Darcy, receiving their guests with smiles and cheerful words, had delighted her. Now that Will wasn't speaking to her, and the atmosphere crackled with tension whenever they were in the same room, her delight had turned to despair.

'Charles is very anxious for me to see Campton Park as soon as it can be arranged. I believe he has already settled on it without seeing the other estates that interested him.' Jane gave a little laugh. 'He can't talk about much else, and his enthusiasm is infectious.'

'Your uncle thought it would suit you perfectly as well,' Mrs Gardiner said. 'He tells me it has been well maintained, the rooms are well-proportioned, and the grounds are magnificent. There would be nothing much for you to do, other than to move in.'

'It would be so lovely to be close to you, Lizzy.' Jane smiled. 'The estate's location alone is enough to tempt me.'

'Take your time, Jane, and make sure you look at everything that's available before you make such an important decision.'

'Oh, I'm sure we shall.'

Miss Bingley appeared from the treeline on the far side of the lake, approaching them with a smile on her lips. Lizzy felt uneasy when she saw her, especially because she was smiling. Miss Bingley *never* smiled when she was anywhere near Lizzy.

'I thought she was still indoors,' she said to no one in particular.

'Hello, Caroline,' Jane said with a sweet smile. 'Do join us. It's wearing us out just watching the gentlemen punting so energetically.'

'Actually, I'm in the mood for exercise.' She turned her bright smile on Lizzy. 'Mrs Darcy, can I persuade you to take a turn about the lake? You have kept us all so fully occupied this week that you and I have barely had a chance to exchange a private word.'

Lizzy wanted to refuse. There was something almost desperate in Miss Bingley's over-enthusiasm. It was also almost the first time

Lizzy could recall the woman addressing her by her proper title. But there again, Lizzy *was* hostess, and it would be impolite to refuse. What harm could a short walk possibly do?

'With the greatest of pleasure, Miss Bingley. Jane, will you come, too?'

'No, thank you, Lizzy. I'm perfectly comfortable where I am. Besides, someone needs to keep an eye on the young people.'

'I'm too lazy to move as well,' Mrs Gardiner said.

'Very well, Miss Bingley.' Lizzy stood up. 'Shall we?'

Miss Bingley walked at a swift pace and showed no desire to start the conversation she claimed not to have had an opportunity for. Lizzy tried several topics, but when they were met with monosyllabic responses she eventually gave up. She marched along at Miss Bingley's side, her half-boots crunching on the gravel path that skirted the lake. Kitty and Captain Turner drifted past them in a punt, and Lizzy returned Kitty's wave.

It really was the most idyllic summer's day. Lizzy tried to push her suspicions about Miss Bingley's motives to one side so she could properly enjoy it. The lake's surface glistened a dozen different shades of turquoise, disturbed only by a torpid breeze and the young gentlemen's enthusiastic punting. She noticed her family of ducks taking shelter beneath some rushes and paused to try and count the babies, hoping none had fallen victim to the local foxes. They wouldn't keep still long enough, and she eventually gave up, consoling herself with the knowledge there still seemed to be a good number of them.

'Are you in a hurry for any particular reason, Miss Bingley?' Lizzy asked, out of breath as she struggled to keep pace with her. 'It's such a beautiful day. It seems a shame to rush about.'

Miss Bingley slowed her pace just fractionally, her expression taut. 'Excuse me, I like to walk fast.'

Lizzy could remember a time in Hertfordshire, not so very long ago, when walking wasn't a pastime that found favour with Miss Bingley. She had ridiculed Lizzy for walking to Netherfield when the ground was wet and her petticoats had suffered as a consequence. That Lizzy had done so because she was anxious to see Jane, who had been taken unwell while visiting that establishment, didn't appear to impress Miss Bingley.

'Mr Darcy tells me you and Mrs Hurst plan to spend the summer in Brighton,' Lizzy remarked, just for something to say.

'Yes, but our plans are not yet fixed.'

Well, you're not staying here with Jane. 'Brighton is a very fashionable spa, so I'm told. I have never been there myself.'

'Mrs Wickham will be able to tell you anything you would like to know about the town.' Miss Bingley's tone was openly scathing. 'I understand it's a good place to find husbands.'

Lizzy had had quite enough of the woman's incivility. Why suggest they walk together when she clearly took no pleasure from Lizzy's company and spoke only to insult her? 'Presumably that must be your reason for going there, Miss Bingley,' she said sweetly. 'I am so glad Lydia has been able to give you the benefit of her advice.'

Miss Bingley was walking slightly ahead of her and so the only way Lizzy could tell that her barb had struck home was through the slight stiffening in her shoulders.

They reached the summerhouse on the far side of the lake without exchanging another word. It was obscured from the sight of those on the lake and the terrace beyond by the tall stand of trees that stood in front of it, in full leaf at this time of year.

'If you're tired, we could rest for a moment here,' Miss Bingley suggested.

Lizzy was so very tired – the inevitable consequence, she supposed, of lack of sleep, her delicate condition and the rigours of throwing a week-long house party. Even so, she had no desire to prolong her time with Miss Bingley.

'I am not tired and would much prefer to continue.'

'Oh no, I insist. You look very tired indeed.'

Lizzy was too startled to protest when Miss Bingley grabbed Lizzy's forearm in a firm grip and almost dragged her towards the summerhouse. She didn't stop when she reached the steps leading to the wooden veranda, meaning Lizzy must either climb them herself or risk being dragged up them. Her heart rate increased and she felt afraid. There was a wild look in Miss Bingley's eye that probably had something to do with her sudden superhuman strength. She was definitely up to something.

'Miss Bingley, please release my arm. You're hurting me.'

'Here we are.' Miss Bingley threw open the door to the main room in the summerhouse and walked through it. She still held Lizzy's arm, forcing her to either go along with her or wrench herself free. The latter course of action was more appealing, especially since every bone in Lizzy's body rebelled at the thought of following Miss Bingley. She was definitely unhinged and was no longer attempting to disguise the fact. Even so, she decided to wait until she was inside. Miss Bingley would have to release her then, at which time Lizzy would simply leave. She had had quite enough of this and Miss Bingley could find her own way back to the house.

'Here we are,' Miss Bingley said for a second time. 'Isn't this nice?'

Lizzy sensed another presence in the room. She felt a patent reluctance to turn towards whoever it was, but did so anyway, and gasped.

'You!' Mr Wickham was the last person she had expected to see on Pemberley's land, but part of her still wasn't surprised. 'What are on earth are you doing here?'

Before she could turn on her heel and leave, the door slammed behind her. Miss Bingley was gone and she was alone with the one man her husband would never forgive her for associating with.

* * *

Caroline threw back her head and laughed aloud as she scurried back to the house. It had been *so* easy to get Eliza to follow her. The woman was so desperate to be accepted by society's elite that she gladly swallowed her pride, endured insults, and still came back for more. Caroline felt no guilt in duping her. She only had herself to blame for presuming to be Mr Darcy's equal. The expression on Eliza's face when she saw Wickham had been priceless. Caroline would never forget it.

The first part of her plan had gone as smoothly as clockwork, which included keeping Mrs Wickham out of the way. She had attached herself to Caroline almost continuously since they had become 'allies' and Caroline had selflessly provided her with a sympathetic ear into which she could pour her endless stream of complaints. Caroline knew Mrs Wickham would have joined them on their walk around the lake if she heard Caroline issue the invitation to Eliza. That could not be allowed to happen. It was vital to the success of Caroline's plan that Mrs Wickham knew nothing of her husband's presence on the estate.

Caroline had managed to keep Lydia Wickham out of sight by gifting her one of her own exquisite gowns to wear for the party that evening. Sacrifices had to be made when one was conducting a war, Caroline thought, fleetingly regretting the loss of the beautiful teal silk. Mrs Wickham would be occupied with a needle for the rest of the day, adjusting the gown to fit her smaller frame since she had no maid to attend to the matter for her.

'Perhaps one of the ladies' maids would do it for me?' Mrs Wickham had said.

'Oh no, it's probably better not to ask. Your sister will only hear of it and forbid you to accept a gift from me. You know how sensitive she can be.'

'I certainly do!'

'Besides, all the servants are busy preparing for the party.'

'Well then, I shall just have to do it myself.'

Of course you will.

Now all she had to do was ensure that Mr Darcy came upon his wife and Wickham, alone in a compromising position, and her work was done. Only the young people had taken to the punts. Mr Darcy, Charles, Colonel Fitzwilliam and Mr Hurst were playing billiards, but the gentlemen were in the habit of joining the ladies on the terrace for the latter part of the morning. Caroline's timing ought to be perfect.

She discovered that it was when she approached the terrace and observed her brother, Mr Darcy and Colonel Fitzwilliam conversing with Jane and Mrs Gardiner. The younger set were still on the lake.

'Oh, Mr Darcy, there you are.'

'Where's Lizzy?' Jane asked.

Botheration. She'd forgotten about Jane seeing them leave together. 'She stopped to speak with one of the gardeners, and I said I would come on back ahead of her. But I came past the summerhouse on my way and saw something peculiar there.'

'Peculiar in what way?' Mr Darcy asked.

'Well, I couldn't be sure who it was precisely, but there was definitely someone in the main room. A man. I saw his face as I walked past the window. I wouldn't have thought anything about it because I assumed he had a reason to be there, until he tried to conceal himself from me.'

Mr Darcy didn't seem unduly concerned. 'Did you recognise him?' he asked.

'Well, it can't be one of your guests since they are all accounted for.' Caroline lifted her shoulders. 'He might well be one of your servants, Mr Darcy, but you have so many that it is impossible for me to recognise them all.'

'Probably youths from the village,' Mr Darcy said. 'It's happened before. However, I had best check it out. If you will excuse me.'

'I'll come with you,' Colonel Fitzwilliam said.

Caroline fell into step with them. 'I can show you where I saw him.'

'There's no need, Miss Bingley,' Mr Darcy replied. 'You have already walked the distance once.'

'Oh, I insist.'

Caroline wouldn't miss this defining moment for any price – especially after she had gone to so much trouble to arrange it.

* * *

A combination of anger and anxiety rioted inside Lizzy, making her feel dizzy. Miss Bingley befriending Lydia now made perfect sense. She had only used Lydia in order to get close to Wickham, and had then persuaded him to come here to cause trouble between her and Will.

She had succeeded better than she could possibly know.

Lizzy clung to the ridiculous hope that Lydia knew nothing of Miss Bingley's desperate plan. In spite of her own perilous situation, Lizzy wouldn't wish to think Lydia had sunk quite that low. Lydia was many things, but she had never been wilfully deceitful.

'I can't speak to you, Mr Wickham,' she said, turning towards the door. 'You ought to leave Pemberley at once. You know you are not welcome here.'

He quirked a brow. 'Not even by you?'

'Especially not by me. You forfeited the benefit of any doubt when you threw my husband's generosity back in his face and quit the regulars.'

'Ah, Darcy has done a good job of poisoning your mind against me.' He flashed a charming smile as he leaned against the door, arms crossed over his chest, making it hard for her to quit the room until he chose to move out of the way. 'There was a time when you enjoyed my society.'

'That was before I understood your character.'

'If you knew the truth you would be less quick to judge.'

Lizzy sighed. 'Let's not waste our energy with verbal sparring, Mr Wickham. I know what you tried to do with Georgiana. You did the same thing with Lydia, except there was no financial compensation on that occasion, and you most certainly would not have married her had it not been for... however, we won't dwell upon my sister's narrow escape from disgrace.' Lizzy shook her head, wishing she didn't feel so tired. Her fatigue was dulling her thought process. 'I cannot find it in my heart to spare sympathy for a man who has brought his misfortunes upon himself.'

'Georgiana was in love with me.'

'Georgiana was an insecure young lady who looked upon you more as another brother.'

Wickham chuckled. 'I can assure you her feelings towards me were anything other than brotherly.'

'The fact that you are so proud of your ability to charm innocent young ladies only paints you in a worse light.'

'You are even more attractive than I remembered, especially when riled.' Wickham sighed. 'You were my first choice, you know. Had things been different, had Darcy treated me fairly, then—'

'Enough! I will not remain here a moment longer and listen to your twisted attempts at justification. Please allow me to pass.'

'It pains me to dismiss any desire of yours but unfortunately, I can't do that.'

Lizzy's alarm intensified when she took in the steely set to his features. 'You mean to imprison me?'

'Miss Bingley went to a lot of trouble to get you here. Disappointing her would be a sorry way to repay her efforts.'

Lizzy treated him to a withering glare. 'How much is she paying you?'

'What a very vulgar question!'

'I'm speaking to a very vulgar person.'

'I fully expect your husband to pay me a very great deal, once he finds us here together. You know how he is. He will do anything to avoid a scandal that might attach itself to the Darcy name.'

'Before or after he has blown your brains out?'

'You forget I am a trained soldier. I could best him in any duel, if he was foolish enough to call me out.'

'You weren't a soldier for long enough to hone your skills.'

'Let us hope, for your husband's sake, you never find out if that's true.'

'I hate to disappoint you, but your plan will never work. Darcy and I understand each other too well for him ever to believe I joined you here of my own free will.'

'Logic might persuade him to think along those lines, I'll grant you. But, you see, Darcy has never been logical when it comes to me. He has always resented me because his father and I were so close, and he felt excluded.'

Lizzy laughed. 'Is that what you really believe?'

'It's what I know to be true. His father enjoyed my society because I was never so full of self-importance as your dear husband, and I knew how to make old Mr Darcy laugh at the world.'

'That illusion must be a great comfort to you.'

'Oh, it's no illusion. Had Mr Darcy lived longer, there is no telling how much he would have done for me. Your husband knew that, of course, but chose to disregard his father's wishes out of spite.'

'Or because you tried to despoil his sister, perhaps?'

'That would not have been necessary had Darcy honoured his father's wishes,' Wickham replied savagely.

Lizzy could see he really believed what he said. Appreciating now just how deranged his thinking was, she became truly frightened and clasped her fingers together to prevent them from trembling. He really didn't intend to let her pass him. He was far larger than her, would easily be able to stop her from leaving by using his physical strength, and she didn't doubt he would do so. Her only other means of escape was the window. It would require her to climb out of it, and then drop several feet on the other side. In her condition, she probably ought not to attempt it, but she had no intention of remaining there waiting for Miss Bingley to return with Will, and goodness knows who else in tow, to 'accidentally' find her and Wickham together. Why, oh why, had she agreed to walk with Miss Bingley when she had known all along it was a far from innocent invitation?

'And you imagine I won't scream loud and long as soon as I hear my husband getting close?'

'Oh,' he replied, sending her a smouldering look combined with a wicked smile she found deeply offensive, 'I know precisely how to prevent that from happening.'

Lizzy could see he was enjoying himself enormously and refused to add to his pleasure by revealing her anxiety. 'What does Miss Bingley hope to gain from all this?' she asked.

But Lizzy already knew. Her twisted logic had persuaded her to believe Will wouldn't countenance an unfaithful wife – especially if she chose to be indiscreet with Wickham, of all people.

Unfortunately, she was very probably right.

'I don't think Miss Bingley likes you very much, Mrs Darcy,' Wickham said in a mocking tone.

'The feeling is entirely mutual.'

'Then we agree on something. She has a very high opinion of herself and lacks common decency—'

'Pots and kettles spring to mind,' Lizzy said sweetly.

'Quite so, but sometimes it is necessary to join forces with the devil to secure justice.'

'Justice?' Lizzy made a scoffing sound at the back of her throat, casting glances around the room as she did so, looking for something, anything, she could use as a weapon against Wickham. Unfortunately there was nothing. 'The woman is completely mad.'

'Very possibly, but in this case she's right. If Darcy sees you alone with me, you will have lost him. He despises me for being all the things he is not and doesn't have a forgiving nature.'

'You are quite wrong, you know,' Lizzy lied. 'We have discussed you often, and he is perfectly aware I thoroughly disapprove of your character.'

'And yet, here we are.'

'Here we are.' The window it would have to be, Lizzy decided. She would make a dash for it but would probably never get through it before Wickham pulled her back. Still, that would remove him from in front of the door, and she just might be able to slip out that way in the confusion. 'Fortunately Jane and my aunt heard Miss Bingley invite me to walk with her. How will she account for having left me alone with you?'

Wickham seemed a little less smug. 'Oh, I am sure she will think of something convincing. She's nothing if not inventive.'

'You have put a lot of effort into plotting my "downfall", but have you stopped to consider how it will affect Lydia? Your scheme will see her alienated from her two oldest sisters, since you know Jane will take my part.'

'I shall no longer require Bingley's help, once your husband has given up what's due to me.'

'Ah, I see.'

And Lizzy did see, all too clearly. She and Jane had never discussed specifics, but Lizzy got the impression Lydia had frequently applied to the Bingleys for financial help, and received it. Money ran through Wickham's fingers like shifting sand, and he would be a fool to test even Jane's good nature indefinitely. His burning desire to embarrass Will had robbed him of any common sense he might once have possessed, and he appeared perfectly prepared to burn that particular bridge.

Wickham had kept her talking for quite a while now and Lizzy had no idea how long she had been inside the summerhouse. It seemed like forever. Will might arrive at any moment. He already doubted her loyalty and absolutely couldn't find her here with Wickham. She swirled away from her sister's loathsome husband, threw a chair on the floor to hamper him and made a frantic dive for the window. He actually laughed as he caught her harshly by the arm and pulled her back. She landed hard against his chest and the wind was knocked out of her.

She heard voices outside and opened her mouth to scream. Before any sound emerged, Wickham covered her mouth with his own as he ripped at her bodice. She struggled frantically, trying to turn her head away from his vile lips, but he was too strong for her and her efforts made no apparent impression upon him. She tried to lift a knee and drive it into his genitalia, but he seemed to anticipate her intention and kept his lower body beyond her reach.

The door flew open, and Lizzy sensed Will's imposing presence filling the aperture. She opened her eyes wide and sent him a supplicating look. She was unsure if he even noticed it since his features were locked into a terrifying expression of cold, hard fury.

'Lizzy?'

Wickham released her, but it was too late – the damage had been done. Her happiness was over. It was too much for her. Will glanced her way and the unbridled reproach she saw on his face was her undoing. Her knees buckled beneath her and the last image she saw before losing consciousness was Miss Bingley's smugly satisfied smile.

17

Lizzy blinked her way back to consciousness, unwelcome memories of how she came to be in the summerhouse flooding her foggy brain. She immediately closed her eyes again, not quite ready to face reality yet. Oh lord, what had she done? Trying to explain to Will how she had finished up in a compromising position with Wickham, of all people, made her wish she could have remained comatose for the next fifty years.

But Lizzy was no coward. She would fight to save her marriage, even if there was little hope of regaining Will's respect or of matters between the two of them ever returning to the same happy footing.

She was dizzy and disorientated, and even if she could have summoned the strength to stand, her legs would not have supported her. And so she remained on the floor, repeatedly asking herself how she could have been foolish enough to fall for Miss Bingley's friendly overtures. She had just learned a harsh lesson, and in future – if she had any sort of future at Pemberley after this farrago had played itself out – she would always be guided by her instincts.

She was aware of raised voices and a harsh thump, followed by a string of expletives voiced by Wickham. Then a heavy body hit the floor.

Wickham's body.

She knew it was him because she briefly opened one eye and saw him sprawled full length close to her own position, blood pouring from his nose. Presumably Will had hit him, and that thought afforded Lizzy considerable satisfaction. Keeping her eyes open to see what happened next required too much effort, and so she closed them again almost immediately, thinking how obliged she would be if the earth would have the goodness to open up and swallow her whole. Someone crouched beside her and felt for her pulse. A large coat was draped over her – Will's coat – presumably to conceal her ripped bodice. She would have recognised the unique aroma that clung to it anywhere. Then a strong pair of arms swept her from the floor. Will again.

'Is she all right?' she heard Colonel Fitzwilliam ask.

'She's still unconscious,' Will replied curtly.

Lizzy wanted to reassure them, but she couldn't seem to find her voice. It was so comfortable snuggling against Will with her eyes closed, momentarily feeding from his strength when she had so little of her own to spare. He made her feel safe and secure, just as he always had when he had still cared about her. The moment she revealed she was awake, she would be asked to explain herself, and she wasn't ready to do that yet. It was her word against Miss Bingley's and Wickham's, and if it came down to a verbal battle between her and Caroline Bingley, Lizzy could not guarantee that she wouldn't follow Will's example and resort to physical violence. The lengths the woman was prepared to go to in order to have Will for herself was beyond anything even Lizzy, who had never liked or trusted Miss Bingley, would have imagined her capable of.

No, it was far better to remain incommunicado for now.

'Oh, Mr Darcy, I'm *sooo* sorry.' Miss Bingley's voice oozed fake sincerity. *Don't fall for her lies, Will!* 'If I had known what was happening here then... well, I would never have interfered.'

'It is not your fault,' Will replied curtly. 'Excuse me, I need to take my wife back to the house. Fitzwilliam, stay here for now and make sure Wickham doesn't escape. I have not finished with him yet.' *Oh God, I have never heard him sound so hostile.* 'I shall send a couple of footmen down to take over from you.'

'Of course,' Colonel Fitzwilliam said. 'Take all the time you need.'

'I will come back with you, Mr Darcy,' Miss Bingley purred. 'Perhaps I can be of service in some way.'

You have already done more than enough.

'As far as the rest of the company is concerned,' she heard Will say to Miss Bingley, 'my wife fainted as a result of heat exhaustion, nothing more.'

'Oh, of course, I fully understand the need for discretion.' *Of course you do, you conniving witch!* 'People will become curious, but I shall keep your secret.'

Lizzy's head rubbed against Will's shoulder as he strode along with her in his arms at breakneck speed. Presumably he didn't want to touch her for any longer than was absolutely necessary.

'I intend to take Mrs Darcy into the house by a side door so as not to attract attention. Oblige me, Miss Bingley, by returning to the terrace and joining the rest of the party. I shall be there myself directly.'

'What do you intend to do about... well, about what we just saw?'

Yes, what?

'This is where we need to separate,' Will said brusquely.

'Until later then.' Lizzy would have bet fifty pounds that Miss Bingley took the opportunity to touch Will in some way. Lizzy didn't trust herself to open her eyes and check for herself, preferring not to know. 'I am so very sorry, Mr Darcy.'

'I must go,' Will replied, his tone still resonating with anger.

He had walked back to the house so fast Lizzy wondered if she still ought to be unconscious. Presumably all the jolting would have brought her round again. Never having fainted in her life before, she was unsure. She felt Will climb the stairs, peeped at his countenance from beneath her lowered lashes, and quickly closed her eyes again. The chilling cast to his features made her insides churn and regret spiral through her in nauseating waves. She couldn't bear to see the disappointment, the heart-rending despair, in his expression. God in heaven, she prided herself on her intelligence but had been outwitted by a jealous jade with an inflated opinion of her own worth.

She heard Jessie's voice, felt herself being placed on her bed and a cold compress being held to her forehead. She couldn't feign sentience indefinitely and reluctantly opened her eyes. Will's dear face hovered mere inches from hers, his expression still icy, his eyes dark with anger.

'Are you hurt?' he asked.

Yes, she wanted to reply. *Your coldness cuts like a knife.* 'No, I don't think so.'

'Jessie is here. I must go down to luncheon and set everyone's minds at rest about your condition.' He ground his jaw as he stood up. 'I will keep the ladies clear so you can recover in solitude.'

'Will, I... you need to understand—'

'Later.'

And with a terse nod, he left the room.

* * *

'I don't understand, Mr Darcy,' Jane said over luncheon. 'Why precisely is Lizzy indisposed? She was perfectly well earlier, just a little tired, but nothing more.'

'She has been over-exerting herself in this warm weather,' Mr Darcy replied. 'Arranging this party has been too much for her, but she's resting now and there is no cause for concern.'

'Oh, I see.' But Jane's face was clouded with concern. 'Perhaps I should go to her at once.'

'She's asleep,' Mr Darcy replied with a marked lack of his habitual civility.

Caroline smothered a smile and remained silent, taking pleasure from Eliza's vacant chair at the foot of the table and all that it implied. Colonel Fitzwilliam had entered the room after everyone else was already seated and nodded curtly to Mr Darcy. For reasons that escaped her, Caroline suspected the colonel was fond of Eliza, too. Now that he had seen her true character, presumably he would agree with his aunt, Lady Catherine de Bourgh, who was sensible enough to violently disapprove of Darcy's unsuitable wife.

'When can I see my niece, Mr Darcy?' Mrs Gardiner asked.

'I shall check upon her as soon as we have finished luncheon,' he said in a commendably calm tone. 'If she is feeling sufficiently rested then of course you can see her.'

Caroline longed to smooth out the deep grooves that had appeared on his forehead with soft fingers and reassure him with loving words. An honourable man, he must feel Eliza's betrayal deeply, and blame himself for falling for her questionable charms. She wanted to tell him the scandal would die down, and she would help him recover from the shame of it.

Patience, she told herself, aware her time had almost come, and Darcy was all but hers.

'Shall the party go ahead tonight?' Mrs Wickham asked.

'Lydia!' Jane and Mrs Gardiner said together.

Darcy sent Mrs Wickham a chilling glance, and she had the grace to look slightly ashamed. 'We shall see,' he said.

Darcy was *such* a gentleman, Caroline thought, her admiration for him increasing as she observed the competent manner in which he fielded the questions being thrown at him by Eliza's relations. She was perfectly sure he entertained no deep feelings for the woman he had so rashly married. Even so, having caught her in the embrace of the man he despised most in the world must have been a humiliating experience for a gentleman with Darcy's rigid moral standards.

Caroline wanted to tell him it was sometimes necessary to be cruel to be kind but, obviously, that wasn't possible. He must never learn of her part in all of this or he wouldn't turn to her for succour. Eliza would try to place the blame on her, of course, but Mr Darcy would never believe that. And then he *would* look to her. Where else could he find comfort and consolation? She was here and couldn't possibly leave as planned – not now when Darcy had never had greater need of her. He knew her well and trusted her absolutely. She was his natural – his only – choice.

Caroline hadn't anticipated that Mr Darcy would put aside his dignity and use his fists on Wickham. The depth of his violent proclivities *had* surprised her, given that he couldn't possibly love his wife. She supposed his reaction meant he wouldn't consider buying Wickham's silence, and Caroline couldn't blame him for that. Why should he expend a single shilling in defence of Eliza's tarnished reputation? He might have reacted differently if others had witnessed Eliza and Wickham together in such compromising circumstances. Unfortunately there had been no time to arrange that without casting suspicion upon herself. Caroline would just have to pay the five hundred guineas she had promised Wickham.

The sacrifice of part of her fortune was a small price to pay when set against the ultimate prize of Mr Darcy's lasting affection.

There was tension in the dining room, the conversations desultory. Even Lydia Wickham had little to say for herself. Caroline could tell everyone was very keen to know the truth about Eliza's mysterious illness but were too polite to probe. Darcy was relying upon her and Colonel Fitzwilliam to keep the truth to themselves, and Caroline certainly had no plans to disappoint him in that respect.

The young gentlemen proposed a long walk that afternoon, but Jane was disinclined to act as chaperone, clearly more concerned for her sister's welfare. Not that her concern would do any good because Eliza's fate was well and truly sealed. In the end, games on the terrace were agreed upon, and Georgiana and Kitty led the procession from the dining room in order to make the necessary arrangements.

'How can I be of help, Mr Darcy?' Caroline asked when they were briefly alone. 'Surely there is something I can do?'

'Thank you, but no.' He sounded rather terse with her, but she couldn't blame him for that. 'Excuse me, I have arrangements to make and must then check upon my wife.'

Of course you must! What Caroline would give to be a party to *that* particular interview, she thought, rejoicing at the manner in which Mr Darcy's lips were pulled into a tight grimace as he left the room.

* * *

The pain in Wickham's head had little to do with Darcy's fist making such brutal and unexpected connection with it. If he hadn't been so angry to be caught unawares he would have smiled at the thought of the oh-so-correct Darcy's passions being aroused to the extent he willingly resorted to fisticuffs. Lizzy had that effect on men, it seemed, stirring even the fastidious Darcy to behave like a street brawler. Wickham had lived with his virulent jealousy ever since he had learned of the union, furious that Darcy would be the man to experience *all* of Lizzy's charms.

That jealousy reignited now, making him forget the throbbing pain from his broken nose, and the humiliation that burned through him like poison. *He* had recognised Lizzy for the feisty firebrand she clearly was. Darcy had actively disliked her when he first arrived in Hertfordshire. Presumably that situation had only changed when Darcy recognised Wickham's interest in her – an interest that, unlike his other passing fancies, had never waned – and had usurped him for no other reason than he could.

Cold, hard fury radiated through Wickham as he sat on the wooden floor of the summerhouse, guarded by two burly footmen. They looked down their noses at him as though he was something they had just scraped from the bottom of their boots. They had yet to speak a word to him, or offer him so much as a bowl of water in which to bathe his injuries. Blood stained his neckcloth and seeped into the lapels of his best coat, but Darcy's servants seemed neither to notice nor to care.

How had matters come to this sorry pass? Not so many years ago, coves such as these footmen ran to do his bidding at Pemberley, keen to serve him because Wickham was the master's favourite. He would have arranged for their dismissal if they'd dared to look upon him with anything other than the greatest respect or were slow to respond when there was something he needed. Wickham sighed. Thanks to the untimely demise of old Mr Darcy, those days were long gone.

He had been so sure he would finally get the better of Darcy on this occasion, which was his sole raison d'être. He couldn't be expected to settle to a career until he righted all the wrongs that had been visited upon him, and Darcy was no longer in a position to blight Wickham's attempts to improve himself.

Miss Bingley had seemed an unlikely godsend. She was at least as ruthless as Wickham when it came to getting what she wanted. She also happened to be at Pemberley at exactly the right time, in the perfect position to cause maximum damage. When Darcy had had an opportunity to think it through, he would realise he had no choice but to pay for Wickham's silence. He touched his broken nose, winced and mentally increased the amount he would demand.

Darcy wouldn't keep Lizzy here, Wickham realised as he continued to mull the matter over. Every time he looked at her he would recall seeing her in Wickham's arms, and that would be anathema for a proud man like Darcy. Besides, he wouldn't want Lizzy having anything to do with Georgiana now that she had been 'tainted' by association with him, Wickham. He rubbed his chin and ignored his aching nose, suddenly smiling in spite of the pain it caused him to do so. Miss Bingley was even cleverer than Wickham had given her credit for being. She knew Lizzy would be sent away in disgrace. Then Miss Bingley would find out from Jane where she was and finish what she had started.

Unless Wickham missed his guess, Miss Bingley intended to deal with her rival permanently – only then would Darcy be in a position to marry Caroline Bingley, which was obviously what she wanted. Darcy would never try for a divorce. It would require a private bill in Parliament, citing adultery as his reason. With Colonel Fitzwilliam's support, he could provide the necessary evidence, but society would have a field day, whispering about his inability to keep his new wife satisfied, and that would be Darcy's undoing.

Wickham paced the summerhouse as he thought it through. If he was right about Miss Bingley's intentions, she was nothing short of crazy. But then so was trying to get Lizzy to meet with him here in the summerhouse, and yet she had managed it. Miss Bingley wasn't quite right in the head, and there would be no stopping her now. Wickham thought about the look of utter disgust on Lizzy's face when he had kissed her, and his admiration for her turned to derision. She was about the only person alive whom he would have helped in any way he could without trying to profit from the experience. With her disdain and her arrogant assumption that she was now somehow better than him, she had put paid to his mild obsession with her once and for all. He absolutely would not be looked down upon by a woman whose background was as unremarkable as hers.

Wickham continued to pace and quietly seethe. If Miss Bingley wanted to do away with Lizzy, she would need someone reliable and discreet with the right contacts to act as her go-between. It would need to look like suicide, of course. Lizzy was stricken with remorse and couldn't live with the disgrace she had brought upon herself and her family. No one would question that.

On second thoughts, instead of arranging for someone to do the job for her, Wickham would do it himself. He would enjoy seeing the look on Lizzy's face when she realised what was about to happen. She wouldn't be quite so superior then. Perhaps she might even beg. Wouldn't that be amusing. If he was better placed, he would even do it for nothing. As it was, it would cost Miss Bingley a vast deal more than five hundred guineas.

Wickham's mental perambulations were interrupted when he heard a noise outside. Someone was speaking to the footman guarding the door. Shortly thereafter the door in question opened and Darcy stood there, smartly attired, aloof, and looking in control of himself again. Wickham clambered awkwardly to his feet and

sent him a teasing smile – no small achievement given the damage
Darcy had inflicted upon his face and the pain it caused him to
move his lips.

'A carriage will be here in ten minutes to take you back to
Lambton,' Darcy said coldly.

'How obliging.'

'It is not for your benefit, but for your wife's.'

Wickham stifled a groan. 'There's no need to involve her. Lydia
knows nothing of this.'

'I am very glad to hear it. Even so, she can't stay at Pemberley
now.'

'She can't stay at Long's cottage either. Would you see her sleep
on the streets?'

'Don't put ideas into my head.' Darcy sent Wickham a damning
look, his stance emphasising the power, strength, and control he
currently enjoyed over him. 'You and your wife will stay at the inn
tonight. You and I have unfinished business.'

'Ah, at last you see sense.'

'I will send for you tomorrow, after my guests are gone.'

So he *did* intend to pay. Wickham tried to keep the triumph out
of his expression. 'Why can't we settle things now? I'm sure you
have no wish to see me again and—'

'And you have no wish to explain to your wife why your nose is
broken, or why she's been expelled from my house.' Darcy openly
sneered at him. 'You should have thought of that before trying to
compromise my wife.'

'I didn't have to try.' Wickham smiled. 'She was completely
willing.'

Darcy's features might as well have been set in stone for all the
reaction he showed, but Wickham knew his barb must have struck
home. Darcy had seen Lizzy in Wickham's arms with his own eyes.

Oh, she would deny being there through choice, but Darcy was a proud man and would never believe her.

'Mrs Wickham will soon arrive. I suggest you tell her the complete truth about your activities. It's bound to come out sooner or later.'

Darcy swivelled on his heel and left the summerhouse. Wickham barely had an opportunity to revel in his success when he heard the sound of wheels on gravel. The footman opened the door and ushered Wickham towards the carriage.

* * *

'My dear, whatever are you doing here?' Lydia clasped a hand over her mouth. 'And what on earth has happened to your nose?'

'Mr Darcy caught me unawares,' he replied, his voice sounding nasal and justifiably peeved.

'Oh, how brutal of him. Just because he found you here at Pemberley, I suppose.' Lydia frowned. 'Why *are* you here?'

'I had business to attend to,' he replied curtly.

'Business?' Lydia frowned as the carriage moved off at a spanking pace, jolting Wickham's bruised body whenever the wheels bounced through a rut. 'I don't understand. Why did you not warn me to expect you?'

'I had business with one of the keepers who used to work for my father,' Wickham replied, hoping Lydia wouldn't ask what business that could possibly be. 'I happened to see your sister walking in the grounds. We were talking together in the summerhouse, and Darcy came upon us and reached the wrong conclusion.'

'Oh, that would explain Lizzy's absence from luncheon and Mr Darcy's foul mood.' Lydia sent him not the sympathetic glance he had been expecting, but a damning one. 'You really shouldn't have come to Pemberley. I've been expelled now. I was given no time to pack my clothes, and probably won't be allowed to go back if you have upset Mr Darcy. I have been told the rest of my things will be packed up and sent on.' She frowned. 'But sent on where? We have nowhere to live.'

Lydia's self-centredness infuriated Wickham. 'You worry about your clothes rather than your own husband?'

'You're obsessed with Pemberley and have to let it go.' Lydia touched his shoulder. 'I know you have been treated badly but, for the love of God, use your sense. You have nothing to fight against Mr Darcy's wealth and influence with, and now I've been evicted and can do nothing to work on Lizzy.'

'I am your husband, and I don't need your advice on how to behave,' he replied coldly. 'It is your duty to do as I say.'

'And it's your duty to support me. So far you haven't done a very good job of that.'

'Because I've been wronged—'

'Enough! I don't want to hear another word about Mr Darcy's ill-usage of you.'

Lydia had *never* opposed him like this before, and she had chosen the wrong moment to start. 'I don't think you realise just how badly situated we are at the moment,' Wickham said in an icy tone. 'Still, my fortunes are about to take a turn for the better. Darcy will have no choice but to buy my silence, if he doesn't want the world to know what a doxy he married, that is.'

'Don't talk about my sister like that!' Lydia cried indignantly.

Wickham was furious and slapped her cheek with considerable force.

'Argh!' She clutched the side of her face. 'How dare you strike me!'

Wickham's body vibrated with anger. 'I will do a damned sight more than that if you ever question me again.'

'You can't expect me to sit back and do nothing when you are trying to ruin my sister's life.'

'You're my wife, and it's about time you started acting as such. Forget your sisters and put your full support behind me from now on. Are we clear?'

Instead of the instant capitulation Wickham had expected, Lydia turned away and refused to either look at him or speak to him for the remainder of the short journey into Lambton.

18

'Here you are, Mrs Darcy.' Jessie held a spoonful of broth to Lizzy's lips. 'I'm sure you will feel much better if you managed to take just a little.'

'Take it away, Jessie. I'm not hungry.'

'But, madam—'

Lizzy was heartbroken and weary to the bone, but she wouldn't be able to sleep. Miss Bingley and Wickham had hatched their plan too well for her ever to know peace of mind again. Will would never believe she was an innocent pawn in their wicked scheme. Every time she recalled the rigid set to his jaw, the concentrated fury in his eyes as he carried her back to the house, her spirits plummeted even lower. A gut-wrenching pain ripped through her like a sabre, twisting her insides into a vicious knot. It would be impossible to convince him of her innocence, but she would never forgive herself if she didn't at least try. She would tell him the complete truth, and if he wanted to send her away after that to live in seclusion and disgrace, then so be it.

Her stomach tumbled when the door opened. She knew without looking up that it would be her husband.

'Leave us,' he said curtly to Jessie.

It took an extreme effort of will to look up at him as he crossed the room to join her. His air of tightly controlled strength and power had always enthralled her and did so now, in spite of her dire situation. There was a diamond-hard gleam in his dark eyes, and his lips were tightly compressed, his disappointment in her on plain show.

The moment of truth had arrived. Lizzy sat up and squared her shoulders, meeting his hostile gaze head on.

'Will, I—'

'Shush.'

To her utter astonishment he sat on the edge of the bed, brushed the hair away from her brow in the way he often had in the past, and peered intently at her face, his harsh expression replaced with one of deep concern.

'How do you feel?' he asked.

She gaped at him. 'Why would you care, given what you just saw?'

He confounded her when he threw his head back and barked a mirthless laugh. 'I may be a little quick to judge when it comes to anything to do with Wickham, but even I can recognise a deception when I see one.'

'I don't understand.' Lizzy's mouth fell open. She hastily snapped it closed again. 'You were so angry with me when you thought I was supporting Wickham's cause. And yet when you find me in a compromising situation with him, you act... well, as though you think I'm blameless. As though it meant nothing to you. As though—'

'I didn't act as though it meant nothing. I struck him.'

'So you did.' Lizzy's lips quirked. 'Very hard. I think you broke his nose.'

'Ah, so you *were* awake. I thought as much.'

'I was too embarrassed to open my eyes.' She grasped his hand and examined his grazed knuckles. 'You ought to put a dressing on that.'

'Nonsense. I want to look at the scrapes so I can enjoy the satisfaction of recalling how they came to be there. I have wanted to hit that man for years, and you provided me with the perfect excuse.'

'Oh.' Lizzy couldn't think of anything else to say.

'Are you so afraid of me you really couldn't open your eyes?'

'Not afraid of you, but petrified you wouldn't believe that I hadn't arranged to meet with Wickham.' She shook her head. 'I was so angry with myself, and so afraid of losing you.'

Will ran a hand distractedly through his hair. 'Oh, Lizzy!'

'Besides, I enjoyed being carried back to the house by you.' Lizzy swallowed against the ache in her throat, overcome with emotion. 'I thought it would be the last time you ever touched me, you see.'

'Lizzy, my love, I am so sorry for my behaviour yesterday. I deserve to be horsewhipped for what I did to you.' The bitter anguish in his smile, the burning torment in his eyes, caused Lizzy's breath to catch in her throat. 'Can you find it in your generous heart to ever forgive me?'

Lizzy wondered if she had hit her head when she fainted. It was the only way to account for her husband's conduct. 'Did I just hear you properly? Are you actually asking for *my* forgiveness?'

'I am perfectly willing to grovel, if it will help my cause.' His eyes, burning with an unfathomable emotion, drilled into hers. 'I'm nothing without you, my love.'

'I forgive you with gladness in my own heart, but there is really nothing to forgive.'

'I disagree. I have been acting like a jealous oaf. All sense of reason leaves me when I have to deal with Wickham.' He shook his head. 'I can't seem to help myself.'

Lizzy arched a brow. 'I still don't believe you walked into that summerhouse and immediately thought I was innocent.'

'Well, initially, when I first saw you in his arms... God, Lizzy, I felt like the bottom had fallen out of my world. If I ever thought you no longer loved or respected me, I think I would...' Will shook his head, too overcome to complete his sentence. 'Anyway,' he continued, clearly making a huge effort to control his emotions, 'I never want to experience that feeling ever again.'

'And nor shall you,' Lizzy replied, reaching up to run her fingers through his hair. 'Wickham has done his worst and failed to come between us.' Lizzy summoned up a smile. 'No one else would dare to try.'

He grabbed one of her hands and kissed each finger in return. 'Your goodness makes me feel thoroughly ashamed of myself.'

Lizzy laughed. 'I am definitely not a good person, Will, and I don't think you would like me nearly so much if I was.'

'Well...'

'How did you overcome your feelings... when you entered the summerhouse, I mean, so quickly?'

'Fortunately, common sense prevailed. I remembered all we had been to one another in this room, recalled how ardently you surrender to me, and I knew you couldn't possibly be so fickle as to turn to another man.' Will managed a hollow laugh. 'But seeing his lips on yours, his body pressed against you... Then I saw you struggling, trying to deploy your knee and, well, in a moment of clarity, I knew what had really happened.'

'He kept moving. I couldn't get anywhere near him with my knee,' Lizzy complained, disgruntled at the memory, yet alight with joy because Will understood and didn't blame her.

'Now, tell me how you feel? I was mad with worry when I saw you looking so pale back there in the summerhouse.'

'Now that I know I have your forgiveness, I feel wonderful.' She touched his dear face. 'Ready to conquer the world.'

'Conquering Wickham once and for all will be enough for me. Tell me what happened.'

'I was duped into going into the summerhouse. Wickham was already there and wouldn't let me leave. I tried, but I couldn't get past him. Then I heard you coming and Wickham grabbed me.' Lizzy gulped. 'I struggled, but I couldn't get away. He was too strong for me.' She shook her head, tears blurring her vision. 'I knew how it would look to you and didn't imagine you would forgive me, even though it was not my fault.'

'Tell me what Miss Bingley did to get you there alone with Wickham.'

Lizzy widened her eyes. 'You realise it was her?'

'I knew you wouldn't have put yourself in that situation voluntarily. Since you voiced your concerns about her, I have been observing her behaviour towards me, which got me wondering. Then there was her inexplicable friendship with Lydia to take into account. I remember her being verbose in her disapproval of her back in Hertfordshire and saw no reason for that situation to have changed, unless—'

'Unless she used her to get to Wickham.'

'Precisely.' Will ground his jaw. 'Is that what she did?'

'Yes, I think so. Miss Bingley invited me to walk with her today. I should have refused because I knew there was something not quite right about it. She usually does everything she can to avoid my society, you see.' Lizzy sighed. 'I was stupid. Anyway, Wickham was convinced you would buy his silence when you caught us together. He also admitted Miss Bingley had come up with the entire scheme.'

'Such desperation.' Will shook his head. 'But I still don't understand why she imagined I would cast you aside.'

'I keep telling you that you don't show your feelings in public.' Lizzy shifted her position and rested her head in his lap. 'She interpreted your lack of emotion as indifference and regret. She decided you had married beneath yourself, and she needed to get rid of me so she could have you instead.'

Will grunted. 'She's demented.'

'I agree, but her fragile mental state makes her very dangerous.' Lizzy slid her fingers inside his coat and ran them across his waistcoated chest. 'What are we going to do about her? What can we do about her, come to that? We have no proof.'

'I wasn't angry with you, Lizzy,' Will said. 'Not really. It was just Wickham coming back into my life again, so soon after I thought I'd got rid of him, that made me lose my temper. That and the fact you were right, of course.'

'Right?' Lizzy blinked. 'About what?'

'My father.' Will's savage expression returned. 'He and I had a severe disagreement about Wickham shortly before he became ill. We didn't have the opportunity to mend the rift before he died.'

'I'm sorry.' Lizzy touched his lips with the fingers of one hand. 'That must play on your conscience. No wonder you're so sensitive to any mention of Wickham. It brings back memories of your father.'

'And that our last words were spoken in anger.' Will nodded. 'Yes, it does.'

'Why did you argue about him?'

'As you know, Wickham has a very pleasant manner and knows how to deploy it, when it suits his purpose. As you rightly pointed out in Kent, I have always been more awkward and, I suppose, fully aware of who I am. Some might look upon that as arrogance.'

'You followed your father's example and knew no better.'

'Perhaps.' Will curled his upper lip. 'Wickham was respectful and subservient, and yet lively and witty in my father's presence.

The pater was quite taken in by him, but I had seen aspects of Wickham's true character at school and more especially at university. He was quite wild, and I knew he would never dedicate himself to any career. I tried to warn my father that he had given Wickham expectations above his situation in life. Father accused me of being jealous and we quarrelled quite violently.'

'It can give you no satisfaction to have been proven right.'

'Or that you picked up on my father's weakness for the rogue?' Will flashed a bleak smile. 'None whatsoever.'

'If your father was so fond of him, I'm surprised he didn't make proper provision for him in his will.'

'Wickham claims he told him he planned to but died before he could do so. He expected me to fulfil wishes my father never once mentioned to me, and that was the original cause of our rift. Matters deteriorated beyond redemption when he almost persuaded Georgiana to elope with him.'

'I'm sure Wickham wished all sorts of ills upon you.' Lizzy shuddered. 'With you out of the way, he might have expected to inherit Pemberley itself.'

'He did more than wish me ill.'

Lizzy's head shot up. 'What do you mean?'

'I can't prove it, but I had several close brushes with death during my university days, and Wickham was present at each one of them.'

Lizzy gasped. 'What did he do to you?'

'I can't actually show he did anything, that's my problem. Once, we were home for the holidays and swimming in the lake. It's very deep in the middle, but we are both good swimmers and had no reason to worry about that. We were diving for rocks, seeing who could hold their breath longer and bring up more.' Will paused, staring off into the distance, clearly reliving an unpleasant memory. 'I was coming up on one occasion when something tugged at my ankle. I couldn't shake it free and was running out of air. I felt myself passing out and kicked violently, managing to free myself just in time.'

'And you think Wickham held you down?'

'Not at the time, no. He had already surfaced and showed genuine concern for me. He said I must have caught my ankle in the tangle of lily pad roots beneath the surface and I saw no reason to disagree.' Will paused. 'Not at the time, anyway. It was the first incident, and I hadn't started to doubt Wickham's integrity at the time. Subsequently I have often wondered about it.'

'There were other occasions?'

'Several. One I particularly remember. Four of us had gone to dine in halls at another college. We drank too much and rode back fast, worried about missing our curfew. My horse bucked me off, and I could have been badly hurt.'

'Riding accidents happen.'

'This was no accident. Someone had placed a burr beneath my saddle.' Will scowled. 'The only problem was, upon examination, burrs were found under all the other saddles too, but not where the rider's weight would make it so uncomfortable for the horse that he tried to dislodge his rider. We thought it was just students at the college we had visited playing pranks.' Will shrugged. 'Young men do that sort of thing.'

'Wickham was clever. There was no way you would have suspected him if all the horses were tampered with.'

'Exactly.'

'I don't have a high opinion of Wickham,' Lizzy said pensively, 'but I didn't think him capable of actual murder.'

'I hate to disagree, my dear, but I think there are few things he is incapable of.'

'After the events of the day, I'm in no position to argue.' Lizzy sighed. 'Poor Lydia, to be stuck with such a man. I know she brought it upon herself, but still.'

'Talking of whom, I have sent him and your sister to the inn in Lambton and told them to await word from me. I won't have Lydia under this roof, acting as the go-between for her husband and Miss Bingley.'

'I understand. I have no wish to see her here either, although I suspect she knew nothing of Miss Bingley's plans.'

'No, I'm sure she did not. Wickham probably thinks I will eventually pay him off, but that I will never do. Fitzwilliam knows you weren't there with Wickham through choice, and he's the only other person, apart from Miss Bingley, who witnessed the event.'

'What about Miss Bingley, Will? If we expose her treachery then Mr Bingley and Jane will be devastated. Worse, Mr Bingley will have to choose between you and his sister and, knowing how honourable he is, he will feel obliged to stand by Miss Bingley. I hate to think of you losing your best friend.'

'That will never happen.' Will ground his teeth. 'But still, my blood runs cold when I think of what she tried to do.' He glanced at Lizzy through haunted eyes. 'Did she really imagine she would succeed?'

'Presumably so. I think she justified her behaviour, at least in her own warped mind, by telling herself she was acting in your best interests.'

'She can't be allowed to get away with it.' Will looked angrier than Lizzy had ever seen him before. 'But without any evidence, there's little we can do. She will simply deny it.'

'Even if she sees that you and I are not at odds?'

'Especially then, and she will rely upon you not wishing to upset Jane.'

'Yes, I'm sure she will.'

'It's a mess.' Will leaned down and brushed his lips against

Lizzy's forehead. 'There has to be something we can do, but I can't think straight when all I want to do is kiss you witless.'

A small smile tugged at Lizzy's lips. 'Then what is preventing you?'

Will's devastatingly wicked expression filled Lizzy with glorious anticipation. He kissed her with heart-stopping precision, sending spirals of heady sensation cascading through her as his hands greedily explored her body. When he finally released her, they were both breathing heavily.

'I have missed you so much, my love,' he said softly. 'The last two nights, sleeping alone, has felt more like two years. I was a fool to allow my dislike of Wickham to come between us.'

'I am so glad we understand one another again, and that you've told me the entire history regarding Wickham and your father. It helps me to understand the depths of his depravity.'

'Much as I would like to remain here and make slow, passionate love to you, your sister and aunt are very anxious about you. If I don't let them see you soon, I suspect they will burst in on us uninvited.'

Lizzy laughed. 'There's no need for them to do that. I shall go down and take tea with them and reassure them about my condition for myself.'

'No, you will not. You have had a nasty experience and need to recover your strength.' He fixed her with a stern gaze. 'Do not make me play the part of the domineering husband.'

'But I enjoy it when you dominate me.'

'I'm serious, Lizzy.'

She laughed. 'So am I.'

Lizzy's hand instinctively went to her stomach. She did need to rest, but not for the reason Will supposed. Now was the time to tell him, except she refused to share the news when the spectre of Wickham and Miss Bingley still hung heavily over their heads.

'The return of your admiration is all I need to restore my health. Without it I-I...'

'Lizzy, what is it?' Will caught a fat tear on his forefinger as it slid down her face. 'What have I done to upset you?'

'I thought I had lost you, Will,' she sobbed. 'My heart was breaking.'

'You will never lose me, my darling. Never think such a thing.' He held her against him as she cried. 'We will show the world just what a formidable pairing we are, you just wait and see if we don't.'

'Which is precisely why I must go down and take tea,' Lizzy said, her tears drying. 'Miss Bingley won't be expecting that. Nor will she anticipate seeing me at your side when we greet our guests this evening.'

The corners of his mouth lifted into a glamorous smile. 'Your courage never fails to inspire me, Mrs Darcy.'

'It doesn't take courage to be brave when one holds a winning hand.'

'We shall enjoy this evening, but we must still decide what to do about Miss Bingley.'

'We could just allow her to leave and say no more about it,' Lizzy suggested. 'That way Jane and Mr Bingley need never know.'

'It might be the only answer, although it doesn't make me happy. What if she does something similar again?'

'I think it's you she has always wanted,' Lizzy replied. 'She was convinced the two of you would eventually marry, and it would only be a matter of time before you offered for her. She thought herself entirely suitable and genuinely believed you admired her because it was what she wanted to believe. It was one of the reasons she was so anxious to separate her brother from Jane. She saw your interest in me before I knew of it myself. She was determined that Mr Bingley would marry Georgiana, hoping where one union took place, another would soon follow.'

'Good heavens,' Will said, looking genuinely shocked.

'That being the case, I don't think she will ever obsess about anyone else the way she does about you.' Lizzy sighed. 'As to her mental condition... well, that's another matter. I can't help thinking she needs help to recover.'

'She does indeed, but I don't see how we can suggest it without causing fatal damage to her relationship with Bingley, and his with us. I won't allow you to become estranged from your favourite sister, no matter what.' Will lifted her head from his lap and returned it to her pillows. 'But now, if you are absolutely determined to go down, I shall ring for Jessie to attend you.'

'Thank you.'

'Don't thank me. I deserve no such consideration.' He stood up and then bent to kiss her again. 'I shall see you later, my love.'

'Will you not join us for tea?'

'Oh, I don't think so.' He sent her another of his wicked smiles. 'Let Miss Bingley wonder why you look as though you don't have a care in the world. That ought to give her pause.'

Lizzy laughed. 'You are a very devious husband.'

'And you are the best wife a man could wish for. I don't know what I have done to deserve you.'

'Well, you can show your appreciation by smiling at me in public tonight.'

Will laughed aloud. 'After all the difficulties my reserved behaviour has created in our lives, I think I can safely promise to do that much.'

* * *

'I wonder what can be keeping Mr Darcy,' Jane said, frowning. 'He's been with Lizzy an awfully long time.'

'I am sure there's no reason to be concerned,' Mrs Gardiner replied, looking very concerned indeed.

Caroline smothered a smile, resisting the temptation to correct Mrs Gardiner and inform her there was every reason in the world for concern.

'Ah, here's tea,' Louisa said, sending Caroline a reproachful glance, as though *her* behaviour was wanting in some way. 'Right on time.'

The tray was placed on the table in front of the ladies, along with plates of delicate sandwiches and a selection of cakes. Georgiana and Kitty were still practising their archery with the young gentlemen. In Eliza's and Georgiana's absence, it was unclear who should don the mantle of hostess and pour. Jane hesitated with her hand hovering over the teapot, but Caroline spoke before she could lift it.

'Oh, allow me to do the honours,' she said.

'Thank you, Miss Bingley, but there's no need to inconvenience yourself.'

All heads swivelled towards the speaker. Caroline's outraged gasp was drowned out by the cries of welcome issued by Jane and Mrs Gardiner. Eliza! What the devil did she think she was playing at? The nerve of the woman! She had the temerity to actually join them, acting as though nothing in the world was wrong.

If Caroline hadn't been so shocked, she might almost have admired her cunning, to say nothing of her skills as an actress. She must be feeling desperate, but it would be impossible to guess as much from looking at her. She stood in the open doorway, wearing a gown of sprigged muslin and a ridiculously bright smile. Her gaze clashed with Caroline's and didn't waiver. Caroline felt a moment's anxiety, wondering if she had somehow convinced Mr Darcy she had not deliberately colluded with Wickham. No, that was impossible. She had seen for herself just how furious Darcy had been to catch her with the man. Heavens, he had even knocked him to the floor with his bare hands. Even so, Caroline couldn't hold the woman's stare and was the first to look away.

'Lizzy, we were so worried about you!' Jane got up and hugged her sister. 'Are you feeling better?'

'Much better, thank you. I am sorry to have neglected you.'

'You look much more like your old self,' Mrs Gardiner said, examining her niece's face closely.

Eliza sat behind the tea tray and lifted the pot. Caroline, having recovered from her shock, decided there was no cause for concern. Presumably Darcy had agreed she could stay until the party ended. He was too considerate to send her away before that and be left to face her angry relations' questions. He wouldn't want to cause too much of a scandal, she supposed. Eliza, the scheming minx, obviously planned to use that time to reintegrate herself, and to try and discompose Caroline. Caroline wanted to tell her not to waste the energy. Mr Darcy would never forgive her for what she had done, and that would spell the end of Eliza's brief sojourn as mistress of Pemberley.

'I hope you managed to get back to the house all right after our walk, Miss Bingley. I am so sorry we were separated.'

Caroline gaped at her, unsure how to respond. Jane, a concerned frown invading her features, saved her the trouble.

'You fainted, Lizzy. Don't you remember? Caroline raised the alarm, and Mr Darcy carried you back.'

'Oh, did he? I am much obliged to you, Miss Bingley. I can't imagine why I fainted. I'm not usually the type to swoon.'

'It was a very warm day,' Mrs Gardiner said.

Caroline looked away, taking a moment to regain her composure. She noticed Georgiana and Kitty heading their way, escorted by their gentlemen, presumably because they had seen Eliza's arrival.

'Lizzy,' Georgiana said. 'Are you all right? We didn't know what to do for you.'

'I'm perfectly well, thank you, Georgie.'

Georgie. Caroline curled her upper lip disdainfully. How typically common of Eliza to shorter Georgiana's name. Goodness alone knew what Mr Darcy made of that, but at least he would not have to put up with it for much longer.

'We are glad to see you back with us,' Kitty said, taking a seat at the table and accepting the cup of tea her sister handed to her.

'You look a little warm, Kitty,' Eliza replied.

'Oh, archery is a warm pastime.'

'I-indeed,' Captain Turner said. 'W-w're happy to s-see you looking better, ma'am.'

'Thank you, Captain. It certainly was not *my* intention to cause so much anxiety.' Eliza looked directly at Caroline as she spoke.

'Where is Lydia?' Mrs Gardiner asked. 'I haven't seen her since luncheon.'

'Wickham has arrived in Lambton, apparently, and Lydia has joined him there.'

Jane appeared surprised, but not as surprised as Caroline was at Eliza's willingness to mention Wickham's name without even blushing. Really, she had absolutely no shame.

'She might have said goodbye,' Mrs Gardiner remarked mildly.

'Oh, you know Lydia and Wickham.' Eliza shrugged as she passed round the cake stand. 'They have a habit of popping up when one least expects them to. I dare say we haven't seen the last of them yet.' She looked directly at Caroline. 'What say you, Miss Bingley? Shall they appear at Pemberley, do you suppose?'

19

It would take a better person than Lizzy would ever be not to triumph over the utter astonishment Caroline Bingley had been unable to conceal when Lizzy appeared at tea. Her expression had been absolutely priceless, and Lizzy still didn't know how she had managed to maintain her composure. Even so, it would be a mistake to underestimate Caroline, or assume she was finished making mischief here at Pemberley. After all, they were not dealing with a rational person.

She gazed at her reflection as Jessie dressed her hair, wondering who the creature was who looked back at her with sparkling eyes, her complexion flawless. Lizzy was no raving beauty, but she was perfectly satisfied with her appearance this evening, seldom having looked or felt more desirable. She wore a new ball gown of change-able pale blue silk with a spangled silver overskirt. It was a colour Will had once admired on her. The emeralds again adorned her throat, ears and wrist.

'I think that will do very well, Jessie,' Lizzy said when her maid pinned her last curl into place.

'You look a picture, ma'am.'

'Thanks to your skill.'

There was a tap at the door.

'See who that is please, Jessie.' She heard Mrs Gardiner's voice. 'Come in, Aunt,' she called out.

'Am I disturbing you, Lizzy? I wanted a quick word, but if it's an inconvenient time it can wait.'

'Not in the least. We will be more comfortable in here.' She smiled at Mrs Gardiner, picked up her gloves and fan and gestured towards the small sitting room that adjoined her bedroom. 'That you, Jessie, that will be all.'

Lizzy's maid bobbed a curtsey and withdrew.

Mrs Gardiner stood back and examined Lizzy closely. 'You look quite lovely,' she said.

'Thank you, Aunt. A new gown tends to work wonders for one's confidence.'

Mrs Gardiner arched a brow. 'Do you have reason to lack confidence?'

'All the time.' Lizzy laughed as they took seats in front of the fireplace. 'Every time I meet a person who has lived in the district for any amount of time, I feel as though I'm being compared to the old Mrs Darcy and found wanting.'

'Nonsense.' Mrs Gardiner patted her hand. 'I have heard nothing but good things said about you since I've been here.'

'That's because no one would dare to say anything derogatory in your hearing.'

'Oh, Lizzy.' Mrs Gardiner laughed as she took in her surroundings. 'This room is delightful. You really are lucky.'

'I know that very well.'

'Not that you don't deserve to be. I'm so glad you and Mr Darcy have resolved your squabble.'

Lizzy elevated both brows, truly astonished. 'Was it that obvious?'

Mrs Gardiner flashed a wan smile. 'Only to someone who knows you as well as I do. I hated to see the two of you at odds, especially since it is obvious you're deliriously happy with one another most of the time.'

'You see a lot.'

'It's none of my business, Lizzy,' Mrs Gardiner said, unnaturally serious, 'but did your disagreement have anything to do with Lydia? Is that why she has left without saying goodbye?'

Lizzy didn't respond immediately, wondering how much she ought to tell her aunt, if anything at all. She considered the trouble her uncle had taken to track Lydia down when she eloped with Wickham, and how disappointed he had been when Will had insisted upon making all the arrangements and footing the expense to bring the wedding about. Mrs Gardiner was discreet and had earned the right to know.

'Not Lydia, but Wickham.'

'Oh dear.' Mrs Gardiner shook her head and appeared quite upset. 'I thought that might be the case.'

'And Miss Bingley as well.'

Mrs Gardiner's head shot up. 'Hence, her reason for asking you to walk with her this morning?' Lizzy nodded. 'I didn't think it was strange until after you had gone, and then it was too late to do anything about it.' Mrs Gardiner shook her head. 'I should have been quicker on the uptake and followed after you.'

'There wasn't any reason for you to do that, Aunt.'

'There was every reason, Lizzy. Miss Bingley has barely spoken a civil word to you the entire time she has been here. Then, all of a sudden, she acted as though you were bosom friends and insisted upon walking with you.'

'Well, if you put it like that—'

'She will never forgive you for marrying Darcy, and will never like you.'

'That's certainly true.'

Lizzy prepared her aunt for a shock and told her all, omitting the personal details Will had told her about his relationship with his father. Mrs Gardiner listened with a look of growing horror on her face.

'Thank goodness Mr Darcy saw through the wicked ruse. When a gentleman's jealousy is aroused, common sense seldom prevails.' She shook her head. 'I don't care for Miss Bingley. She thinks herself superior to the rest of us—'

'Which is probably why she did what she did. She thinks she is saving Mr Darcy from his own folly.'

'Possibly, but I still can't believe she is quite that evil, or Wickham quite that desperate.'

'Unfortunately, Aunt, I don't share your high opinion of human nature and have no difficulty believing either of them perfectly capable of colluding for their own individual purposes. Indeed, I was on the receiving end of their machinations,' she added, wrinkling her nose as she recalled the vile feel of Wickham's lips forcing themselves on hers. 'And so I can say with absolute certainty, they are. Wickham was disgustingly pleased with himself. He boasted quite openly about the way they had duped me.'

'No wonder Miss Bingley seemed so horrified when you appeared at teatime, looking as though you didn't have a care in the world.' Mrs Gardiner smiled. 'She looked as though she had seen a ghost.'

'Yes, I will confess I enjoyed her reaction, for which I hope you don't blame me.'

'Not in the least, but be careful, Lizzy. Miss Bingley probably thinks you acted out of desperation. She won't believe your husband has forgiven you.'

'Yes, I realise that.' Lizzy, aware that time was getting on, picked up her gloves and pulled them on, smoothing out the wrinkles as she went. 'But if I can just get him to smile at me in public tonight, which he has promised to do, then she will have to accept that all hope is lost.'

Mrs Gardiner nodded. 'He does still conduct himself very formally when in company.'

'Yes, so I have been trying to make him understand. We both think that is what persuaded Miss Bingley to launch her desperate scheme, so he has no choice but to agree with me.'

'It must be hard for him. I imagine his father taught him how to behave, and his manners are deeply ingrained.'

Lizzy flashed a mischievous smile. 'Yes, but I shall undo all his father's bad work if it's the last thing I ever achieve.'

Mrs Gardiner laughed. 'I am glad your fighting spirit has re-emerged, and I have every confidence in your success.'

'Thank you.' Lizzy sighed. 'Anyway, Miss Bingley will be gone from here tomorrow and, since my husband knows I am the wronged party, there is nothing more she can do to drive a wedge between us. He will never believe anything she tells him.'

'But she will get away with her attempts to separate you.' Mrs Gardiner looked troubled by that prospect. 'I suppose you are prepared to allow that to happen, for Jane's sake, but it still doesn't seem right.'

'Precisely. But without actual proof, there is nothing more that can be done.'

'No, I suppose not.' Mrs Gardiner fell into momentary contemplation. 'What of Lydia and Wickham?'

'Mr Darcy won't do a thing for Wickham now, obviously, and so he must make his own way. I feel badly for Lydia. She's head-strong and foolish, otherwise she wouldn't have finished up married to Wickham under such questionable circumstances. However, our mother must bear much of the blame for the way Lydia turned out. She spoiled her youngest child from the day she was born, treated her as a favourite and failed to correct her wild behaviour.'

'Quite so. I am delighted with the way Kitty conducts herself now that she doesn't use Lydia as her example.'

'Lydia will just have to make the best of a bad job, and there's nothing more to be said about that.'

'Lizzy, where are you?'

'In here.'

Will entered Lizzy's sitting room, stopping short when he realised she wasn't alone.

'Don't mind me, Mr Darcy,' Mrs Gardiner said, standing. 'I was just about to leave.'

'I'm interrupting.'

'Not in the least,' Lizzy said. 'Is it time to go down?'

'Yes, indeed.'

'Then I ought to go and find my husband,' Mrs Gardiner said. 'Please excuse me.'

Will opened the door for her and then returned to Lizzy.

'Are you ready?' he asked.

Lizzy shuddered. 'As I ever will be.'

'You look beautiful,' he said softly, taking her hand, kissing the back of it and then placing it on his sleeve. 'And I promise to smile at you until my jaw hurts.'

'I can't ask any more of you than that,' Lizzy replied, already feeling slightly better about the evening ahead of her.

* * *

Caroline stood at the side of Pemberley's magnificent ballroom, quietly seething. Her moment of triumph had turned into an unmitigated disaster. She could scarce believe her eyes, but Mr Darcy actually appeared to have forgiven his wayward wife. The house party guests were all assembled in the drawing room when their host and hostess joined them. Eliza looked reasonably well, in a rather coarse sort of way, in a fashionable ball gown. But it was Darcy's behaviour that caused a leaden weight to drag Caroline into the depths of despair. He actually smiled at Eliza, not once but constantly. If Caroline hadn't seen it with her own eyes, she never would have believed it possible.

What in the name of the devil could Eliza possibly have done to make Darcy smile? Worse, Eliza was making no effort to disguise just how much she was enjoying her triumph at Caroline's expense. Her sparkling gaze rested upon Caroline just long enough for her to feel the full force of her failure, before moving on as though Caroline was unworthy of her notice.

Caroline had never felt more humiliated.

Neither of the Darcys spoke a single word to her during dinner. Not that she had any interest in conversing with Eliza, but Darcy's incivility cut to the quick. His manners were punctilious, and Caroline would never have imagined he could behave so negligently, no matter how strained the circumstances. Tonight it was as though he didn't have any guests, and he appeared to have trouble tearing his gaze away from his wretched wife, seated at the opposite end of the table between Colonel Fitzwilliam and Major Halstead. Darcy kept sending her speaking glances that pointedly ignored the rest of the party. Each time Caroline caught him doing so, she died a little more inside.

After dinner, he and Eliza had greeted the rest of their guests, laughing and relaxed, no tension in evidence. Worse, the dancing had started and Caroline was without a partner. Darcy had stood up with Mrs Gardiner, Eliza with Colonel Fitzwilliam. Why would he wish to dance with the woman when he had seen her in Wickham's embrace? Caroline shook her head. It made no sense at all.

'We shall be gone from here tomorrow, and you can put it all behind you, my dear. It would probably be best if we didn't accept any more invitations to Pemberley. I hate to see you so upset.'

Louisa's voice snapped Caroline out of her reverie. The last thing she wanted was sympathy, especially from her own sister, and she replied with more asperity than she had intended. 'I have no idea what you mean, Louisa. I am having a perfectly lovely time.'

'What happened today, Caroline? Why did Mrs Darcy faint?'

'I'm sure I have no idea. She does not confide in me.'

'Well, she seems to have recovered remarkably well.' Louisa fell quiet for a few minutes and the sisters watched the dancing in taut silence. 'We shall leave here after luncheon tomorrow, if that suits you. We can take our time travelling back to London, leave Mr Hurst to his own devices there, and then we shall be at leisure to make our way on to Brighton. I believe I have found a cottage for us to take.'

'You found it, or do we have Mr Henley to thank?'

'Ah, a waltz,' Louisa said, throwing back her head and then glancing around her, as though looking to catch the eye of a suitable partner. 'I do so enjoy waltzing.'

Caroline straightened her spine, clinging to the desperate hope that Mr Darcy had been waiting for this moment to notice her. It would make her efforts all the sweeter if she were to be swept onto the floor in Mr Darcy's strong arms, in front of his wife's relations and supporters, no less.

She gasped when Darcy indeed stepped onto the floor – with his wife. The smile he sent her as the music started and their feet moved in perfect harmony sent a chill of despair through Caroline. That smile was so capricious, invested with such deep passion, Caroline wanted the floor to swallow her up. How could she have got it so very wrong? She shuddered when the entire ballroom burst into spontaneous applause as the Darcys circled the floor completely alone.

Other couples joined them when they had completed a full circuit, but Caroline's humiliation endured. She slipped through the doors to the terrace and stood there alone, looking up at the stars patterning a cloudless sky, wishing herself a million miles away, wishing Mrs Darcy a painful and prolonged death.

Her brother found her a little later. 'Caro, what are you doing out here all alone?' he asked, frowning at her.

'How many times have I asked you not to shorten my name?'

'Don't be so stuffy. Abbreviated names are a sign of affection.'

'I have been thinking, Charles. Derbyshire isn't so very fashionable.' Caroline tapped her foot on the flagstones, not caring about the welfare of her delicate dancing slippers. 'And it's a long way from London. I am not persuaded it's the best place for you and Jane to settle.'

'Why ever not?' Charles elevated his brows. 'You were very keen on the idea at one time.'

'It suits Mr Darcy. He's taciturn and enjoys being isolated. You are very different and you would soon tire of the county.'

'Nonsense, you're just feeling out of sorts. Jane and I love the area.' He held out his hand. 'Come back inside and dance with me. A cotillion is just forming up.'

So, she thought, as she allowed Charles to lead her back inside, *I am reduced to accepting my brother's pity*. How did matters come to this sorry pass?

20

'You were wonderful tonight, my love.'

Will appeared in Lizzy's bedchamber seconds after she dismissed Jessie. It was as though he had been waiting on the other side of the connecting door, listening. Lizzy was still sitting at her dressing table. Will pulled her onto her feet and into his arms. Warmth from his body seeped through the thin fabric of her robe and curled around her heart.

'Thank you. I think it was a success.'

'I know it was.'

'Did it hurt so very much to smile for the entire evening?' Lizzy teased.

'Looking at you made it easy. Just knowing you are my wife makes me want to smile all the time. However, I caught a few people looking at me askance, as though they thought I had indigestion.'

Lizzy laughed. 'You will be plagued by tenants calling for favours once word of the changes gets out. They will attempt to take shameful advantage of your good humour.'

'They are certainly welcome to try.' Will kissed the end of her nose. 'However, if *you* wish to take advantage of me, that would be another matter entirely.'

Lizzy sighed. 'So many sacrifices. I cannot imagine what has come over you.'

'You have come over me, my love. Over me, in me, part of me. Forgive my jealous tirades if you possibly can and never tire of me.'

'Oh, I think I can safely promise you that will never happen.'

'I shall keep you to your word, Mrs Darcy.'

'I depend upon it, sir.'

'What were you and your aunt in such animated conversation about earlier?'

'She wanted to know why Lydia had really disappeared. As she pointed out, Lydia doesn't have it in her to walk out on a party.'

Will grunted. 'That is certainly true.'

'Anyway, given the part my aunt and uncle played in bringing Lydia's wedding about, I felt she deserved to know the truth. I hope you don't mind my having told her.'

'Not in the least.'

'Poor Mrs Gardiner. She was very upset.'

Will shrugged. 'She knows as well as anyone Lydia and Wickham are a law unto themselves.'

'Yes, she does.'

Will scooped her into his arms and carried her to the bed. Lizzy laughed as he did so. 'What's so funny?'

'I was thinking about Miss Bingley. She didn't know what to make of my performance tonight.'

'So I noticed.'

'Did she try to talk to you about the summerhouse?'

'I avoided her all the evening, as did Fitzwilliam at my particular request. Neither of us spoke to her, much less asked her to dance.' Will's jaw firmed. 'It was an unpardonable slight and she must suspect we know what she did. I just wish there was more I could have done to show my displeasure.'

'She will assume I used my feminine wiles and somehow persuaded you to forgive me.'

'Then use them, woman! Don't disappoint my best friend's sister.'

His body half-covered hers as Lizzy leaned up to kiss him.

'We won't have any more trouble from Caroline Bingley once she leaves here tomorrow,' Will said when Lizzy finally allowed him to speak. 'She will assume that even if I believe you, there is no evidence to prove what she did.'

'Unfortunately she's right about that.' Lizzy sighed. 'It's so unfair.'

'Don't think about it any more.'

Will ensured that she didn't by distracting her with roving lips and marauding hands, invading every square inch of her body with skill and expertise, lifting her to unimaginable heights of pleasure. Lizzy surrendered to him with joy in her heart, willing herself to give her husband her undivided attention. Even so, a small part of her brain continued to feel guilty about Lydia, whose future was now far from certain.

* * *

Lizzy woke to find Will already gone. She must have been more tired than she realised because he always woke her with a kiss, which inevitably developed into something more passionate. If he had kissed her that morning, she had been unaware of it.

Delighted the party was over, Lizzy's pleasure was marred by the thought of Wickham and Miss Bingley getting away with their heinous behaviour. She looked about her sumptuous chamber, reminding herself she had won. It ought to be enough, but Lizzy abhorred duplicity, especially since Lydia – who was guilty of nothing more sinister than poor judgement – would suffer because of it.

She smiled at Jessie when she came in with her breakfast and applied herself to it, thinking through the things she had to do that morning. She had just finished dressing when a housemaid delivered a message from Will, asking her to join him in his library at her convenience.

Wondering what it could be about, Lizzy lost no time in going downstairs. When she entered Will's room, she found a man she had never seen before in there with him. He was respectably dressed, but his attire wasn't that of a gentleman.

'Ah, Lizzy.' Will stood up and smiled at her. 'This is Long, who was once a keeper here at Pemberley.'

Lizzy's heart rate accelerated when she made the connection. This was the man whom Wickham had been lodging with in Lambton, and he had presumably come to plead Wickham's cause. Long bowed respectfully to Lizzy and waited for her to seat herself before he resumed his own chair.

'Long, perhaps you would tell Mrs Darcy what you just told me,' Will invited, resuming his seat behind his desk.

'Young Wickham,' he said without preamble. 'His father had great hopes for him, and I had great respect for his father. That's why I allow Wickham to stay at my cottage whenever he's in the locality.' Long sniffed. 'Begging your pardon, ma'am, but my daughter enjoys his society, too. She's been widowed these three years and—'

'I understand, Mr Long,' Lizzy said, sharing a swift glance with Will. 'Please continue.'

'Can't rightly say I was too pleased to see him again so soon.

Thought he was carving a career for himself in the army. Anyway, he turned up, said he'd decided to follow in his father's footsteps after all and planned to take up estate management. By then I was starting to doubt his constancy when it came to any career at all, but it was really none of my business. Until... well, until I came home unexpectedly the other day and found him in intense conversation with a lady. A lady what was a guest up here at the big house.'

'Had you seen the lady before, Mr Long?' Lizzy asked.

'Oh aye, she had come to my cottage with Wickham's young wife.'

'I see.' Lizzy nodded at Will, satisfied there could be no doubt as to the lady's identity. 'Pray continue.'

'I didn't see what business a fine lady like that had being in my cottage, and I didn't like it above half. It didn't smell right, begging your pardon, ma'am.'

'Not at all. You were perfectly right to be suspicious, Mr Long.'

'I listened outside the back door, curious to know what was going on, but I couldn't hear what they said.' Long scratched his head. 'It was like they were bartering over something or other. Then I peeped through the window, saw pen and paper being fetched, and my girl was asked to witness whatever it was that was written after they signed it.'

'How extraordinary.' A burst of anticipation spiralled through Lizzy. 'Did you ask your daughter what she had witnessed?'

'No, I knew better than that. She's right taken with Wickham. She believes all the rot he spills into her ear.' Long shook his head, causing his jowls to wobble. 'If he was up to something he shouldn't have been, she wouldn't have given him up. Instead, I waited for Wickham to go out yesterday and then searched the space where he sleeps up in the loft.'

'And Long found this beneath the mattress,' Will finished, handing Lizzy a folded piece of paper.

Lizzy's hands shook as she opened it, hardly daring to hope. But there it was, clear as day. The full particulars of the scheme Miss Bingley and Wickham had hatched, signed by them both, witnessed by Maria Allwood.

'Five hundred guineas,' Lizzy said, shaking her head. 'That's a king's ransom. She must have been feeling very desperate.'

'So it would seem.'

'Does she actually have access to those sorts of funds?' Lizzy asked.

'Yes,' Will replied. 'She took control of her own fortune when she came of age. Bingley mentioned it to me, and wasn't too happy about it, but she insisted. She would need to apply to Bingley's man of business for its release, of course, and I'm sure questions would be asked as to its purpose, but—'

'But she would come up with a plausible explanation.'

'Precisely. Thank you, Long.' Will stood to indicate the interview was at an end. 'I appreciate your bringing this to my attention. Your loyalty won't be forgotten.'

Mr Long looked embarrassed by the praise. 'I'm a Pemberley man through and through, Mr Darcy, never doubt it. I don't take kindly to plots against the Darcy family being hatched beneath my roof, especially when they involve a man who, excuse me, ma'am, is playing fast and loose with my girl's affections when he's already married to another.'

'I admire your principles, Mr Long,' Lizzy said, standing also. 'It was wrong of Wickham to put you in this position. You have every right to feel aggrieved.'

Will rang the bell, and Simpson materialised to show Long out.

'Well, Lizzy,' Will said when they were along again. 'I think we now have all the proof we need.'

'Yes,' Lizzy agreed. 'But what shall you do with it?'

'Confront Miss Bingley,' he replied with determination, ringing the bell again. 'Simpson,' he said when the butler responded. 'Send Miss Bingley my compliments and ask her to join me here. Only when she is in this room, ask Mrs Hurst to join us as well.'

'At once, Mr Darcy.'

'What are you up to?' Lizzy asked.

'You'll see, my love.' He stood up, leaned over her chair and kissed her. 'No one who attempts to undermine my marriage, or paint my wife in a bad light, can expect to get away with it.'

'Why do I get the impression you have been planning to confront Miss Bingley all along?'

Will's laugh owed little to humour. 'Oh, I was. Were it not for the party I would have done so last night. It's a good job I refrained because by waiting I now have all the evidence I need to prove Caroline Bingley's duplicity.'

* * *

Caroline slept badly, still at a loss to explain Mr Darcy's extraordinary behaviour the previous evening. Rather than being disgusted by his wife's conduct and distancing himself from her, he went out of his way to remain at her side. He hadn't spoken one word to Caroline the entire evening, nor had he danced with her. Colonel Fitzwilliam had followed his lead. She would give much to know what was going on. The Mr Darcy she thought she knew had far too much pride to hang on to a wife who was unfaithful. He might, she supposed, wish to avoid the scandal of a divorce, but she couldn't imagine him wanting to have Eliza under his roof for a moment longer than necessary, a daily reminder that he had been played for a cuckold.

Caroline absently directed her maid as she set about the packing. Not that she required any direction, but Caroline refused to go downstairs until she absolutely had to for fear of encountering Eliza. She still clung to the hope that last night had been a big charade on Darcy's part, put on for the sake of appearances. He had only just married, after all, and would find it distasteful to admit to local society that his wife had played him false before the ink on their wedding certificate was even dry. No, he would send her to live in seclusion somewhere while he attended to the humiliating matter of obtaining a divorce. All Caroline needed to know was *where* he'd send her; then she could finish what she had started.

The more Caroline thought about it, the more convinced she became that she had hit upon the right – the only – plausible answer. It would also account for Darcy's inexplicable smiles. He was angry and upset with his wife but didn't want anyone to know it, causing him to overplay his hand. Darcy would send for Caroline at any moment to ask precisely what, if anything, she knew about Eliza's secret tryst with Wickham.

As though summoned by the strength of her own thoughts, a maid delivered a request from Mr Darcy that she attend him at her convenience. Caroline smiled, already feeling much better. She checked her appearance in the full-length glass and then tripped lightly down the stairs. She tapped on the door to Darcy's library, never having entered the room before, curious to see his elegant inner sanctum. His deep voice bade her enter and she did so immediately, only to stop dead in her tracks when she saw Eliza seated beside the fire, looking very composed and completely unconcerned about Caroline's arrival.

'You wished to speak with me, Mr Darcy,' she said, completely ignoring Eliza.

'Please take a seat, Miss Bingley.'

Mr Darcy directed her to a seat facing his wife, and she had no choice but to take it. Darcy himself sat beside Eliza, causing Caroline's confidence to stutter.

'How can I help you, sir?' she asked when several seconds of tense silence had elapsed.

Before Darcy could respond, the door opened again and Louisa was shown in.

'Mr Darcy,' she said. 'Mrs Darcy. Caroline.' She frowned. 'What is all this about? Is something amiss?'

'You will have heard from your sister that my wife and Mr Wickham were found in a compromising position in the summerhouse yesterday?'

Caroline gasped. How could he refer to that outrageous event in such a composed manner?

'Well, yes,' Louisa replied. 'But I didn't believe it for a moment. I'm sure there must be a perfectly reasonable explanation.'

'And yet Miss Bingley assured me of her silence,' Darcy said in a languid tone.

'My sister and I have no secrets from one another.' Caroline was furious that she felt the need to defend herself. She hadn't been the one to betray her wedding vows, nor would she ever betray Mr Darcy once they were together.

'I hesitate to disagree, but that isn't precisely true, Miss Bingley, is it?' Darcy fixed her with a penetrating gaze. 'Lizzy only finished up with Wickham because you arranged for him to be there.'

Caroline laughed. 'I'm sure that is what she told you. Your wife is jealous of me and has never liked me. I *am* surprised you leant her words any credence.'

'Caroline,' Louisa said quietly.

'You deny it, Miss Bingley?' Mr Darcy asked.

'Well, of course I do. What possible reason would I have to

cause such mischief? And how could I, even if I wished to? I had no idea Wickham was in the district.'

'You befriended Mrs Wickham for precisely that purpose.'

Louisa's mouth fell open, but she snapped it shut again, shot Caroline a probing glance and said nothing. Caroline's mind was racing. Eliza had obviously convinced Darcy that she, Caroline, had arranged the assignation with Wickham, but why did Darcy seem so totally convinced she was being truthful? No man liked to be played for a fool, but even so, he had too much pride to cling to any woman unless he was convinced of her constancy.

Caroline tossed her head. 'I did no such thing and resent your implying that I did.'

'Miss Bingley, let's stop playing games.' Darcy's voice had turned hard and decisive. 'I *know* you are responsible for trying to cause trouble, and I can prove it. However, I would prefer it if you would admit it without my having to do so.'

'I am sure you would.' Caroline folded her hands in her lap and met Mr Darcy's gaze head on. 'But there is nothing for me to admit. I understand you are hurting, Mr Darcy, but you really can't blame me for your wife's loose behaviour.'

Caroline glanced at Mrs Darcy as she spoke, hoping to see her wince at her harsh judgement. To her disappointment, she remained perfectly calm.

'Mrs Hurst, I asked you to join us in the hope that you would be able to persuade your sister to do the right thing.' Mr Darcy spoke to Louisa with a degree of politeness that was absent from the comments he had just addressed to Caroline. 'If you really have no secrets from one another, perhaps she confided in you.'

Louisa shared a glance between Caroline and Darcy. 'I know nothing of this, but I do know my sister. I don't believe she is capable of causing such mischief, but if she is, I hope she would have the grace to admit to it.'

Damnation. Louisa didn't sound too convinced of Caroline's innocence. Worse, Darcy showed not the slightest inclination to condemn his wife. Caroline inwardly groaned, aware she had underestimated the hold Eliza had somehow established over Darcy. All she could do now was maintain her innocence in the hope of salvaging at least some of her dignity.

'There is absolutely nothing to admit,' Caroline insisted.

'I think you have almost convinced yourself you speak truthfully,' Mr Darcy said, shaking his head and looking very concerned. 'Even if your unlikely friendship with Mrs Wickham didn't condemn you, your sudden desire to walk with Lizzy at the exact time she had supposedly arranged to meet Wickham in the precise location you just happened to walk in most certainly would.'

'I feel for you excessively, Mr Darcy.' Caroline shot Eliza a condescending smile. 'You are so desperate to defend your wife's behaviour you are seeing conspiracies where none exist.'

Darcy shook his head for a second time, reached behind him to his desk and produced a piece of paper. Wordlessly, he threw it in front of Caroline. She took one look at it and gasped, recognising it as the agreement she had signed with Wickham.

'Five hundred guineas,' Darcy said. 'You really were desperate.'

* * *

Lizzy had watched the drama with Miss Bingley unfold without saying a word, expecting to enjoy her revenge. Instead she felt truly sorry for a woman whose mind was unbalanced and who had been caught out in an immoral deception.

'Caroline?' Mrs Hurst leaned over her sister's shoulder to read the promissory note and then stared at Miss Bingley with total astonishment. 'You actually did this?'

The elegant Caroline Bingley lost her composure completely at that point, suddenly becoming a wild, unrecognisable creature. She clawed at her own hair, sending the pins holding it in place scattering across the floor. Her mouth hung open, and her eyes blazed with either anger or madness – Lizzy wasn't entirely sure which.

'Someone had to do something,' she yelled. 'I told you we should have done more to prevent Charles from marrying Jane. Not that I have anything against Jane, but the connection put us far too close to the wretched Bennet clan.' Miss Bingley pointed an accusatory finger at Lizzy. 'She bewitched Mr Darcy, made him forget who he is and what responsibilities rest upon his shoulders. I could see he regretted his hasty marriage the moment I arrived here, so I acted for his sake.'

Mrs Hurst glanced at Lizzy and gave an imperceptible shrug. Lizzy could see she was genuinely confused and very concerned about her sister. 'Caroline, calm down and take a moment to be thankful that no permanent harm was done by your misguided actions. You owe Mr and Mrs Darcy an apology, at the very least.'

Caroline burst into tears. 'Never!'

'Then allow me to apologise for her,' Mrs Hurst said, stroking her sister's back and looking close to tears herself. 'She is obviously unwell. I should have noticed before now. The signs were there, but I chose to ignore them.'

'The fault is not yours, Mrs Hurst,' Will said. 'But I fear the remedy must fall to your lot.'

'Anything I can do to repair the damage. What do you have in mind?' she asked.

'My wife's first consideration is for her sister, as I am sure yours is for your brother.' Mrs Hurst nodded. 'The knowledge of what she tried to do would destroy Bingley, and I'm sure none of us want that.'

'No,' Mrs Hurst said quietly, patting Miss Bingley's hand as she continued to sob. 'That would serve no useful purpose, especially with Jane in such a delicate state.'

'Quite.' Will took a deep breath. 'I understand you and Miss Bingley were planning to remove to Brighton.'

'Yes, but now I'm not sure if we—'

'My suggestion is that you go ahead. Take her away from here and give her mind time to recover. I know a physician who might be able to help her. I would be glad to give you his name.'

Lizzy knew Will was asking a lot, expecting Mrs Hurst to take on the care of her damaged sister but, to her credit, she didn't hesitate.

'Thank you, Mr Darcy. She doesn't deserve your compassion.'

'Just take good care of her and make sure Jane and Bingley never find out what she did. That will be thanks enough.'

'That I will.' Mrs Hurst turned towards Lizzy. 'You have my apology, ma'am,' she said with dignity.

Lizzy knew Mrs Hurst didn't much like her either, and so that apology must have cost her a lot. 'Thank you, Mrs Hurst,' she replied.

'Come along, Caroline,' Mrs Hurst said with forced joviality. 'We need to be ready to leave directly after luncheon. Although, now I think about it, it might be better to get on the road straight away.'

Will opened the door for them, and the two ladies walked through it, Miss Bingley leaning heavily on her sister's arm, now as quiet and docile as a child. Lizzy didn't envy Mrs Hurst the task she had taken on.

'Well, my love,' Will said, returning to his seat and clasping one of Lizzy's hands in both of his. 'At least we are done permanently with Miss Bingley's society. She will never come to Pemberley again.'

'That might be difficult to explain, if Mr Bingley purchases an estate in the locality.'

'Let's not concern ourselves with that for now.' Will sighed, looking troubled. 'We still have other matters to resolve.'

'Mr Wickham?'

'Precisely. He sits in the inn at Lambton at my expense, waiting to be summoned, probably still hoping I will purchase his silence.'

'What do you intend to do about him?'

Will sighed. 'I have absolutely no idea.'

21

So, Lizzy thought, *the time has come to discuss Wickham*. Much as she wanted to help Lydia, Lizzy wasn't prepared to risk her marriage in order to plead her case. Not that there was anything she could possibly say to help her sister. Now that she knew the extent of Wickham's spiteful actions against her husband, she understood just how distasteful it must have been for Will to have anything to do with the man at all. Lizzy would just have to live with the guilt she felt about Lydia and hope Wickham's failed efforts to extract money from Will would make him stop obsessing about perceived injustices and look to his own future.

There was a tap at the door, and Lizzy braced herself for another visit from Miss Bingley. Instead her aunt and uncle came in.

'I hope we are not interrupting,' Mr Gardiner said.

'Not in the least,' Will replied, standing to offer them both a seat.

'I will not waste your time, Mr Darcy,' Lizzy's uncle said. 'My wife told me of the trouble Wickham tried to cause yesterday.' He shook his head. 'The extent of the man's depravity knows no bounds. May I ask what you plan to do about him?'

'Lizzy and I were just discussing that very subject, but we have reached no firm decisions yet.'

'Well, if you're willing to hear it, I might have a solution that will rid you of the man once and for all.'

Will's expression of surprise probably reflected Lizzy's own. 'By all means, share your thoughts with us, sir.'

Mr Gardiner did so. Lizzy found it impossible to hide her surprise, and gratitude, towards her uncle. She exchanged a glance with Will and could see that his thoughts mirrored her own.

'That is so very generous of you, Uncle!' she cried, moved to tears. 'But are you absolutely sure? I mean, Wickham has not shown himself to be trustworthy, in spite of all the help he has been given so far. It would take a huge commitment on your part that might very well be thrown back in your face.'

'I thought of the idea yesterday when Mrs Gardiner told me of Wickham's latest exploits. I've slept on it and am still determined to make the offer, but only if you are happy about it, Mr Darcy.'

'Why, Uncle? Wickham does not deserve your kindness. Besides, I doubt whether he will accept. He will consider it beneath him.'

'Lizzy, your husband prevented me from being of service to my niece at the time of her wedding. He bore all the expense, while I took all the credit for it. That never sat comfortably with me. Now the time has come to redress the balance by doing something for her, and the worthless rogue we compelled her to marry.'

'Well, Mr Gardiner,' Will said. 'If anyone can knock a sense of responsibility into Wickham, I am persuaded it's you. Thank you, sir. I accept your offer. It sounds to me like the perfect answer, although I would advise you not to put too much faith in Wickham's constancy.'

Mr Gardiner shook his head emphatically. 'That I certainly will not do.'

Lizzy impulsively hugged the Gardiners. 'Thank you, both of you. I don't know what I have done to deserve such caring relations.'

'It is we who are the fortunate ones,' her aunt replied, tears in her eyes.

'I shall wait until after luncheon, see off those who are leaving, and then summon the Wickhams,' Will said, grimacing. 'Shall you mind remaining another night and leaving in the morning?'

'No, no, we will leave as soon as we've spoken with the Wickhams,' Mr Gardiner replied. 'You and Lizzy deserve to have your house back.'

* * *

'Allow me to do all the talking,' Wickham said to Lydia as the carriage sent to collect them conveyed them down the long Pemberley driveway.

'What do you imagine Mr Darcy wishes to say to us?'

'I have absolutely no idea. But if he wishes to pay me off, you will *not* put up objections.'

'If he does so because you were caught with Lizzy then I most certainly shall.' Lydia put up her chin and matched her husband's determined gaze. 'I don't care two figs what happens to us. I won't allow you to be dishonest.' She glared at him. 'Well, are you going to hit me again, to try and make me obedient? You might as well save yourself the trouble, because it won't work.'

Wickham realised he shouldn't have hit her. Something had changed in Lydia since he'd done so, and he was no longer quite so sure he could control her.

'For the love of God!' he cried. 'It's easy to tell you have never gone hungry, or had to think where the next shilling will come from. If you had, you would have a more realistic attitude.'

'You are perfectly capable of working for a living, like so many other gentlemen must. Resorting to stratagems and deceptions is unworthy of you.'

'Yea gods, why couldn't Darcy have sent for me alone. This is a most inconvenient time to develop a conscience, Lydia.'

'Is that what you think I have done?' Lydia shrugged. 'Perhaps it has always been there, but I've had no use for it before now. Then again, perhaps I just love my family too much to see it torn apart.'

'I am your family now.'

'So you are, and I have every faith in your ability to provide for us both,' she replied, sounding unconvincing in her supposed belief.

When they arrived at the house, Simpson conducted them inside, looking down his long nose at them. Wickham had known the man since he had been an under-footman and was determined that he would speak to him with respect.

'The place has not changed much, Simpson.'

'Indeed.' Simpson walked in front of them, disapproval radiating from his ramrod-straight back.

Wickham refused to be deterred. 'How have you been?'

'Perfectly well.'

'Where is everyone?' Lydia asked.

'Most of the guests left after luncheon,' Simpson replied, apparently willing to address Lydia in more than just monosyllables. Not that Wickham particularly cared if a butler disapproved of him, but still, his attitude rankled. 'Wait in here.'

Simpson opened the door to the small salon, waited until they seated themselves and then withdrew.

'This used to be Georgiana's favourite room,' Wickham remarked. 'It has been redecorated.'

'That's probably because Lizzy uses it now.'

They were kept waiting for more than ten minutes, deliberately, Wickham was sure. If Darcy thought that would discompose him then he had badly miscalculated. No offer of refreshments was forthcoming, which didn't surprise him. Returned to his rightful place beneath Pemberley's roof at last, Wickham didn't care about tea, but was annoyed to find himself taut with nerves. All his old resentments resurfaced as he reminded himself that he never should have been expelled from the house in the first place. If only old Mr Darcy had lived for just a little longer...

It was typical of Wickham's luck that the son defied his best efforts to do away with him, and yet the old man disobliged him by dying before his time. All of Wickham's expectations were now pinned on the forthcoming interview with Darcy and so he tried to remain calm and prepare his mind for the battle ahead. Presumably Lydia would be left in this room, perhaps with her sister, while Darcy and Wickham conducted their business in private. That would be for the best. Lydia was not being as supportive as she should be, but provided she didn't get to see Darcy, Wickham was sure he could contain the situation and walk away from it suitably enriched. He reminded himself that he couldn't lose. If all else failed, he would call in Miss Bingley's pledge.

The door opened. Wickham glanced towards it and saw Mr and Mrs Darcy walk through it together. He hadn't expected them to be on speaking terms, but he swallowed down his surprise as he stood to greet them. Might as well keep this civil. His confidence took a further knock when Mr and Mrs Gardiner also joined them. Lydia kissed her sister, and then her uncle and aunt, easing the tension. Darcy merely scowled at Wickham and ignored Lydia completely.

'Let's get this over with,' Darcy said, sitting beside his wife on a couch, having first ensured that Mr and Mrs Gardiner were comfortably seated. 'To save time, Wickham, we know what you and Miss Bingley did.'

'Then you have the advantage of me.'

Wickham casually crossed his legs, his head whirling at the firm conviction behind Darcy's words. He couldn't possibly know. Lizzy had somehow convinced him without any actual proof, but it was her word against his. It was difficult to appear elegant and disinterested when one had a crooked, swollen nose that was already turning black and blue. He was also aware that his words sounded nasal and distorted, all thanks to Darcy. God, how he hated the man!

'Absolutely.'

Darcy threw the document Wickham and Miss Bingley had signed on the table between them. Wickham's breathing hitched. He tried to hide his discomposure, but suspected that he failed. How the devil had that fallen into his possession? Long, of course. He had caught Wickham and Maria together the previous day and had not approved. He was also a strong supporter of Pemberley. The devil take it, there went his five hundred guineas and the satisfaction he would have taken from helping Miss Bingley rid herself of Lizzy. Was no one loyal any more?

'What is this?' Lydia grasped the document before Wickham could stop her, read it and gasped. 'You colluded with Miss Bingley? She was going to pay you five hundred guineas if you... you... with my sister.' Lydia looked genuinely distressed. 'I had no idea about this, Lizzy, and I would have told you at once if I had known.'

'I know that, Lydia,' Lizzy replied. 'Don't distress yourself.'

'But I *am* distressed. How could you?' she asked, turning blazing eyes upon her husband. 'Are you so very desperate?'

'You have gone too far this time, Wickham,' Darcy said in an icy tone. 'Were it left to me, I would turn you away to starve and never

hear your name mentioned again. Fortunately for you, there are
still those willing to look out for your interests.'

'As your late, revered father was.'

'You have had everything from me that my father promised you
and more besides.' Darcy turned towards Lydia's uncle. 'Mr
Gardiner, the floor is yours.'

Mr Gardiner. What the devil did this have to do with him?

'Wickham, I have a proposition for you that, if you accept it, will
enable you to earn an honest living.'

'I am listening.'

'As you know, I have a number of warehouses in Cheapside. I
import all manner of merchandise, which is kept there and sold on
to traders. In short, I require someone to manage the entire
operation.'

Wickham sneered at him. 'You want to turn me into a
shopkeeper?'

'I advise you to listen and to keep a civil tongue in your head,'
Darcy said in a mordant tone. 'After the trouble you tried to cause,
not many people would have the generosity of spirit to think of
your welfare.'

'Presumably you left debts behind you in Newcastle?' Gardiner
asked.

'Well, perhaps a few—'

'It is as I thought. Draw up a complete list and if you agree to
my terms, those debts will be discharged against future earnings.
There is a small apartment that goes with the position I am offering
you, Wickham, ideal for the two of you. You will learn the business
from the bottom up beside some of my more trusted employees. No
money will pass into your hands until all your debts have been
worked off.'

'Out of the question.'

'You have other possibilities?' Darcy asked.

'I can do better than that.'

'We would be in London,' Lydia pointed out.

'But not in a position to be seen in society,' Mrs Gardiner said. 'You will have no funds for that.'

'Yes, Aunt, I understand,' Lydia said. 'And I, for one, am very grateful to you for your generous offer.'

Lizzy and Mrs Gardiner exchanged an incredulous glance. Wickham felt like partaking in it. Lydia had truly astonished him with her mature response. He almost felt respect for her and might well have done so had she not been acting directly against his interests. She absolutely should not show any enthusiasm for Gardiner's offer. It was an opening gambit. There would be something better being held back, he just knew it. No one could seriously expect a man with Wickham's education to accept such a lowly position.

'Whereas I find it completely unacceptable.'

Darcy stood up. 'Then this interview is at a close. You can make your own way back to Lambton and get on with your life, Wickham. Don't let us keep you.'

He had to be bluffing. Lizzy would never allow her precious sister to be thrown to the wolves. He remained in his seat and sent Darcy an appraising glance.

'I am ready to hear your real offer now.'

'There is nothing more, Wickham. Did you really imagine you could use my wife to get at me, and that I would reward you for it?'

'If you wish to accept my offer, then you may travel to London with us in our carriage,' Mr Gardiner said. 'But you need to decide now. We leave within the hour. Oh, and one more thing. If I discover, or even suspect, that you have entered a single London establishment that permits gambling, then our arrangement comes to an immediate end.'

'You cannot possibly mean—'

'I can and I do,' Mr Gardiner replied firmly. 'I don't need

another warehouse manager, and were it not for my niece I would not have made you this offer. In other words, you need me a great deal more than I need you. It's up to you to decide.'

Everyone looked towards Wickham, waiting for him to speak, but there was very little he could say. He knew he was beaten, for the time being anyway, and really didn't have a choice.

'Very well,' he said with as much grace as he could muster. 'Thank you, sir. I accept your offer and look forward to serving you well.'

* * *

Lizzy contrived a few minutes alone with Lydia while her luggage was brought down, before she left for London with her aunt and uncle. She wanted to be sure Lydia knew this really was Wickham's last opportunity to make something of himself. She looked at her youngest sister, expecting at any moment for there to be tears, tantrums or complaints that Lizzy ought to do more for her. Lizzy must be more tired than she realised because instead she could have sworn Lydia looked embarrassed and apologetic. That couldn't possibly be right. She couldn't recall a single time in Lydia's seventeen years when she had seen fit to apologise about anything.

'I really didn't know what Wickham was planning to do.' She shook her head. 'Nor did I realise Miss Bingley had befriended me just to get to Wickham.'

'I know you did not. I don't blame you for any of this, Lydia.'

'Still, I should have been suspicious when Miss Bingley singled me out.' She shook her head. 'She and I have never had anything to say to one another before. I was foolish... about many things.' There were tears in Lydia's eyes. 'Can you ever forgive me?'

Lizzy opened her arms, and Lydia flung herself into them, crying softly on Lizzy's shoulder.

'It's all right,' Lizzy said, stroking Lydia's back. 'Things will work out, provided Wickham makes the most of the opportunity our uncle is offering him. It's up to you to make sure that he does. Mr Gardiner is being very generous, you know.'

'Oh, I do know. Never fear, Lizzy, my eyes have been opened, and Wickham will behave himself this time. It's not as though he will be in the army, out of my sight, so I shall be able to ensure he conducts himself as he should.'

Lydia removed herself from Lizzy's arms and wiped her eyes. There was something different about her when she looked up at her sister, an air of resolution which probably shouldn't have surprised Lizzy. Lydia wasn't stupid, and a year of marriage to Wickham, listening to his constant refrain about ill-usage and unfulfilled expectations, must have forced her to withdraw the blinkers. Never having enough money, being overlooked by the people she would expect to socialise with because Wickham didn't quite measure up to their standards, and always hiding from debt collectors would have consolidated her doubts about her husband's character.

In short, Lydia had grown up.

'He doesn't deserve my protection,' Lydia said, 'but it would upset me if Mama and Papa learned what he did. Do you imagine our aunt will tell them?'

'Not if I ask her not to. I can understand why you wouldn't want your husband to lose our parents' respect, even if he doesn't deserve it.' The sisters held hands as they walked towards the door, more in accord with one another than Lizzy would ever have imagined possible. 'As long as he does as he should, all will be well. Mr Gardiner is a man of influence, never lose sight of that. If Wickham pulls his weight and is prepared to work hard, then he could still make a comfortable future for you both.'

'You will write to me, Lizzy.' Lydia suddenly looked very young and vulnerable. 'Mr Darcy has no reason to think well of me, I quite understand that, but I do so enjoy hearing from you.'

'Of course I will.'

Lizzy knew it really would be up to Lydia to keep Wickham honest. Her heart ached for her silly, impetuous, yet kind-hearted sister. No one so young should have so much responsibility thrust upon her. But at least Lydia appeared to appreciate the precariousness of her situation and had realised what a wastrel she'd married, which might just be enough to save them both. How many times during the course of history had a strong woman kept the man she loved on the right path? And Lydia did love Wickham still, Lizzy could sense it, even if he had lost her respect and she no longer harboured illusions about the man himself.

'Does Jane know?'

'No, and we would keep it that way. It would upset her, especially in her delicate condition, if she knew what Miss Bingley did. Mrs Hurst has undertaken to look after her sister, and we must trust her to ensure she gets well again.'

'Why did she do it?'

'Miss Bingley?' Lydia nodded. 'Because she thought I'm not good enough for Mr Darcy, I suppose, as well as being an unsuitable mistress for Pemberley. She thought he had always intended to marry her, before I bewitched him and took him away from her.'

Lydia pulled a face. 'She must be three-farthings short of a shilling.'

'Very likely.'

'You are ten times better than she is, Lizzy, and Mr Darcy is very lucky to have you.'

'That is a very generous thing to say, Lydia. Thank you.'

'It's true, and I wish... well, never mind what I wish. It's too late for regrets, and I shall just have to make the best of things.'

'Lydia, if you really don't want to—'

'No, Lizzy, don't say anything.' Her laughter sounded forced. 'You know me. I always find a way to... well, to get my way.'

'Yes.' Lizzy squeezed Lydia's hand. 'That's certainly true.'

'Is Kitty here? I would like to say goodbye.'

'It would probably better if you didn't. Besides, she and Georgie made themselves scarce immediately after luncheon. Major Halstead and Captain Turner have just left, you see.'

'I was unkind in the things I said to Kitty about Captain Turner. To be honest, I was a little jealous.'

Lizzy elevated her brows. 'You were?'

'Certainly. Kitty has the sense to set her cap at a man of means. I should have done the same thing instead of being swayed by good looks and charm.'

'Well, it might all be for naught. I believe the captain left without expressing any intention of returning with Major Halstead when he calls to see Georgie.' Lizzy sighed. 'There are difficulties between him and his father that need to be resolved. Let's hope he has the backbone to go after what he wants for himself, which is, I believe, our sister.'

'And I am perfectly sure Kitty wants the captain. I do hope she gets her heart's desire.'

'As do I,' Lizzy agreed, surprised this new Lydia could spare a thought for Kitty when her own future looked so precarious.

The sisters had made their way to the front steps, where the Gardiners' carriage awaited them, the horses stamping their feet, anxious to be off. Lizzy and Lydia embraced. When they separated, Lydia made a very proper curtsey to Mr Darcy.

'Thank you for everything, sir,' she said.

Lizzy, engaged in wishing her aunt and uncle adieu, could see

Will was truly surprised by Lydia's display of maturity. He responded to it with more civility than he had shown her the entire time she had been beneath his roof.

'Please say goodbye to Jane and Mr Bingley for me, Lizzy, and Kitty too, of course.' Lydia stepped into the carriage. 'I would have liked to have seen them for myself, but it can't be helped.'

It could have been, but Will had made sure he sent for the Wickhams while Jane and Mr Bingley were off viewing Campton Park. Lizzy wanted to explain Wickham's new position to Jane without Lydia there to answer any of Jane's questions inappropriately. Keeping secrets definitely wasn't one of Lydia's strengths.

'This is very generous of your uncle, but will it work?' Will asked Lizzy as they waved the carriage away.

'Surprisingly, I think it will, but only because Lydia will ensure that it does. She, at least, realises how fortunate her husband is to have been offered yet another chance to prove himself.'

'Well, let us hope you're right,' he said, taking Lizzy's hand and leading her back inside.

22

Two hours later, Lizzy was in her small sitting room, enjoying having Pemberley more or less to themselves again and mulling over all that had occurred. Will joined her there, one of his devastating smiles flirting with his lips – the type of smile that never failed to lift her spirits and stir her passions.

'Well,' he said, sitting beside her. 'Thanks to your relations, things turned out better than I could have imagined.'

'True, but then if it weren't for me and my family, the situation wouldn't have arisen in the first place.'

'Never blame yourself, Lizzy,' Will replied passionately. 'All you are responsible for is agreeing to be my wife. I am still unsure what I did to deserve that honour.'

Lizzy laughed. 'How can you say that after all the trouble my family have caused you?'

'Very easily.' He framed her jaw with his long, elegant fingers, running the pad of his thumb across her lips. 'There is nothing I would not do to retain your love and good opinion, my darling. Never doubt it for a moment.'

Now, Lizzy thought. Now was the moment to tell him her news.

Before she could formulate the right words, Will leaned over, effort-lessly lifted her from the couch and settled her on his lap.

'Will! Anyone might come in.'

'Let them. Why should I not worship my wife beneath my own roof whenever the fancy takes me?'

Lizzy sent him a sultry smile. 'Now that you mention it, I can't think of a single reason. Please feel free to continue with your worshipping.'

'Especially when she looks at me like that,' Will growled, nuzzling her neck.

'Georgie and Kitty are both feeling a little lovesick, I think,' she said when Will finally stopped trailing delicate kisses down her neck.

'I don't think Georgiana has reason to doubt Halstead's constancy, even if I am still unsure about him.'

Lizzy laughed and ran a finger idly down his forearm. 'You would doubt any man who looked romantically upon your sister.'

'Perhaps.' Will paused to kiss her deeply. 'But whether or not Turner finds the strength to stand up to his father is altogether another matter.'

'I believe he will. He had a lot to prove to himself. He has achieved that ambition and now has the confidence and strength of character to let his father know he is his own man.' Lizzy snuggled up against Will's chest. 'Anyway, time will tell.'

'Which leaves poor Fitzwilliam.' Will frowned. 'I don't envy him. He has to marry for money, and my aunt's determination to have him for her daughter will make him a rich man.'

'Provided he's prepared to put up with your aunt's interference.'

'Quite.'

'Actually, he spoke to me about it and I suggested he stand up to her, offer her an ultimatum.'

Will looked astounded. 'You did not!'

'Certainly I did. He is a gentleman of strong principles and would be miserable if he subjected himself to Lady Catherine's tyranny. He has breeding, charm and respectability enough to find himself a wealthy wife elsewhere, even if her riches don't come close to matching those offered by the Rosings estate. I think he will always feel less of a man if he doesn't lay down his own terms, especially since he is aware Lady Catherine is only acting out of spite towards you.'

'You're probably right.' Will laughed and ran a hand across Lizzy's breasts. 'I would give much to be a party to that conversation, should Fitzwilliam take her on.'

'As would I.'

'Bingley and Jane are taking their time,' Will said after a short pause.

'Jane must like what she sees.' Lizzy turned to look at Will. 'Did you manage to do anything about the vacant estate manager's position?'

'Yes, I sent word to Porter, the current incumbent, telling him that Wickham wasn't qualified to fill the position, and that I could not offer him a character.'

'And your word will be sufficient to ensure Porter doesn't recommend him for it, should he be foolish enough to revive that aspiration?'

'Oh yes. I received a reply from Porter this morning. Seems he had already cooled to the idea of Wickham taking over from him. Reading between the lines, I gather it was Porter's young wife who was enthusiastic to see Wickham appointed. She persuaded her husband to throw his support behind him, but Porter now wonders why she did that.'

'Ah, I see.'

'Quite.' Will flexed his jaw. 'Porter is extraordinarily protective of his wife, with good reason, I suspect, in Wickham's case.'

'That's good. I should hate for Mr Bingley to be bothered by Wickham. The truth would then come out and create all the difficulties we have worked so hard to avoid.'

'I don't think Wickham will try it, especially given the change in Lydia's attitude.'

'Yes, at least one good thing has come out of this farrago.'

'You were worried about your sister, even after what Wickham and Miss Bingley tried to do to us?'

'Don't be angry, Will. I can't help feeling loyal, but I never would have done anything to help them. You must know that.'

'I would think less of you if you didn't feel a strong sense of duty towards your family.'

'It's lovely to have Pemberley more or less to ourselves again,' Lizzy said, relaxing against the solid wall of Will's chest, feeling comfortable and completely happy.

'You did extraordinarily well this week, especially given the problems Miss Bingley created as well as Lydia's unexpected arrival. I was never more proud of you.'

'Thank you.' She leaned up and brushed her lips against his. 'Your approval is all I have ever craved. Well, that and acceptance as mistress of Pemberley.'

'That you undoubtedly have. All of my staff are already devoted to you.'

'I hope they are. I have worked hard to earn their trust.'

They remained where they were for some time, perfectly comfortable in the quiet room, only the ticking of the long clock disturbing the serenity of the moment. The doors were open directly to the terrace and sunshine streamed through them, falling upon husband and wife embracing on the settee.

'Well, whatever happens with the Wickhams, at least Lydia shows no signs of increasing,' Will said absently. 'And for that we ought to be grateful. Lydia is barely more than a child herself, and Wickham is in no position to support a child.'

'Unlike two of her sisters' husbands.'

'Quite. Bingley is perfectly able to... Just a minute.' Will broke off and fixed Lizzy with a probing gaze. 'Did you just say *two* of her sisters' husbands?'

Lizzy sent him triumphant smile. 'I believe I did.'

'Lizzy!' He grasped her shoulders and looked at her with longing in his eyes. 'Are you sure? Why didn't you say something before now?'

'Yes, I am perfectly sure, and I didn't tell you because you would have insisted upon cancelling the party and treating me as though I was made of porcelain.'

Will's smile challenged the sunshine streaming through the open doors as he pulled Lizzy into a tight embrace, plastering kisses over her face and neck. 'I have been so rough with you in the bedroom. Why did you allow it? I could have harmed our child.'

'No, Will, you could not.'

'And then, what Wickham did to you. The shock might have been enough to—'

'Shush, it wasn't.' She placed her index finger against his lips. 'We are absolutely fine. But it does mean I won't be able to go to London for the season.'

'Certainly you shall not. I wouldn't hear of it.'

'I rest my case about your protectiveness,' she said smugly.

'What sort of a man would I be if I didn't worry about you? However, regarding the season, I shall make arrangements for Georgiana to be chaperoned and remain here with you.'

'Perhaps Georgiana would prefer to remain here as well.'

'Hmm, we shall see.'

Will was still grinning as he pulled Lizzy into another embrace. 'Ah, my love, you have made my life complete. A child of our own.'

'Well, I can't take all the credit for that.'

Will kissed her again, softly and yet with desperate passion. The door opened and Simpson stood there, almost dropping the salver he bore when he found the master and mistress of Pemberley so intimately engaged. Simpson was so correct Lizzy suspected he would be shocked into giving notice. Instead he turned to leave and, catching Lizzy's eye as he pulled the door shut, he actually winked at her.

ABOUT THE AUTHOR

Eliza Austin is the Regency romance pen name of prolific, bestselling author Wendy Soliman. Wendy has written historical romance, revenge thrillers and cosy crime.

Sign up to Eliza Austin's mailing list for news, competitions and updates on future books.

Follow Eliza on social media here:

 facebook.com/wendy.soliman.author
 x.com/wendyswriter
bookbub.com/authors/wendy-soliman

ALSO BY ELIZA AUSTIN

Pemberley Presents

Miss Bingley's Revenge

Lady Catherine's Demands The

Daring Miss Darcy

Kitty Bennet's Ruin

You're cordially invited to

The home of swoon-worthy
historical romance from the
Regency to the Victorian era!

Warning: may contain spice

Sign up to the newsletter
https://bit.ly/thescandalsheet

Boldw**oo**d

Boldwood Books is an award-winning fiction publishing company seeking out the best stories from around the world.

Find out more at www.boldwoodbooks.com

Join our reader community for brilliant books, competitions and offers!

Follow us
@BoldwoodBooks
@TheBoldBookClub

Sign up to our weekly deals newsletter

https://bit.ly/BoldwoodBNewsletter

Milton Keynes UK
Ingram Content Group UK Ltd.
UKHW042049110724
445481UK00004B/165

9 781836 031901